THE SHERLOCK OF SAGELAND:
THE COMPLETE TALES OF
SHERIFF HENRY, VOLUME 1

W. C. Tuttle

THE SHERLOCK OF SAGELAND

THE COMPLETE TALES OF SHERIFF HENRY, VOLUME 1

W.C. TUTTLE

AFTERWORD BY

SAI SHANKAR

ALTUS PRESS
2015

EDITED AND DESIGNED BY
Matthew Moring

PUBLISHING HISTORY
"Henry Goes Arizona" originally appeared in the February 23, 1935 issue of *Argosy* magazine (Vol. 253 No. 5). Copyright © 1935 by The Frank A. Munsey Company. Copyright renewed © 1962 and assigned to Steeger Properties, LLC. All rights reserved.

"With the Help of Henry" originally appeared in the March 23, 1935 issue of *Argosy* magazine (Vol. 254 No. 3). Copyright © 1935 by The Frank A. Munsey Company. Copyright renewed © 1962 and assigned to Steeger Properties, LLC. All rights reserved.

"The Sherlock of Sageland" originally appeared in the April 27, 1935 issue of *Argosy* magazine (Vol. 255 No. 2). Copyright © 1935 by The Frank A. Munsey Company. Copyright renewed © 1962 and assigned to Steeger Properties, LLC. All rights reserved.

"The Diplomacy of Henry" originally appeared in the July 6, 1935 issue of *Argosy* magazine (Vol. 256 No. 6). Copyright © 1935 by The Frank A. Munsey Company. Copyright renewed © 1962 and assigned to Steeger Properties, LLC. All rights reserved.

"About the Author" appears here for the first time. Copyright © 2015 Sai Shankar. All rights reserved.

THANKS TO
Joel Frieman, Gerd Pircher and Sai Shankar

ISBN
978-1-61827-190-7

Visit *altuspress.com* for more books like this.
Printed in the United States of America.

TABLE OF CONTENTS

I

HENRY GOES ARIZONA

Henry, old large-nosed trouper, had a flair for comedy, but when he inherited a ranch and a relative's debts, his was a tragic rôle .

CHAPTER I

A LEGACY

HENRY HARRISON CONROY stopped at the bottom of the steps, which led up to the manager's office, and squinted thoughtfully at the darkened foyer.

The word had been passed to him at the door of his dressing room that he was wanted at the manager's office at once.

Henry Harrison Conroy was about five feet six inches in height, rotund, fifty-five years of age, with a sparse growth of taffy-colored hair on his head. His face was moon-like, the muscles sagging quite a bit now, and adorned with a huge, putty-like nose, which was forever red. In dress he was a typical down-at-the-heel vaudevillian, an old-time tragedian in manner.

Finally he went up the stairs, like a condemned criminal going up the thirteen steps to the dangling noose. Slowly opening the door, he entered the office.

Jack Bentley, manager of the Alcazar, sitting at his desk, chewing an unlighted cigar, looked up quickly from the report of yesterday's business. He shifted the cigar, grunted softly, and turned back to the figures.

"Sit down, Conroy," he said kindly.

The old actor sank into a chair and searched his pockets for the cigar he knew he did not have.

After several minutes of silence Bentley shoved the paper aside, picked up a telegram, and looked at Conroy. "Came this morning, Conroy," said Bentley.

1

"To cancel my act?" queried the old actor.

Bentley nodded, chewing viciously on his cigar.

"I'm sorry, Conroy," he said. "It wasn't any of my—I mean, I didn't say a word about your act. I like you. You've been a credit to the profession—always. A hell of a lot of tank actors would have starved if it hadn't been for you. Oh, I know; I've heard things. Your act was getting past until Tipton kicked out. And because it was you, they gave you a chance as a single. But this telegram—want to read it?"

Henry Harrison Conroy shook his head.

"I felt it coming, Bentley. The world is getting so sophisti-cated that they fail to see any humor in a red nose. As you might say, I have been beaten by a nose."

The clown was still trying to laugh. But Bentley knew. It meant the end of things for Henry Harrison Conroy. Old at fifty-five, born and raised in the only profession he knew, gen-erous to a fault, and as improvident as a child.

"You might try the legit again, Henry," he said thoughtfully.

"It is kind of you, my boy."

"Oh, you'll strike something. You are the only one of the Old

"Arrest me?" queried Danny, straightening in his saddle.

School who hasn't bragged to me that they were with Booth or Barret."

"I was never with Booth," said Henry softly.

"With Barret?"

"Yes; grin and bear it—all my life."

Henry got heavily to his feet and picked up his hat.

"Do you happen to have a copy of *Variety?*" he asked.

"I certainly have. Oh, say, wait a minute. I was busy when the mail came, and—here's a letter for you."

"No doubt a belated admirer, asking for a photo and an autograph—of my nose."

Slowly the old actor opened the envelope and drew out the enclosure. Leaning closer to the light from the window, he squinted his small eyes and carefully read the letter. He shifted the letter and looked past it, a queer expression on his face. After blinking several times, rather violently, as if distrusting his vision, he read the letter again.

Slowly he folded the letter, carefully replaced it in the envelope, put it in his pocket, and turned to Bentley. "No more dogs," he said whimsically.

"What about dogs?" asked Bentley.

HENRY SHRUGGED his shoulders.

"Oh, just no more dogs. You see, for fifteen years I've been following a dog act. Once it was monkeys. That time, when I came on, they thought it was an encore. Bentley, do you realize how damn hard it is to follow a dog act—with a nose like mine?"

"I hate dog acts," said Bentley.

"They're all right," said Henry slowly. "I've met a lot of nice dogs in my time. Poor old Tipton used to say—oh, well, what's the use? But, Bentley, do you know anything about cows?"

"Cows?" Bentley looked curiously at the old trouper. "Thinking of starting a cow act? I've never seen a trained cow."

"Neither have I."

"What made you mention cows, Henry?"

"It seems," replied Henry soberly, "that I've got a lot of them."

"A lot of cows?"

"I suppose some of them are bulls. It seems reasonable to suppose that it would be co-educational, if I might be permitted to use that expression."

"I think you need a drink, Henry," said the manager seriously.

"Possibly I do. But have you ever heard of Tonto City, Arizona?"

"No, I never have."

"Have you never heard of Wild Horse Valley, Bentley? Surely you must have heard of that valley?"

"No, I never have."

"I have. Bentley, I own what is known as the J Bar C cattle outfit, located in Wild Horse Valley, near Tonto City. An uncle of mine, whose name was Jim Conroy, has died and left me this inheritance. A law firm of Tonto City asks me to come at once and take over my inheritance. That was the letter I just received."

"A cattle ranch!" exclaimed Bentley. "Why, Conroy, such things are worth big money. You'll be rich!"

Henry Harrison Conroy nodded slowly.

"Rich," he said softly. "Just when I hit the bottom. No more dogs ahead of me. But," he smiled whimsically, "if it was a dog ranch I'd know how to handle it—I've known so many mutts."

"I think we both need a drink," said Bentley, closing his desk.

"I have drunk for a lesser reason," said Henry. "But can you visualize me in a big hat, leather pants, and a trusty gun on my hip. I—I wonder if there are any squaws in Tonto City."

"Thinking of the *Squaw Man*, Henry?"

"That's right. Let us adjourn to a rummery, my boy. No more dogs. Egad, that is wonderful!"

"I'm glad for you, Henry," said Bentley. "It is wonderful. Of course, you will miss the crowd and the applause and—"

"I shall only miss the crowds, my boy," interrupted Henry gently. "Remember—only the crowds. But I shall have my cows. As I understand it, they moo—not boo. They eat vegetables—but do not throw them. All in all, my boy, it will be a relief."

"Oh, you never got hit with many vegetables," laughed Bentley.

"That is true. But most of them were badly aimed. I remember one particular egg—or is an egg in that condition particular? No matter now—those days are past!"

CHAPTER II

ARMED, SOBER, AND SUSPICIOUS

"**THE BLETHERING OF** a drunken old sot," complained the prosecuting attorney of Tonto City, "listened to by an idiotic jury."

Cornelius Van Treece, known as "Judge," the "drunken old sot," drew himself fully erect, his pouchy old eyes snapping.

"I resent your implications regarding that jury," he said. "As for myself, sir, I may be a drunken old sot, as you say; but I am the one who tore your case into shreds and saved young Danny Regan from the rope. In my opinion, sir, you are a damn poor excuse for a prosecutor. Good day, sir."

And the "Judge" went unsteadily across the narrow street, his wrinkled old cutaway coat flapping in the breeze, one hand clapped over the sagging crown of his ancient derby. Danny Regan was waiting for him in front of the Tonto Saloon.

Danny was twenty-three years of age, a lithe, well-built young cowboy, with a mop of red hair, freckles, and a wide, white-tooth smile. His eyes were very blue under the brim of his big hat, and there was a Celtic tilt to his nose. Danny had been in jail for over four weeks, facing a murder charge, and he had lost some of his color.

After a ten-day trial, the jury had been out only fifteen minutes, bringing in a verdict of not guilty as charged. There was no doubt that the vagabond lawyer had influenced the jury, but his masterly handling of the defense had wrecked the case for the prosecution.

"The prosecution is still out of sorts, Danny," said the Judge.

"Thanks to you, Judge," replied Danny. "You beat 'em bad."

"No thanks to me, son. After what you've done for me?"

"I didn't do that much, Judge."

"No? Remember that night in Gold Valley, when that gang decided that I was a detective sent in there to stop high-graders from stealing ore? Well, I haven't forgotten it. You got me out of there alive, brought me here, and welcomed me to your little home. Not a dollar to my name—and a dozen human wolves thirsting for my blood. You've shared with me since then, and it is damn little good I've been to you. This was my chance to save you—and, by gad, I'm thirsty."

They walked into the saloon, where Ricky Dole, foreman of

the J Bar C, was having a drink with Slim Pickins and Tug Evans, two of his cowboys. Ricky was in charge of the ranch now, waiting for Henry Harrison Conroy to put in his appearance and claim the outfit.

Danny had heard that Ricky had lost a sizable bet on the jury's verdict. Ricky turned his head and looked at Judge.

"If I ever murder a man," said Ricky, "I'm sure goin' to hire you to defend me, old-timer."

"Murderers are not always tried for murder," replied Judge, and went with Danny to the far end of the bar.

"I reckon that'll hold yuh, Ricky," chuckled Slim.

"What did he mean?" queried Ricky, who was not too bright.

"He said yuh wouldn't need a lawyer unless yuh got caught."

"Yea-a-ah? Meanin' that I ain't been caught yet, eh? I'll knock his ears up through his old hat."

"Use yore brains," warned Tug Evans softly. "You make any sort of a pass at the old man, and Dan Regan will kill yuh too dead to skin. If I know anythin' about human nature, that kid is honin' to turn you over to an undertaker. And you ain't got brains enough to realize it. Have a drink and forget it."

"T'morrow is another day," said Ricky.

Danny bought a drink for Judge and threw a dollar on the bar.

"Have a couple more and then meet me later over at the store, Judge," he said softly. "I'm goin' over to see Leila for a minute."

Danny crossed the street and went down the block to a little millinery store, where Mrs. Jane Harper and her daughter, Leila, kept house and made hats for the women of the cow country. Business of that nature was pitifully small in Tonto City, but they managed to exist.

LEILA WAS waiting for Danny, and her eyes filled with tears as he took both her hands and they looked at each other. Leila was twenty, tall and slender, with nice features, dark wavy hair, and big dark eyes. Her mother came from back of the store. In her youth she had been beautiful, too; and traces of it still remained. But privation and trouble had aged her far beyond her years.

Danny shook hands with her, awkwardly, silently.

"I'm glad," she said wearily. "Glad they found you not guilty, Danny."

"Thank yuh, Mrs. Harper," said Danny. "I reckon I had the best lawyer on earth. Of course, I never killed Jim Conroy. Not that he didn't have it comin' to him."

Mrs. Harper nodded grimly. "He did," she said simply.

"Well, let's forget him," said Danny briskly. "I'm sure glad to get him off my mind."

"It is hard to forget," said Mrs. Harper, "that he put us where we are. He set out to break Lon Harper; set out to own all of this valley for himself. Lon wasn't strong enough to fight back— and when he died Jim Conroy fought me."

"Forced yuh out for eighteen thousand dollars—and then smashed the bank," added Danny grimly. "I hope he enjoys the money, where he is livin' now."

"It can't be proved," sighed Mrs. Harper. "All I *know* is that my money was in the Tonto Bank just thirty-six hours, when the bank was robbed of every last cent. If Jim Conroy didn't do it, who did?"

Danny shook his head. "I hear that Conroy willed the J Bar C to another Conroy, who is due here any old time. Ed Walsh made out the will for Jim Conroy about a month before he was killed."

"I wonder if Jim Conroy backed Ed Walsh to buy the Tonto Bank," said Leila. "I've heard that he did."

"Prob'ly," replied Danny. "Conroy wanted to own everythin'. Mebbe he busted the bank so he could buy it mighty cheap. Well, I've got to get Judge and go back to the ranch. If I wait too long he'll get drunk and start a fight—God bless him."

"I know I shall never laugh at his funny face and funny old

clothes again," declared Leila. "I heard his talk to the jury, and, Danny, I even forgot that you were on trial. It was wonderful. Why, he made the jury cry—and the judge; I saw him wiping his eyes."

"I wasn't laughin'," said Danny soberly. "Anyway, I hope the new owner of the J Bar C will give us small ranchers a chance to make a livin'. I'll be runnin' in to see yuh soon, folks."

"Take care of yourself, Danny," said Leila anxiously.

"Oh, everythin' is all right now," he grinned.

As Danny left the little store the stage arrived from Antelope, thirty miles east of Tonto City. Sitting on the seat with Barney Eastland, the old stage driver, was Henry Harrison Conroy, getting a near bird's-eye view of the land of his inheritance. His nose was very red, his eyes watery from looking great distances, and his usually immaculate linen was generously sprinkled with Arizona dust.

HE CLIMBED ponderously from the stage seat, walked heavily to the outer edge of the sidewalk, gripping his gold-headed cane, and looked with whimsical eyes upon the main street of Tonto City, which was not very long, not very wide, and certainly not straight.

"Do yuh want me to put yore baggage inside the office?" asked the driver.

Henry turned and looked him over quizzically.

"I don't even see any dogs around," he said.

"I asked yuh if yuh—"

"Oh, I suppose so," interrupted Henry. "Put it any place."

"It says Theater on it," remarked the driver. "We ain't got none."

But Henry was interested now in the approach of Judge, who was coming across the street. He was a trifle uncertain in gait, it seemed, but carried a certain dignity that was not unnoticed by Henry Harrison Conroy.

"Sir, I welcome you to Tonto City," said Judge. "I, sir, am Cornelius Van Treece—at your service."

"And I, sir, am highly honored," replied Henry. "My hand."
They shook hands solemnly. Judge's eyes were owl-like.

"I take it that you are a stranger in a strange land, sir."

"The point is well taken, my friend," replied Henry. "Is there a place where a weary wanderer may rid his tonsils of a three-ply coat of alkali dust and again become normal, at least to a degree that he may enjoy the beauties of his surroundings?"

Judge nodded solemnly. "There is, my friend; follow me."

Danny heard part of this conversation, watched them single file over to the Tonto Saloon, and turned to Barney Eastland.

"Who the devil is that, Barney?"

"Name it and take it," growled Barney. "I've had that to contend with all the way from Antelope. I told him every lie I ever heard about this valley, and he believed every one. But he won't remember one of 'em. Not him. Why, he couldn't even remember my name. I told him it was Eastland, and he kept callin' me Munch—Munchhoozen or Munchowzen. I done corrected him a dozen times, but it didn't do any good. All his baggage has got Theater on it. Mebbe he's goin' to put on one of them medicine shows."

"He's got a bigger nose than Judge has," smiled Danny.

"Yeah, and a damn sight redder. Oh, I forgot to congratulate yuh on gittin' turned loose, Danny. That's fine—I'm shore glad. Wins me twenty dollars from Ricky Dole, too. It don't make a bit of difference whether yuh killed Jim Conroy or not now; they can't try yuh for it again."

"No," replied Danny, "it don't make any difference—except that I didn't shoot him, Barney."

Danny went across to the Tonto Saloon. Henry and Judge were at the bar, while Ricky, Slim and Tug grouped together, staring and listening to the conversation of the two men. All three of the cowboys were drunk enough to invite rough horse-play.

"Where's the masquerade?" asked Ricky loudly.

Henry turned his head slowly and looked upon the foreman

of the J Bar C. Judge Van Treece was talking, and Henry turned back to him.

"Must be one of Judge's lodge brothers," said Tug.

"What lodge is that?" asked Slim.

"Brothers of the Busted Beaks," snorted Tug.

HENRY TURNED and looked upon the three cowboys. "Gentlemen," he said slowly, "my nose has been laughed at by millions. It has always been my stock in trade; so instead of annoying me, it is very gratifying. Go right ahead."

"Kind of a cocky old pelican, ain't he?" drawled Slim. "I wonder how him and Judge would look doin' a dance together."

Slim's fingers tightened around the butt of his gun as Danny's voice drawled from the doorway, "I'd think twice before I done that, Slim."

Slim jerked around and looked at Danny.

"Yuh see," explained Danny, "they ain't doin' you any harm."

"Where'd you get any license to horn into this?" demanded Ricky.

"I've got six of 'em, Ricky," replied Danny, "and every one of 'em says that there ain't goin' to be any dancin' done."

"For a feller that's jist out of jail, it seems to me—" began Ricky, but changed his mind and ended there.

"Acquitted, yuh mean," reminded Danny. "And that acquittal cost you quite a little money, I hear."

"That's no skin off yore nose!" snapped Ricky.

At that moment Edward Walsh, banker and attorney at law, came in. Walsh was tall, thin to the point of emaciation, and walked with a peculiar shambling gait. His face was long, bony, and he habitually wore his glasses midway of his long, thin nose. He looked quickly at the cowboys, but concentrated his gaze upon the back of Henry Harrison Conroy, who was just now drinking a toast to his new friend, Judge Van Treece.

"I beg your pardon," said Walsh, touching Henry on the arm, who squinted into the bar mirror at Walsh's reflection.

"And now," said Henry ponderously, "that the formalities have been observed, what in the devil are you begging my pardon for?"

"You are Henry Harrison Conroy?" asked the lawyer.

"Ah, yes. Thank you for the reminder. And you?"

"I am Edward C. Walsh, the attorney at law."

"Attorney at law? Oh, I remember. You wrote me. Well, well! It is truly a small world. Have a drink?"

"I do not indulge, Mr. Conroy."

"This," said Henry, indicating the bar bottle, "is not indulgence—it is damnation. But perhaps you do not damnate. I thought I had sampled every kind of whisky on this globe; and here I find at least three ingredients in one bottle of which I have never tasted before. Verily, there *is* something new under the sun. My dear Van Treece, I salute you."

"How soon may I expect you at my office?" asked Walsh. "There are matters to be discussed, you know."

"Ah, yes. Well, as soon as possible, we shall be over to see you. No doubt my colleague knows the location of your office."

"This must be a private conference," said Walsh.

"My unasked advice would be," said Judge, "for you to go armed, perfectly sober, and deeply suspicious."

Henry shut one eye and looked at Walsh, who glared at Judge.

"Drunken sot!" snorted Walsh, and walked out of the saloon. At the doorway Ricky Dole grasped Walsh's arm.

"Is that—that the owner of the J Bar C, Ed?" he asked.

"Damn him—yes!" snapped Walsh.

"Hell's delight!" grunted Ricky, and walked over to the hitchrack with Slim and Tug.

Judge caught sight of Danny and insisted on introducing him to Henry.

"It was my pleasure," said Judge, "to act as his counsel in a trial which ended today, and acquitted my friend of murdering your esteemed uncle. Or was he esteemed by you, sir?"

"That will depend," replied Henry, a trifle thickly. "My uncle was merely a name that I must confess I had forgotten. It seems that I am his only living relative. Therefore, as I understand it, I am the last of the line of Conroys. After me—nothing. I must turn posterity over to the other Conroy branches to do with as they please. Not that it makes the least difference now, but I should like to hear something of this Uncle Jim."

"He was a crooked old snake," said Danny seriously.

"Let's have another drink," suggested Henry.

CHAPTER III

MISSING RECORDS

ABOUT THIRTY MINUTES later Henry Harrison Conroy entered the Tonto Bank, his hat tilted over one eye, his cane held jauntily. This had been his stage entrance—and he was still the actor. Walsh led him to his private office, where he proceeded to explain about the untimely death of Jim Conroy, and to explain exactly what Henry had inherited.

"Your cash deposit amounts to exactly eighteen hundred dollars, Mr. Conroy. You have approximately twenty thousand acres of land, twelve hundred head of cattle, sixty to seventy-five head of horses, and all the necessary equipment incidental to a ranch of that size.

"Against all this, we hold Jim Conroy's personal note for the sum of eighteen thousand dollars, which is secured by a second mortgage on the J Bar C. The first mortgage is for ten thousand dollars, and expires late this fall. This was originally for twenty-five thousand, but has been cut to ten thousand."

Henry Harrison Conroy fingered his nose thoughtfully.

"Correct me if I am in error," he said slowly. "I have eighteen hundred dollars in cash, twelve hundred head of cattle, some sixty head of horses, and considerable land. I owe twenty-eight thousand dollars to the bank. Is that correct?"

"Exactly, Mr. Conroy."

"Then," said Henry softly, "why in hell didn't you send me a bill for the balance, and save me the necessity of coming all the way out here?"

"Of course," added the banker, "there will be the current bills, which have accumulated since your uncle died; such as food, salaries for the cowboys and the cook. Possibly some other small items."

Henry sat there, staring down at the carpet.

"My uncle was killed, was he not?"

"Murdered in cold blood. Dan Regan was tried for the murder, but was acquitted today. Regan had trouble with Jim Conroy in the Tonto Saloon. Hot words passed, I believe. Your uncle had a vitriolic tongue. Young Regan rode away ahead of your uncle, who was shot down on his way home."

"I'd like to find his murderer," said Henry as he got to his feet.

"May I ask why?" queried the banker.

"You may, sir," replied Henry, adjusting his tie. "I should love to give him a good hiding with my cane for letting me into such a situation. I give you good day, sir; it's about all I have left to give away."

"FRIJOLE BILL" CULLISON had been the cook and housekeeper for the J Bar C many years. Frijole was sixty years of age and admitted forty. He was five feet three inches tall, would not weigh over a hundred pounds, made his own whisky from prunes, and would fight a wild cat. He wore a pair of huge mustaches, which gave him the appearance, as Slim Pickins said, of a walrus disappointed in love.

Frijole was a natural born liar; but he was not lying as he sat on the porch steps at the J Bar C ranch house, his flour sack apron folded in his lap, and told Henry Harrison Conroy all about Jim Conroy and the Wild Horse Valley.

Henry sat at ease in a broken-down rocker, nursing a badly sunburned nose.

"So my uncle aspired to be the King of the Valley, eh?" mused Henry.

"Well," replied Frijole, "he figgered on goin' higher 'n' that, of course; but he believed in workin' himself up."

"I see. Sort of starting at the bottom. A very wise move."

"Yessir, he shore was ambitious."

"And the King abdicated in favor of the Fool," muttered Henry.

"What'd yuh say?"

"Nothing. You say he bought out a widow's ranch, paid her in cash, and when the bank went busted—"

"It was robbed," corrected Frijole. "Busted into at night, and they took every damn cent in the place. It broke the bank. That was when Walsh took it over. I dunno who backed him; but the widder, Mrs. Harper never got her money back. She's got a pretty daughter, too. Ricky Dole was stuck on her, but she turned him down for Danny Regan, I hear."

"Ah, yes; Danny Regan. Quite a lad, that Danny Regan."

"Tougher 'n hell. Him and Jim Conroy hated each other. He was one little rancher that Jim Conroy couldn't scare."

"Do you believe Danny killed Jim Conroy, Frijole?"

"I dunno. Mebbe he did. Jury says he didn't—and that's good enough for me."

"Do you know Van Treece?"

"Judge Van Treece? Yeah, I know him. I heard him at the trial. And don'tcha ever git an idea that he ain't smart.

"He saved Danny Regan. But he's a drunken old bum, jus-sasame."

"I see. But it seems rather strange that my revered uncle did not keep a set of books."

"Books?"

"Well, some sort of a record. It is the usual thing, I believe."

"You mean, somethin' to show how he stood?"

"Yes."

"Wait a minute."

Frijole went into the house, and came out in a minute, bringing a small, dog-eared notebook, which he gave to Henry.

"I found this under his bureau, after he was buried," said Frijole. "It's got writin' and figures in it. Yuh see, I ain't got no college education; so it don't mean much to me."

"No college, no interest," muttered Henry as he began examining the much-thumbed book, which seemed to contain a jumble of notes and figures, with no indication of continuity, as few pages were dated. Apparently Jim Conroy wrote or figured on any page where the book happened to open at the time.

About in the middle of the book was a dated item which read:

> *Sold to Crenshaw and Co., 522 head at 60. Cut back 37 head at Antelope.*

Near the back of the book was another item:

> *Sold to Crenshaw and Co., 318 head at 62. Cut back 31 head at Antelope.*

These two items were dated about five months apart, and the latter was dated about two weeks before Jim Conroy was killed.

"What is a cut-back?" asked Henry.

"Well, I'll tell yuh," replied Frijole wisely. "Usually a cut-back is a cow that the buyer don't want. Most always they cut back so many head at the shippin' corrals."

"Are the shipping corrals at Antelope?"

"Yeah. We have to herd to Antelope, 'cause we don't have no railroad here."

"I discovered that," said Henry dryly. "You don't mind if I keep this book, do you?"

"I reckon you've done inherited it," smiled the cook. "Walsh tells me that you inherited everythin'."

"**MR. WALSH**," replied Henry, "has a sense of humor. Frijole, I'm wondering."

"Yeah? Wonderin' what?"

"I'm wondering what debts the meek are going to assume when they inherit the earth."

"I ain't gave it much thought," replied Frijole.

"No, I don't suppose you have. But it doesn't matter."

"Anyway," said Frijole, "I've got bread in the oven."

"Just a moment," said Henry, halting Frijole at the doorway. "Frijole, you have no doubt heard me discussed by the cowboys. Just what is their opinion of me as a boss of the J Bar C?"

"Not very damn good," replied the cook.

"I see," said Henry, nodding slowly. "I appreciate your frankness and I—I wish you luck with your bread."

Henry walked down to the stable, where he found Oscar Johnson, horse-wrangler, wood-cutter, and general handy man, repairing a harness.

"Would I be intruding upon your labors if I asked you to take me to town in the buggy?" asked Henry meekly.

"Sure," replied Oscar.

"Good," said Henry.

"Not good," denied Oscar. "Ricky tell me he is the only one to give me orders. He is boss."

"I see. What would happen if you disobeyed him?"

"Ay get fired."

"Right. And if you don't obey me, you get fired. Think it over."

Oscar appeared to be thinking deeply; then:

"Ay am in a hell of a fix," he decided.

"Perfectly marvelous situation," agreed Henry indifferently.

"Ay will harness up the team," decided Oscar.

"We all, at times, show flashes of wisdom, Oscar; and you've made your flash. And if Mr. Dole reprimands you, send him to me."

Henry went straight to the Tonto Bank, where Walsh met him with a hearty handclasp.

"And what do you think of the J Bar C, Mr. Conroy?" he asked, trying to beam over the tops of his glasses.

"I have conflicting emotions," replied Henry. "By the way, do you know if my uncle kept any books on his business?"

"I don't believe he did."

"For instance," said Henry, "his bank deposit book is new, and it appears that the only amount on it is a transfer of balance from a former book which I have not been able to find."

"Yes, I believe that is true," agreed the banker. "But we do not retain the old book."

"I see. Of course, I have discovered some records made by Jim Conroy, noting sales and such things, giving amounts, dates, and all that. It seems that he kept a record of cattle sales and the sale prices, including dates. These, I believe, could be verified through the buyers."

"I—I don't know anything about those things," said the banker. "Oh, yes, I wanted to ask you if you wished to have us continue to handle the legal affairs of the J Bar C. Your uncle was perfectly satisfied with our methods, and we would be glad—"

"No doubt you would," interrupted Henry. "But, as a matter of fact, I have—er—retained an attorney to represent my interests."

"Indeed!"

"Yes; I have engaged Judge Van Treece."

"Van Treece? Why, my dear man—"

"An estimable gentleman with a vast knowledge of law, and who has one of the most wonderful thirsts I have ever met. Good day, sir."

"Now," said Henry to himself as he crossed the street, "I shall have to take the matter up with Van Treece."

WHILE HENRY was at the Tonto Saloon buying a drink for

Oscar and himself, Ricky Dole and Slim Pickins rode into town and tied their horses at the Tonto hitch-rack.

Ricky scowled at the sight of the team and buckboard.

"What the hell's that rig doin' here?" he muttered. "If that damn Swede—"

"Walsh is wavin' to yuh from the bank, Ricky," said Slim.

"Yeah; all right. You lope over to the saloon and see if Oscar is there. I'll be over in a minute."

Ricky joined Walsh, who led the way to his private office.

"How are you and the new boss makin' out?" asked Walsh.

"Aw, he's as loco as a shepherd," replied Ricky. "Ain't got sense enough to pour sand out of his boots."

"I wonder," said the banker, and proceeded to tell Ricky of his conversation with Henry Harrison Conroy.

"What records is he talkin' about?" asked Ricky.

"Maybe he found something."

Ricky gnawed his lower lip.

"I think he's lyin'. But what's his idea of hirin' Van Treece? I wouldn't trust that drunken old liar."

"He's shrewd, Ricky."

"Don't I know it? Records." Ricky frowned thoughtfully. "If Jim Conroy kept any records, I never seen 'em. I tell yuh, there wasn't a damn book nor piece of paper left when I got through."

"Then you think he is bluffing, Ricky?"

"Why should he bluff, Ed? What does he know—or suspect?"

"He said he could check up on shipments through the people whose names appeared as the buyers."

Ricky laughed harshly. "I wish I knew what the fool is thinkin' about."

"Don't figure him too much of a fool," advised Walsh.

"I'll watch him," said Ricky.

As they walked out into the bank they saw the buckboard team turn around in the street and go out of town in a shower of dust.

"There they go," said Walsh.

Ricky nodded and walked over to the Tonto Saloon, where he joined Slim.

"Well?" queried Ricky.

Slim laughed shortly.

"They took a couple quarts with 'em and headed for Regan's ranch. Oscar told him you'd fire him for goin' near Regan's ranch; and he told Oscar that if yuh did, he'd fire you and then make Oscar foreman."

"Oh, he did, did he?" snorted Ricky. "The cabbage-nosed old booze hound! Fire *me*, eh?"

"Well, he owns the ranch, don't he?" asked Slim. "He can fire any of us if he feels thataway, can't he?"

"Why was he goin' out to Regan's ranch?"

"I don't know. Anyway, Ricky, he ain't such a bad sort of a coot. He don't know a headstall from a hondo, but that's all right; he'll learn. He admits bein' ignorant."

"Go ahead and love him, if yuh want to," snarled Ricky.

"Aw, don't git runty," advised Slim. "You'll snort once too often, and he'll send you down the trail talkin' to yourself."

"All right," growled Ricky. "Let's get back to the ranch and forget it."

AND WHILE they rode back to the J Bar C, Henry, Oscar and Judge sat on the little porch of Danny's two-room ranch house, taking their liquor from tin cups. Danny was not at home. Judge was clad in a pair of misfit overalls, a torn shirt and a pair of worn boots. His mop of uncombed gray hair stood up like the roach on a grizzly bear.

"To all of us, including the Viking," toasted Henry, lifting his cup.

"A son of Thor!" exclaimed Judge.

"Skoal!" blurted Oscar, who was beginning to doubt his own capacity. Not that he cared especially.

"Spoken like a loyal Swede," applauded Henry. "But, Oscar,

don't get too polluted. Remember that team almost got away from you, after three drinks. I have no wish to bleach my bones on Arizona sands."

"Ay am de best damn drifer in Arizona," declared Oscar. "Did you efer hear me sink?"

"Sink? Did I ever hear you sink?"

"Ay know good Svede songs."

"Oh! Did I ever hear you sing? Is it an affliction, Oscar?"

"It is," declared Judge. "I've heard it. No wonder the Vikings took to the sea."

"We all have our skeletons in our closets, Oscar," said Henry dryly, "and yours must be vocal. Have another drink and forget your song."

"Ay am joost like mockingbirt," insisted Oscar.

Henry sighed deeply. "I may have to let him sing, Judge."

Oscar downed another cup of whisky, blinked heavily, and adjusted himself to fit more comfortably against a porch post.

"End of Act One," said Henry softly, as Oscar emitted a preparatory snore.

"Mockingbirt!" exclaimed Judge softly.

"We all have our weaknesses," reminded Henry. He corked the bottle and shoved it aside.

"Judge," he said seriously, "I have released Edward Walsh as attorney for the J Bar C, and I want you to act as attorney for what is left to be acted upon."

"Me? My friend, have you gone crazy?"

"Gone? Hell, I've been crazy for years. Here is the situation." Henry outlined the financial condition of the J Bar C, showed Judge the notebook and the bank deposit book. Judge got a piece of paper and a stubby lead pencil. After doing some rapid figuring he said:

"You owe the bank twenty-eight thousand dollars, and you've got only eighteen hundred. The value of cattle is problematical. Of course you might sell the entire herd and have considerable money left, after the bank was paid off. That is, if there was a market, which there isn't at the present time. But, judging from this notebook, the J Bar C sold cattle to Crenshaw & Company to the tune of over fifty thousand dollars. What was done with that money?"

"And," replied Henry, "I drove all the way down here with that wild Swede, only to have you ask me the same question I've been asking myself. Let's have a drink."

Danny rode in, while they were having the drink. He swung out of his saddle and came over to the porch, grinning at them.

"Well, Mr. Conroy, how do yuh like ranchin'?" he asked.

"As yet I have failed to ranch, my boy," said Henry. "Have a drink?"

"Thank yuh kindly," replied Danny, "but I rarely drink."

"Danny," said Judge, "Mr. Conroy has offered me the honor of an appointment as legal adviser for the Conroy estate."

"Holy cow!" snorted Danny. "I—I mean, that's great, Judge. Have yuh told Ed Walsh, Mr. Conroy?"

"Yes," replied Henry expansively. "I—I relieved him of all further responsibility."

"How'd he take it?"

"He was still perpedicular when I walked out," said Henry soberly.

"Well, well! So you are goin' to be a lawyer again, Judge. I suppose you will open up an office in Tonto City and hang out a shingle."

"He will not," said Henry firmly. "He will take up his residence at the J Bar C. He is the first lawyer I ever hired, and I'm going to have him right where I can use him."

"That's fine," said Danny. "I'm goin' to miss my old pardner a lot—but I'm glad for him."

"You can come over to see us, Danny," said Judge.

"And meet that J Bar C bunch? Not a chance, Judge."

"What's wrong with the J Bar C bunch?" demanded Henry.

"Oh, I jist don't mix with 'em," said Danny. "When Jim Conroy was alive, me and him didn't hitch at all. He tried to put me out of business. Then me and Ricky Dole got to kinda gnawin' around at each other. No, I'll stay away from there, if yuh don't mind."

"Ricky Dole, eh?" mused Henry. "The handsome foreman. I expect to hear him break into a tenor solo at any moment. By gad, I've an idea, Regan. I'll discharge Dole and make you foreman."

"No, I wouldn't do that. Why, the first thing you know, you wouldn't have any crew at all. Dole has been there for a long time, and—and—well, it wouldn't be right."

"Do you think the rest of the crew would quit?" asked Henry.

"Well, I don't say they all would."

"But enough to make me shorthanded, as they say."

"Yes, I think that's right."

"Good! I'll fire Dole and let the rest quit. My caste is too damn big, anyway. You and Judge move over tomorrow. Let's have one more drink. Oh—oh, the Viking is coming to life."

"Joost like mockingbirt," mumbled Oscar.

CHAPTER IV

A BULLET AT A BANQUET

REGARDLESS OF HOW he felt about it, Ricky Dole, the handsome foreman, accepted his dismissal calmly. Tug Evans decided that he wanted to quit; so Henry gave him a check on the Tonto Bank, and watched the two cowboys ride away.

Henry called Slim Pickins, Oscar Johnson, and Fred Simpson to the house, and explained that Danny Regan would be the new foreman of the J Bar C.

"Suits me," said Slim. "A job's a job with me."

"Same here," agreed Simpson.

"Ay don't give damn," said Oscar.

"You drive as though you didn't," said Henry dryly.

Frijole, the cook, had already sworn allegiance to Henry.

"I jist cook, and I don't care a damn who eats it," he said.

"Let the applause fall where it may," smiled Henry. "Well, I don't need to tell you boys that I don't know a cow from a kangaroo rat. I've never been on the back of a horse—and until they have decided offhand that I'm the boss around here I'm not going to get on any of them.

"This ranch was wished on me. I've been on the stage for forty years, and that is all I know. I thought I was the only comedian in the Conroy family, until I was made the legal heir to this ranch, when I discovered that—well, no matter."

"This here is shore a fine spread, Mr. Conroy," said Slim. "There ain't a better cow outfit in the State."

"God be merciful to the others, then," sighed Henry.

"Yore uncle made plenty money," said Frijole.

"He did, eh? What did he do with it?"

"I dunno. Mebbe he put it in the bank."

"Well, gosh!" grunted Slim. "That there last shipment must have been worth twenty thousand or more. That was only a little while before he was killed. He sold lotsa cows. Sellin' cows was what got the small ranchers sore at him. Why, every time a buyer came into the valley Jim Conroy'd fill his order, even if he had to sell below the market. Things like that soon bust a small cowman."

Henry rubbed his nose reflectively. "I see. And so they measured him for a golden harp."

"He was pretty good on a fiddle," said Frijole.

"They say the same thing about Nero," said Henry. "They might frame up a duet—and let my uncle do the comedy."

"He played by ear," offered Frijole innocently.

Danny and Judge came that afternoon and were installed by Henry, who greeted them expansively. "Welcome to the best cow ranch in the State, gentlemen."

"Not bad," agreed Judge. "I've seen better, but it will do."

"Oh, I expect to improve it," said Henry. "I suppose you are bubbling over with ideas on the betterment of cows. By the way, what does a cow expect?"

"Who knows?" replied Judge soberly. "It is a worthy subject for debate—but not in a sober state of mind. Danny, have you ever attempted to read the mind of a cow?"

"No," laughed Danny. "I don't reckon a cow has a mind."

"You do not believe they expect anything?" asked Henry.

"Oh, food and water, I reckon."

"I see. After all, a human trait. Danny, I'm not presuming to give you any orders. Meet the cows, if you feel inclined. Talk things over with the cowboys, or do what you please; Judge and I are going to hold a conference."

DANNY REGAN found the three cowboys down in the bunkhouse, and they greeted him in a friendly manner.

"The boss fired Ricky, and Tug quit," explained Slim.

Danny nodded and looked them over.

"I want yuh to understand that I didn't bump Ricky out of his job," explained Danny. "Mr. Conroy got the idea—and I kinda think he carries out his own ideas."

"He's all right," said Slim. "He admits that he don't know a thing about ranchin'. We all know how things was between you and this ranch, Regan. But that was between you and Ricky, or you and Jim Conroy. We never was asked to mix into things. Even if some of the things Jim Conroy done wasn't exactly accordin' to Hoyle, it wasn't none of our business."

"This Conroy will give everybody a square deal, I think, Slim."

"He shore tickles me," said Fred Simpson. "All dressed up thataway, packing a gold-headed cane. Danny, does he actually *shine* his nose on purpose?"

Danny grinned and shook his head.

"I don't reckon so, Fred. He told the Judge that he was on the stage—you know what I mean—an actor—for years and years, makin' people laugh with that funny nose."

"Uh-huh," nodded Slim. "And his nose don't know yet that he ain't a actor no more."

"I reckon that's it," chuckled Danny. "Anyway, they're a good pair—him and Judge. They can use words I never heard of—and know what they mean. Judge was a city lawyer before he tried to keep the distilleries workin' day and night."

Danny walked to the doorway and saw Frijole coming, carrying a hatchet.

"You ain't on the warpath already, are yuh?" asked Danny.

"I'm on the chicken path," replied the cook. "He-e-ey! Some of you punchers come and help me. The boss says we're goin' to start this here new ree-gee-me with a banquet; so I'm goin' to kill off Annabel, Clarice, and Powder River."

"Spring chicken?" asked Danny.

"Spring of 1896—and tough. Powder River has done whipped seven coyotes. C'mon, you fellers! Gump stew for supper!"

The three chickens were in the stewpot, when Bill Parton, the sheriff, and Rolling Stone, the deputy, arrived at the ranch. Parton was a big man, slightly gray, hard-faced, and big of hand.

Rolling Stone was an undersized, bandy-legged person, partly bald, and with an overdeveloped sense of humor, which did not always please the sheriff. Neither of the officers had met Henry.

Judging from outward appearances, the conference between Henry and Judge had been a liquid success.

"Sheriff," said Judge expansively, and a bit owlishly, "I wan' you t' meet the grea'est man since Shakespeare. It is my pleasure t' preshent Hennery Conroy. Hennery, thish is Sher'ff Parton."

"Sheriff, the pleasure is all mine," said Henry. "I hope you didn't come out here to stop the show."

"What show was that?" asked the sheriff.

"No matter," replied Henry, holding out an uncertain hand to the grinning deputy.

"My name's Stone," said the deputy.

"**A SOLID** name," said Henry seriously. "Welcome to the J Bar C, gentlemen. You arrive at an opportune time. My chef is now in the act of preparing a banquet, of which I hope you will partake. It signifies a new regime at this ranch."

"I knowed Jim Conroy well," said the sheriff. "A solid citizen."

"Not too solid," said the deputy. "That thirty-thirty went plumb through him."

"Yuh didn't need to make that remark, Rollin'," said the sheriff. "It was his uncle, and yuh ort to show some consideration."

"I wish my uncle had," said Henry sadly. "But we digress. Judge, please find the corkscrew, will you—and a fresh bottle."

It was long after dark, before Frijole decided that the two old hens and the rooster were done. Danny and Frijole were the only sober people on the ranch; so they piled the food on the long table, while Henry stood at one end of the table and made a grandiloquent speech, which nobody heard. Part of it was from Hamlet's Soliloquy, and part from "East Lynne."

"And I," concluded Henry, hammering himself violently on the chest, "am the last of the Conroy family."

"Now look what yuh done!" wailed Rolling Stone. "You've made the sheriff cry."

"All he's done is blubber for the last hour," complained Judge. "If there's anythin' I hate it's a blubberin' sher'ff."

"Be sheated, gen'lemen," said Henry.

"Same to you, par'ner," said Slim owlishly. "We've all been down for five minutes."

There was no silver and fine linens at the J Bar C. The cloth was white oilcloth, and there were no napkins. The knives and forks were steel, and the huge pot of stewed chicken, flanked by catsup and sundry bottles of seasoning, made the centerpiece.

Judge Van Treece sat midway on the right-hand side of the table, and now he stood up unsteadily and grasped a huge spoon.

"I hereby appoint myshelf as official server," he announced. "Hennery, pash your plate."

Crash!

The bowl of stew seemed to explode in the midst of the diners. In fact, everything on the table seemed to explode, while a shattered window-pane added to the flying missiles. Henry went over backwards, chair and all, while Judge went backwards, crashing over his chair to the door, while from outside came the rattling report of a rifle.

Danny was almost to the table, bearing a pot of coffee, which he promptly dropped. For a moment no one seemed to know exactly what had happened. Then Danny swiftly drew his gun and sent a bullet smashing into the big hanging lamp over the center of the table.

ONLY a few short seconds elapsed from the rifle shot until they were in darkness, except for the light in the kitchen. Danny sprang back to the kitchen, blew out the lamp and flung open the door. After a moment or two he ducked outside, but could see nothing in the darkness. He went back in, closed the door, and stepped into the dining room.

"What went wrong?" asked Frijole. "Did somebody shoot through the winder, or did Powder River explode?"

"Don't light a lamp," warned Danny. "Wait'll I cover the window."

Several moments were consumed in covering the window. Then he lighted the kitchen lamp and brought it into the dining room.

"The boss—he got it!" gasped Slim.

"Killed!" snorted the sobered sheriff. "Gawd, look at the blood!"

"Shot his head plumb off!" exploded Rolling Stone.

"No!" gasped Judge, lifting his face above the table. Most of the stew had exploded in his face, and the leg of a chicken was between his collar bone and neck. He fairly dripped stew.

"Didja ever see so much blood?" gasped the sheriff.

Henry, a gory sight, sat up like a mechanical toy.

"The last of the Conroys!" he whispered. "The last."

"Catsup!" snorted Danny. "That ain't blood."

He grabbed a towel out of Frijole's hand and mopped Henry's face. Except for a swelling over his left eye, he seemed to be unhurt.

Henry looked at him, a whimsical smile on his face.

"No tonic," he said calmly. "Comb it dry."

The sheriff was over at the window, examining the broken pane, and now he crossed the room and found where the mushroomed bullet had smashed into the plaster. The ceiling and walls were spattered with stew, and one side of the metal container had a huge hole. Only a piece of the catsup bottle was in evidence.

Henry got to his feet, shaking his head.

"Somebody shot through the window," explained Danny.

Henry looked blankly at Danny.

"Shot through the window?" he queried. "Why?"

"That's what I want to know," rumbled the sheriff.

"There's no use goin' out there in the dark," said Danny.

The sheriff drew him aside, and they looked inquiringly at each other.

Danny shook his head as he said softly:

"It looks like they meant it for Henry Conroy."

"Why in hell would anybody want to kill him, Danny?"

"*Quien sabe?* He was in line with that shot. That stew pot and the catsup bottle must have deflected the bullet."

"Hanging would be too good for 'em," declared Judge. "Look at me! I'm—I'm stewed. Henry, are you all right?"

"I—I seem to have blank moments," replied Henry. "I must

say that a combination of stew and catsup, propelled by a bullet, has a mighty sobering effect. Don't you find it so, Judge?"

"Quite so."

"If yuh don't think them hens was tough, take a look at that bullet," invited Frijole. "Flattened her right out."

"The hen?" asked the deputy.

"Na-a-a-aw—the bullet."

The *pièce de résistance* was scattered and lost, but it did not seem to matter, as appetites had vanished with the stew.

The sheriff seemed very unhappy over the incident. "If somebody done that for a joke, I'd like to tell 'em my opinion of it," he said.

"It does seem like carrying comedy to the nth degree," admitted Henry, as he dug a gob of catsup from his left ear. "I love a good joke, even at my expense—but not at the expense of my life. The perpetrator of that act was a bad actor."

Judge cleared his throat. "A bad actor, indeed," he agreed warmly. "Wasn't it the immortal Shakespeare who said that all the world is a stage?"

"He did," agreed Henry. "But he never said a damn word about a shooting gallery."

"How about me cookin' up a flock of ham and eggs?" asked Frijole. "We're plumb out of poultry."

"That," said Henry, "is the first real sensible thing that has been said since Catsup's Last Stand. You win, Frijole."

"Why don't you say somethin', Oscar?" asked Slim. "All you've done is set there, bug-eyed. Ain't yuh got no ideas?"

"Ay don't give damn about the bullet," said Oscar, "but Ay do love stew. Ay like to keek the pants from the man who shoot hole in the pot."

"The Swedes," said Judge, "have no imagination."

"One did," said Frijole. "He was the one that invented that doojingus key that opens sardine cans."

"Possibly. However, it was merely a quicker way to get at food."

"How about havin''em all fried?"

"Swedes?" asked Slim.

"No, you dumb saddle-slicker—eggs!"

Supper was finished without further incident, and the two officers went back to Tonto City. Ricky Dole and Tug Evans were in a poker game, both half drunk. The sheriff's discreet questioning of Pat Shannon, the saloonkeeper, showed that both of the ex-cowboys of the J Bar C had spent the entire evening in the Tonto Saloon.

"You didn't figure that Ricky was sore enough over losin' his job to try to murder Conroy, didja?" asked the deputy, after they left the saloon.

"You figure a better reason, will yuh?" retorted the sheriff.

"I swore to help yuh uphold the law—not to be a fortune teller," replied Rolling Stone. "But I still think it was a joke."

"Now," said the sheriff, "I know where they got the expression—Joker Wild."

CHAPTER V

MYSTERIOUS MURDER

"IN MY OPINION," said Judge next morning, as he and Henry sat on the porch of the ranch house, "it was a deliberate attempt to murder you, Henry."

Henry flinched visibly at this disquieting statement.

"Somebody," continued Judge, "desires your death."

Henry squinted at the sunlit hills and rubbed his nose, which was already a deep brick color.

"And they'll try it again," finished Judge.

"I'm afraid," replied Henry, "that it will be a case of love's labors lost."

"In what way, Henry?"

"I'll be scared to death before they have another chance."

"You jest, my friend."

"I do, like hell! Jest at murder? Jest?" Henry closed his eyes and leaned back in his chair.

"Who knows? Perchance some local *Hamlet* saying, 'Alas, poor Henry! I knew him, Judge; a fellow of infinite jest, of most excellent fancy—where be your gibes now, your gambols—'"

"A Yorick of Wild Horse Valley," sighed Judge.

"I think," said Henry soberly, "I shall carry a gun."

"And I think," added Judge, "that we shall ask Oscar to hitch up the team; so we may ride to town."

"And for why, may I ask?"

"You may, Henry. Someone inadvertently left the cork out of that last quart, and it was tipped over."

"Summon the Viking at once, Judge. I had sworn never to ride with him again—but what difference the mode of passing? I believe I should as soon die in a buckboard wreck as to have a catsup bottle driven through my vitals."

Oscar was willing to do the driving. He had an all-consuming thirst, and the prospects of getting it quenched were excellent. They met Leila Harper on the street, and she invited them to come into their shop, where Henry met Mrs. Harper for the first time.

"You do not favor your uncle," said Mrs. Harper critically.

"Nor did he favor me, Mrs. Harper," replied Henry dryly. "Still I have met some wonderful people here."

"Yes," added Judge, "and one of them tried to shoot him through the window last night."

"I heard something about that," said Leila. "I don't see why any one would want to kill *you*, Mr. Conroy."

"Sins of the uncle, perhaps," said Henry blandly. "But no matter—I am alive. Mrs. Harper, I have heard some of the things my late uncle is supposed to have done to you; I want to assure you that I do not believe in heredity. I have no ambition to own this valley."

"I am sure the valley will be pleased," said Mrs. Harper. "We were pleased to know that you have made Danny Regan foreman."

"A great boy, that Danny Regan, Mrs. Harper. Wonderful sense of humor."

"Danny knows cattle, Mr. Conroy," said Leila.

Henry looked at her critically and nodded.

"Danny," he said, "uses very good judgment in other things too."

Leila flushed and quickly turned to Judge, who was looking through the window at the main street.

"I notice that the ex-foreman is still in town," he said.

"He and Tug Evans have been drunk ever since they have been in town," she replied.

"Boys will be boys," he told her.

"I know, but—" Leila shook her head.

"But what, my dear?"

"I hear that Ricky is blaming Danny for losing his job."

"Don't worry about that."

"Judge, who tried to kill Mr. Conroy last night?"

"I wish I could answer that, Leila."

"Are you sure it was Mr. Conroy, and not Danny, they shot at?"

"**LEILA**, I wouldn't be willing to give my oath that it wasn't aimed at me, or the sheriff. But the stew pot and the catsup bottle saved Henry Conroy, I'm certain. I suppose the only thing we can do is to wait and—I was going to say, wait until they do kill somebody; so we can be sure. But that isn't sensible."

"I know I'll feel better when Ricky and Tug have left the valley," said Leila.

"They won't stay long," assured Judge. "As soon as their money runs out, they'll hunt for a job."

"Mother and Mr. Conroy seem to be getting on fine," said Leila softly.

Judge grinned slowly, and they went to the back of the room, where Henry was perched on the arm of a chair, talking to Mrs. Harper.

"Well, I suppose we must be going, Judge," he said briskly. "We must find Oscar before he gets to a speed condition."

"Come in again, won't you?" asked Mrs. Harper.

"Thank you," smiled Henry. "Come out and see us. Isn't that the proper thing—trading visits?"

"Not here," laughed Leila. "Come in when you can."

They went back to the buckboard, where Oscar joined them.

"Pretty, isn't she?" said Judge.

"A very pleasant, likable woman," agreed Henry.

"I meant Leila."

"Oh!"

They settled themselves in the buckboard, while Oscar untied the team.

"Do you know, Judge," said Henry, "my knowledge of the cattle ranges was limited to a few Western plays I have seen; but my impression was that white women were so scarce that one naturally married a squaw. Or just one white girl, who married the hero."

"You're not on a stage now, my friend," said Judge. "And what has marriage got to do with it, anyway?"

"I'm sure I don't know."

"Anyway, we're too old to marry, Henry."

"Speak for yourself, will you?"

"You hired me to give you advice."

"When I ask for it—yes. Leave my age out of things."

"Huh! Next thing I know, you'll be playing a guitar."

"Or a harp," added Henry. "Oscar, did you get the liquor?"

"Sure."

Oscar did not try to break any speed records. A mile out of

town the road led around the point of a low hill, on which was the Tonto cemetery, a small cluster of badly kept graves.

"Except for the stew pot," said Oscar, pointing with his whip, "das is where you would be planted."

Henry shuddered slightly. "You have such sweet thoughts, Oscar."

"Sure," agreed Oscar. "Ay am Svede."

"I said 'sweet'! S-w-e-e-t."

"Das all right," nodded Oscar. "Ay don't spell very goot myself."

"And for forty years I tried to think up funny things," sighed Henry.

THAT EVENING Danny decided to ride to Tonto City and see Leila. Judge told him that Leila was worried about what Ricky Dole and Tug Evans might do.

"You better go in and talk with 'em, Danny," advised Judge.

"Sure," agreed Danny. "I'll go. Want to ride in with me?"

"No, not tonight. Henry and I are having an important conference."

"I saw it in the back of the buckboard," nodded Danny. "Please keep the windows covered, Judge."

It was about an hour after dark when Danny tied his horse in front of the millinery store. He could see that both Leila and her mother were disturbed over something, and finally Leila explained.

"Rick Dole came over here an hour or so ago, Danny. He was very drunk. I tried to get him to leave, but he would not. He said he was going to whip you for taking his job away. Oh, he's terrible, Danny. I never argued with him—merely tried to get him to leave. I don't know what might have happened, except that Rolling Stone knew he was here and came after him. They had words, and I thought it might end seriously, but Rolling got him out.

"Rolling came back and asked me if I'd be willing to swear

out a warrant against him; but I didn't want to do that, Danny. I want him to get out of the country. Then Rolling came back with a shotgun and laid it there on the counter. He said, 'If he comes back, hand him a load of buckshot, Leila.'"

"It was a terrible experience," sighed Mrs. Harper.

Danny's blue eyes were as hard as tempered steel.

"If you'll excuse me for a few moments," he said softly. "I—I've got a little errand—"

"No, Danny—don't!" exclaimed Leila. "Don't go over there."

"But," protested Danny, "don't yuh see—I've got to do it."

"No, Danny. We're all right. It might mean bad trouble. You know how he is—and there's two of them, both drunk."

Danny nodded slowly. "I see—both drunk. Mebbe tomorrow they'll be sober. I'll come back tomorrow."

"Let's sit down and talk," suggested Mrs. Harper. "You haven't been here for a good talk in ages, Danny."

They went to the rear, where the Harpers kept house, and sat down to talk over the things that had happened since before Danny had been arrested for killing Jim Conroy. They talked for an hour, or more, when Danny decided it was time to go home.

"Will you take that shotgun back to the sheriff's office?" asked Mrs. Harper. "Neither of us could shoot it—and I'm afraid to have a loaded gun in the house."

Danny wanted to show them how to operate the gun, but they both declined—with thanks.

After telling them good night Danny led his horse down to the sheriff's office, but the door was closed and locked. He did not want to leave the gun outside; so he decided to take it out to the ranch and bring it back next day.

Over at the Tonto Saloon, Ricky Dole and Tug Evans were standing at the bar, arguing over a dice game. Both cowboys were undeniably drunk and quarrelsome. Sitting on the edge of a card table was Rolling Stone, the little deputy. In the parlance of the range, he was "riding herd" on these two. They knew it. At times they looked at him malevolently, but confined their remarks to impersonal statements.

"Do yuh know, Ricky," said Tug owlishly, "I 'member about a feller who was watched by a deputy sher'ff until he got so awful sore that he killed the deputy. 'S a fac'. And they didn't hang the feller, nor they didn't put 'im in jail, even."

"Shouldn't," stated Ricky. "Ought t' give 'im a medal."

"They didn't give 'im no medal," said Tug. "He was nawful good shot, too. They didn't hang him, and they didn't jail him, and he didn't even try to get away."

"MUS' HAVE been a wonnerful place to live," said Ricky. "What happened to him?"

"Sher'ff shot him!" Tug doubled up in a paroxysm of mirth.

"That ain't funny to me," declared Ricky, turning around, with his back to the bar, and glowering at the deputy from under the brim of his big hat.

"Why don't you go home and go to bed, Stone?" he asked.

"Same to you, feller," retorted the tough little officer.

"Yea-a-a-ah?" sneered Ricky.

"Might's well," declared Tug. "Thish place is dead. Let's go over to the hotel and grab a li'l shut-eye, Ricky."

"All right," agreed Ricky. "C'mon, Stone."

"Why should I go?" asked the deputy.

"Why? To see that we don't snore; yo're so particular."

Ricky started for the door, closely followed by Evans, but at the doorway Ricky stepped aside and tripped Evans, who went blundering over the door-sill and out on the porch.

An instant later the roar of a shotgun shattered the quiet of the street, and buckshot screamed through the doorway. Rolling Stone felt one of them tug at his boot top. The bartender dropped behind the bar, knocking down a pile of glasses. Ricky Dole, out of line with the shot, backed heavily against the wall beside the doorway.

The deputy sprang recklessly through the doorway, gun in

hand, and nearly tripped over Tug Evans. It was too dark for him to see any one on the street. Evans was dead—drilled full of buckshot. They carried him into the saloon and sent for a doctor; but they knew it was no use.

Ricky was sobered, but had nothing to say. He realized that only his rough horseplay with Tug at the doorway had saved him from being in Tug's place.

The news spread quickly. Bill Parton, the sheriff, came while the doctor was there, and got the details from his deputy.

Back at their office Rolling told about Ricky annoying Mrs. Harper and Leila.

"I loaned 'em our shotgun," said Rolling.

"You did, eh?" said the sheriff. "Aw, shucks, they never done this!"

"Of course they didn't."

The sheriff put on his hat and went up to Harper's place. Someone had told them what had happened, and Parton could see that both women were greatly agitated.

"Rollin' left a shotgun here, didn't he?" asked Parton.

Leila turned away; but Mrs. Harper nodded.

Parton looked at them thoughtfully. "Where is the gun now?"

Mrs. Harper drew a deep breath, hesitated. Leila turned.

"Danny Regan was here this evening," she said. "We—we gave him the gun to take back to your office."

"Oh!" exclaimed Parton softly. "Leila, how long was it after he left until that shot was fired?"

"He didn't do it," said Leila. "Danny is not a murderer."

"How long, Leila?"

"About fifteen minutes."

"Did you see which way Danny went?"

"He went toward your office, leading his horse. He said he would leave the gun at your office."

The sheriff nodded grimly and walked out. Rolling was still at the office, and Parton told him.

"I was over at the Tonto, and the office door was locked," said the deputy.

"There was buckshot shells in the gun, wasn't there?"

The deputy nodded.

"Hell!" snorted Parton. "I suppose we've got to get Danny."

"Better wait until mornin', Bill."

"He could be out of the valley by mornin'."

"That's what I was thinkin'."

"Uh-huh. Well, all right. Anyway, if he's guilty he's already on his way. How many shells was in that old pump-gun?"

"I don't know," replied the deputy.

The sheriff looked at him thoughtfully.

"You kinda like Danny, don'tcha?" he asked.

"No," replied the deputy, "I never did like Tug Evans."

"Uh-huh," nodded the sheriff. "I thought so. Might as well go to bed."

CHAPTER VI

CORONER'S INQUEST

DR. JOHN CLEMENS, the coroner, was very serious regarding his official capacity. He talked with Ricky Dole, who was cold sober next morning, and Ricky knew that Danny Regan had been in town. The coroner talked with Leila and her mother, who did not think to conceal the fact that Danny had taken that shotgun. To Dr. Clemens it was as simple as two and two. Danny had taken Ricky's job, and there had been a previous rivalry between them over Leila Harper.

After a talk with Rolling Stone, in which the deputy spoke of Ricky annoying Leila and her mother, the coroner's case was complete. He had made up his mind that Danny killed Tug Evans with a shotgun belonging to the sheriff's office.

Doctor Clemens confinded his findings to Paul Baker, the

elderly prosecutor, who was still smarting over his failure to convict Danny for the murder of Jim Conroy, and together they went to see the sheriff.

"You better go right out and arrest Regan," said the lawyer, and added maliciously, "If he hasn't already left the country."

"Are you willin' to charge him with the murder?" asked Parton.

"There's enough evidence right now to hang him."

"I'll bring him in for the inquest."

"Yes, and you better bring him in irons."

"You ain't tryin' to tell me how to run my office, are yuh, Paul?" asked the sheriff. "Hello! It kinda looks like Danny was bringin' himself in. Who the devil is that with him?"

It was Henry Harrison Conroy with Danny. Henry, wearing a big sombrero, bat-wing chaps and high-heel boots, and riding a sway-backed, gray horse, which had been a J Bar C pensioner for years. Buffalo Bill never sat straighter in his saddle than Henry. Danny's eyes were dancing, but his face was deadly serious, and across the fork of his saddle he carried that sawed-off Winchester pump-gun.

"Brought yore gun back, Bill," he said, handing the gun to the sheriff. "I owe yuh for the shells that was in it. We used 'em up on some tin cans at the ranch."

"How—" the sheriff hesitated. "How many shells was in it, Dan?"

Danny turned to Henry. "How many did we shoot?"

"We!" snorted Henry. "I fired one—and the gun kicked me into the watering trough." He eased himself carefully in the saddle. "Danny, which side of this is the exit?"

"Wait—I'll help you down."

"You'll not! *You'll... not... help... me... down.* You got me into this damn outfit. You said I'd have to dress like this, if I intended to be a cattleman. You said I'd have to ride a horse. And now you want to *help me down* right in sight of Tonto City. I'll get down alone, if I have to fall down."

"You might learn Methusalem to kneel," suggested the sheriff soberly.

"How many cartridges were in that gun?" interrupted the lawyer.

Danny looked curiously at him. "What difference does that make?"

"You might tell him, sheriff," said the lawyer grimly.

Parton looked at the shotgun, frowned heavily and looked at the young cowboy, as he said:

"After Mrs. Harper gave yuh this gun last night, where didja go?"

"What's the big idea, Bill? Anythin' wrong with the gun?"

"I'm askin' a question, Danny."

"Well, I went down to yore office, but it was locked; so I got on my horse and went home, takin' the gun with me."

"Can you prove that?" asked the lawyer.

"What's the matter with that jigger, Bill?" asked Danny.

"Somebody murdered Tug Evans with a shotgun last night, Danny."

"Murdered Tug Evans?"

"Shot him in the doorway of the Tonto Saloon."

"Well, I'll be darned!" exclaimed Danny.

"You will probably be more than that," said the prosecutor.

"Wait a minute!" flared Danny. "Why would I kill Tug Evans?"

"You mistook him for Ricky Dole."

"I—don't be a damn fool! They don't even look alike in the dark."

"The shot was intended for Ricky Dole," said the lawyer stubbornly. "Dole started out ahead of Evans, but turned and tripped Evans out through the doorway ahead of him."

DANNY looked at him keenly. "It kinda looks as though Ricky knew somebody was out there."

"I never thought of that angle," said the sheriff.

"Don't jump at foolish conclusions," advised the lawyer. "If you don't arrest Regan on the evidence—"

"Arrest me?" queried Danny, straightening in his saddle.

"What can I do?" asked the sheriff. "If the prosecutor says the word—oh!"

The "oh!" was occasioned, when Danny drew his gun, leaning down close to the sheriff, but watching all three men.

"I'm not goin' to be throwed in jail for somethin' I didn't do," he said coldly. "You had me there a damn long time for somethin' I didn't do—but not again. Unbuckle yore gun-belt, Bill. Just let it drop. Never mind the shotgun—it's empty."

Danny looked at the astonished Henry, laughed shortly and rode swiftly out of Tonto City. The sheriff smiled grimly, as he picked up his gun-belt and buckled it around his waist.

"Yo're a hell of a sheriff!" snorted the lawyer. "Get on your horse and catch him!"

The sheriff looked at him coldly, as he replied:

"You and Doc go back and get ready for yore inquest. If you'd kept yore snoot out of this, Danny Regan would have been here to testify at the inquest. As it is, you'll get along without him."

Henry scratched his nose thoughtfully, as the two men walked up the street.

"Well," he said wearily, "I'll try and get down—even if I know I'll never get up again."

The sheriff watched Henry prepare to dismount.

"Slide yore left foot nearly out of the stirrup," he advised. "That'll let yore left foot drop out easy, when yore right is down. Always play safe with that left foot, 'cause a bad horse might jump away and yore foot might hang up in the stirrup."

"Thank you, officer," replied Henry. "In the event that this equine should awaken and—"

Smack! Henry's left foot slipped, while his right was elevated over the rump of the animal. He made a plunging fall, flung both arms around the animal's neck, and literally did a swing over to the sidewalk, where he came down in a sitting position. The old gray looked at him accusingly, sighed and went to sleep.

"Neat, but not gaudy," panted Henry. "You might say, I got the hang of it very quickly."

"It's quite a trick," admitted the sheriff. "I'll bet there ain't a puncher in this valley that can dismount like that."

"Merely a matter of balance," assured Henry. "Suppose I should buy a drink—would you explain to me what this shooting is all about?"

"I reckon yo're entitled to know as much as I do," replied the sheriff, as they went to the Tonto, where he showed Henry the effects of buckshot on the walls and furniture.

In less than an hour Judge, Slim, Fred and Oscar came to town. Danny had told them, and they came in a body to find out about things. Henry met them, his sombrero cocked over one eye, very unsteady on his unaccustomed high-heels, and very red of nose.

"Welcome to Mysteryville," he said expansively.

"So you got off yore horse all right, eh?" said Slim. "Danny was worried about yuh."

"He didn't need to worry," assured the sheriff who was none too sober. "Henry gets off a horse as completely as any man I have ever seen."

"Merely a matter of balance," assured Henry. "I have complete control of equilibr'm."

"I desire a résumé of what you know about the shooting," said Judge stiffly.

"I reckon you better wait until the inquest, Judge," said the sheriff. "We'll be holdin' it soon."

"Where?"

"Over in that vacant room next to the bank."

RICKY DOLE was around town, cold sober. He seemed to keep away from everybody, and did not care to talk about the shooting. Ricky realized how close he came to being murdered. The inquest was held in a vacant store-room, where they had moved the corpse from the saloon. The curious crowd craned their necks for a sight of the tarpaulin-covered pile on a plain board table at the rear of the room, while the officers prepared for the hearing.

A six-man jury was quickly selected. Ricky Dole was the first witness, cool and collected. His story was simply told. He did not know of any reason why Tug Evans was murdered. Rolling Stone, the deputy, substantiated what had occurred in the saloon, as did the bartender. Mrs. Harper and Leila had been summoned, but only Mrs. Harper was asked to testify. She told of the trouble at the shop with Ricky earlier in the evening, and of Rolling Stone bringing the shotgun, as a defense weapon for them.

She told of Danny's visit, and that she asked him to take the gun back to the sheriff's office.

"Mrs. Harper," said the coroner, "about how long was it after Dan Regan left your place that you heard the shot fired?"

"Possibly fifteen minutes," she replied.

"Danny Regan hated Ricky Dole, did he not?"

"I object to that!" snapped Judge Van Treece. "That is a leading question—and Danny Regan is not on trial."

"He soon will be," said the prosecutor.

"You've heard of the Frenchman's Flea Powder, haven't you, Baker?" asked Judge. "First you catch the flea—"

"Isn't it a fact that Danny Regan took Ricky Dole's position as foreman at the J Bar C?" asked the coroner.

Henry got to his feet and faced the coroner.

"I beg your pardon, sir," he said heavily, "but as a matter of fact, I fired Mr. Dole and hired Mr. Regan. Mr. Regan had nothing to do with it, sir. Men do not *take* positions on the J Bar C—I give them the positions."

Ricky scowled at Henry, his lips shut tightly. The coroner took the stand and testified as to the cause of death. He let the prosecutor sum up the evidence, which really instructed the jury to ask for the arrest of Danny Regan, charging him with first-degree murder.

Henry and Judge walked down the street with Mrs. Harper and Leila.

"My dear lady, you couldn't help testifying," said Henry. "Do not feel bad about it."

"But Danny never shot him," insisted Leila.

"Granted. My dear girl, I do not need proofs."

They stopped in front of the millinery store, as the sheriff came past.

"Oh, he's going after Danny!" choked Leila.

"Don't worry," said Henry softly. "I sent Slim home before the case went to the jury."

"But he can't dodge all his life," said Leila.

Henry Harrison Conroy's lips tightened, and for once in his life he looked anything but a comedian.

"He may not have to," said Henry coldly.

"We might go down there and delay the sheriff a little," said Judge.

"Right," agreed Henry. "If you ladies will excuse us—"

"We shall be back," said Judge, and they hurried.

"Damnable!" snorted Henry. "They are really damnable, Judge."

"Those women?"

"No—these boots!"

AT THE SHERIFF'S office they found Rolling Stone and the sheriff preparing to carry out the orders of the jury.

"There ain't no use hurryin'," argued the deputy. "I seen Slim Pickins pull out twenty minutes ago, headin' for the ranch. If we find Dan Regan by this time next month, I'll be surprised."

"We are really having wonderful weather for murder," said Henry. "I've never seen better. That should be an advertising point for Wild Horse Valley. Why not establish a Better Murder Bureau?"

The sheriff looked curiously at Henry and then jerked around toward the doorway, as they heard the sound of hurrying feet on the wooden sidewalk. It was the prosecutor and the coroner, who came in, all out of breath. They stopped panting. Twice the coroner opened his mouth, like a fish out of water, gasping for breath. Then he blurted:

"My God! The corpse is gone!"

"Gone?" The sheriff stared at the two men.

"Gone!" parroted the lawyer. "We—we looked. The body was supposed to be under that tarpaulin, and all we found was a bundle of old sacks and a couple of old buckets."

"Show me!" snapped the sheriff.

They all went up to the store-room and gazed at the remains.

"We brought the body here last night," said the coroner. "I worked over it until after midnight. Barney Eastland was in here. Baker was here until a short time before I locked up the place. Ed Walsh was here and so was Pat Shannon. Walsh and Shannon were here, when I finished my work. There was no use of an autopsy—we knew what killed him; so I had fixed up the body, ready for burial. I don't know why we happened to remove the tarpaulin a few minutes ago."

The sheriff nodded thoughtfully.

"What is to be done?" asked the coroner.

"What would you suggest?" asked the sheriff. "We're just shy one corpse, that's all."

"*Corpus delicti,*" murmured Judge.

"I've been waiting for you to say that!" snapped the prosecutor.

"Something like a Chinese laundry, eh?" said Henry. "No tickee, no laundry. Only in this case, no corpse, no murder charge."

The sheriff smiled thinly. "I reckon that's right, gents."

"And I'm jist wonderin' how yuh could trail a dead man," said the deputy. "Doc, did you examine him real close? Mebbe he wasn't so awful dead."

"He was dead," replied the coroner gloomily.

"Is that the first corpse that ever got away from you?" asked Henry. "I didn't suppose that a doctor ever let anyone get away dead or alive."

"Of all the fool remarks!" snapped the prosecutor.

"Judge," said Henry, "I really feel the need of a drink. Will you disgruntled gentlemen join us?"

"I do not drink!" snapped the coroner.

"I see," murmured Henry. "Some people get that way without liquor. Come with me, Judge—you, Mr. Parton and Mr. Stone?"

"Yea-a-ah," drawled the sheriff.

"They act as though we stole that body," complained Judge.

"Didn't yuh?" queried the sheriff.

"Certainly not," replied Henry. "I didn't want him alive— much less dead for twelve hours."

"It was sure a good break for Danny—until the corpse is found."

At the saloon they found the rest of the J Bar C boys, and Henry told Fred Simpson to go to the ranch and find Danny.

"Tell him we're entirely out of dead men around here, Fred. Somebody obligingly stole the evidence."

Ricky Dole heard the news, but did not believe it, until he had a talk with Doctor Clemens.

"How do you figure it out, Doc?" asked Ricky.

"Why, the J Bar C outfit, of course. They stole that body."

"Uh-huh. Without the body, yuh can't prove murder, eh?"

"Plenty of men saw the body," replied the doctor, "but not one of them could swear that Tug Evans was dead. I *know* he was dead; but I'd have an awful time proving it to a jury."

Ricky scowled thoughtfully.

"It don't make sense," he said. "I'll be damned if it does."

"What don't make sense?" asked the doctor.

"Regan tryin' to murder me."

"If he didn't, who did, Dole?"

Ricky shook his head and walked away.

It was late in the afternoon, when Danny came to town. Slim came first, to see that everything was all right; and then Danny went straight to the millinery store.

The sheriff had made no pretense of a search for the body. He was satisfied that whoever had stolen the body had placed it in a safe place.

"Yeah, and we'll never find it," declared Rolling Stone, arguing at the Tonto bar.

CHAPTER VII

A SOCIAL CALL

IT WAS THE main topic of conversation in Tonto City; and it seemed that everyone had made up their minds that the J Bar C had stolen the body to save Danny Regan from a murder charge. The veiled accusations sobered Henry, who quit drinking for the time being.

"Grave snatcher!" he exclaimed softly. "My goodness! An entirely new rôle for me."

He sat down in a chair against the wall, tilted his big hat at a new angle, and tried to think clearly. He was very sure that none of the J Bar C outfit knew of the murder, until today. That precluded any chance of them stealing the corpse. Still, as far as he could see, the purloining of the body would only be an advantage to Danny Regan.

If Danny Regan *had* fired that fatal shot, it would have been within the realm of possibility that Danny did return to Tonto City and take the corpse away, in order to destroy any evidence against him. Henry decided to have a heart-to-heart talk with

Danny. Not that he wanted any harm to come to Danny; he merely wanted to know.

Slim had told him that Danny was at the Harpers' store; so Henry went over there, where he was welcomed heartily.

"What's the latest news?" asked Danny.

"The Dutch," replied Henry soberly, "have taken Holland; and the J Bar C are accused of taking Evans."

"Do they think we stole that body?" queried Danny.

"Who else could use him, Danny?"

"But we didn't even know he was dead until today."

Henry sighed and tried to ease his aching feet.

"Why don't you take off those boots, Mr. Conroy?" asked Mrs. Harper.

"Am I registering pain?" he asked in surprise.

"You certainly are," smiled Leila. "Let me help you."

"I'll do it," chuckled Danny.

Henry settled back in his chair, grimacing with relief, after the boots were off.

"Those chaps are over in the saloon," he told Danny. "They're too hot. Ah-h-h-h! This is something like solid comfort. It isn't such a bad old world, after all—if they'd only quit shooting and stealing."

"Tonto City is certainly upset over things," said Leila.

"Especially the coroner and the prosecutor," smiled Henry. "I've never met such zealous officers before."

"This makes the second time they've failed to lead me to the halter," laughed Danny. "But, Boss, how did you get off the horse, after I left in such a hurry?"

"How does anyone get off a horse?" asked Henry. He glanced at Leila, who was choking softly. She wiped her eyes and avoided his glance.

Henry got to his feet and walked to the window, where he peered down the street. Nodding slowly, he went back to his chair, where he sat down. He looked at Leila and suddenly broke into a merry chuckle.

"You saw me from the wings, as it were," he laughed. "You spied on my first attempt at acrobatics. Was it good?"

"Almost impossible!" choked Leila.

"Not at all," dryly. "Merely a matter of balance."

"What did the horse do?" asked Danny.

"Shifted his feet and went back to sleep."

"I don't think it is anything to laugh about," declared Mrs. Harper. "Every man must learn to get on and off a horse."

"My heavens! It isn't compulsory, is it?" exclaimed Henry.

"Don't worry," laughed Danny. "After six months down here, you'll be flankin' calves, ropin' steers and toppin' bad broncs—and like it, too."

"If I live," sighed Henry. "You must consider that, Danny."

"Don't talk like that!" exclaimed Mrs. Harper. She turned to Danny.

"Go over and get Judge; and we will all have supper to-gether."

"I'm scared he's drunk by this time, Ma," replied Danny.

"Not yet," said Henry. "You don't know his capacity."

"Anyway," smiled Mrs. Harper, "he's a gentleman—drunk or sober."

Judge came willingly. He was not drunk.

"I am too mad to drink," he declared. "The whole town is accusing us of stealing that corpse."

"Well," replied Henry, "Tonto City isn't such a big place."

JUDGE was obliged to laugh. "No, it isn't like being accused by a big city, of course," he admitted.

"Let us forget it and enjoy a pleasant supper," said Mrs. Harper.

"A good suggestion," agreed Judge. "It is getting quite windy tonight."

"More paint going away," said Danny. "Every time the wind blows here you can see the sand scour more paint off the buildings."

"Paint!" snorted Judge. "There hasn't been a brush of paint used in Tonto City since the Indians went off the war-path."

"You shouldn't say things against Tonto City," said Henry. "Please remember, it is my home town."

"I don't care if it was the birthplace of Christopher Columbus. The idea of accusing us of stealing a cadaver. It makes my blood boil."

The three men sat together, discussing things, while the two women prepared supper.

"That lamp needs filling pretty badly, Danny," said Judge.

"It is runnin' kinda low," agreed Danny, and went into the kitchen to find the oil can.

"There isn't a drop left," said Mrs. Harper. "You and Leila go to the store and get some, will you, Danny?"

"Sure will, Ma."

"And hurry back, because supper is almost ready for the table."

It was only a few steps up the street to the store, but they were gone a long time. Supper was on the table, when they got back.

"Man, that wind is sure blowin'!" exclaimed Danny.

"Ma, they didn't have a bit of kerosene at the store," said Leila.

"We went to Shannons and they let me have some."

"No kerosene at the store? Jim Groves must be getting absent minded."

"He says he's been robbed," laughed Danny.

"Robbed?" queried Judge. "Blames the J Bar C, I suppose."

"No, he didn't openly accuse anyone," replied Leila laughing.

"You see," explained Danny, "he keeps that barrel of kerosene in a shed behind the store. I don't suppose he bothers to keep it locked. My opinion is that he forgot to order a supply. Supper ready, Ma?"

"Sit right down, everybody. Mr. Conroy, you sit at the head of the table."

"I am honored, Mrs. Harper. Wonderful! A roast of beef—roasted, but not incinerated. Frijole would have been in demand in the days of the ancients, when they specialized in burnt offerings. I asked him if he knew what a rare steak was and he said he supposed it might be one off a buffalo, because they were quite rare these days."

The conversation gradually drifted around to valley happenings, before Jim Conroy was killed; his efforts to force the small ranchers out of the valley, and the robbery, which smashed the Tonto City Bank, and brought financial ruin to the Harper family.

"Edward Walsh was an attorney, before he became banker?" queried Henry.

"Yes," replied Judge. "He was attorney for the bank."

"Did he have enough money to take over the banking interests?"

"He didn't take 'em over. The bank was broke. It did not open for several months, when Walsh started his new financial venture under the name of the Bank of Tonto City."

"Who backed him?"

"I don't believe that has been known, Henry. I have heard rumors that the Bank of Antelope backed him; and that he received financial support from some eastern people. Who knows?"

"**MR. WALSH,** I suppose," said Henry dryly. "I was wondering, if, by any chance, Jim Conroy's money was involved in the refinancing."

"There is nothing to show that it has."

"That's the worst of it, Judge. Mrs. Harper, those potatoes are fit for the gods—and such gravy! I wonder who killed Jim Conroy."

"I'm wondering who killed Tug Evans," said Danny seriously.

"Difficult to say," replied Judge. "The evidence shows that the shooter was intending to kill Ricky Dole—not Evans."

"I—" Henry started to say something, stopped short, staring into space. He blinked thoughtfully, rubbed the back of his right hand on his nose, and finally looked curiously around the table.

"Well, what struck you, Henry?" asked Judge.

"Oh!" Henry smiled dryly. "You see, it is so unusual for me to get an inspiration that—it nearly upset me."

"Are you sure it wasn't a touch of indigestion, Henry?" asked Judge.

"Now you might be right, Judge. I believe it was. Mrs. Harper, those biscuits are the best I have ever eaten. Thank you. No gravy. Hm-m-m! No kerosene."

"Certainly not," said Judge. "Kerosene, indeed!"

Henry laughed and shook his head. "You will pardon me, I hope. You see, I sometimes think aloud. We were speaking about the bank and the banker. Is there a Mrs. Walsh?"

"Walsh is a single man," replied Judge. "That is, as far as we know. He lives in that little cottage directly south of the Tonto Saloon. That is, he abides there, takes his meals at the restaurant, and has a woman come in once in a while to clean up his house."

"He rides a horse, too," said Danny, with a side glance at Henry.

"I must challenge him to a dismounting contest," said Henry. "It should be worth going miles to see. Am I right, Miss Leila?"

"I'm afraid you could never do it that way again," laughed the girl.

"Oh, I believe I could. It is merely a matter of balance, you see. Or would you call it unbalance. I must ask the sheriff his opinion."

After supper Henry insisted on putting on his boots. Judge watched him critically, but made no comments.

"Judge and I are going to make a few social calls," stated Henry.

Judge scratched his mop of gray hair, wondering what Henry meant.

"Want me to go along?" asked Danny.

"No," replied Henry seriously. "If somebody shoots the both of us, it won't affect the future of Arizona."

"Speak for yourself!" grunted Judge. "If there is any shooting to be done, I don't even want to be a witness."

Henry essayed a little dance on his high-heels, picked up his big hat and carefully tied the long chin-strings.

"If the wind ever gets under your hat, it'll choke you to death," warned Judge, as he drew his ancient derby on firmly.

"I suppose. And then they'll swear that the wind came from the J Bar C. Folks, we hope to see you later; and many, many thanks for your charming hospitality. We give you good evening."

Henry led the way across the street and they stopped on the lee side of the blacksmith shop.

"Do you know what you are doing, Henry?" asked Judge.

"I do—so far. Can you find Edward Walsh's residence in the dark?"

"Walsh's residence? Is that where we are going?"

"Go ahead; I'll follow."

They stumbled along in the dark, bumped into a tumble-down fence, hung up on some loose barb-wire, but finally arrived at the small cottage of Edward Walsh. There was not a light showing.

"Apparently he is not at home, Henry," observed Judge.

"That is evident. In fact, I saw a light in the bank, when we went across the street. Is that his stable—there, behind the house?"

"I believe it is."

Henry led the way over there. The door was closed, an unlocked padlock holding the door closed. Henry drew out the padlock, hung it in the staple, and opened the door.

"I sincerely hope you know what you are doing, Henry," said Judge.

"I do—so far."

They entered the stable and the wind blew the door shut behind them. Henry scratched a match and held it up, as they peered around. In the one stall stood a saddled horse. A lantern hung on a wooden peg at the end of the stall, and Henry lighted it.

"I do not feel right about this, Henry," declared Judge. "We haven't any legal—"

"I'm not going to steal his horse!" snapped Henry.

"Then what on earth are we doing here?"

"Taking the equine census of Arizona, Judge. Wait!"

CHAPTER VIII

NO MYSTERY

BEHIND THE SADDLE was tied a slicker, which showed a decided bulge between the tie-strings. Without any hesitation Henry untied the bundle, placed it on the floor and proceeded to unwrap it. Inside were two sacks, approximately the same size.

Henry quickly untied one of them, disclosing a miscellany of food, which included crackers, sardines and a small bottle of whisky. He closed the sack and jerked the strings tight. Then he opened the other sack, disclosing package after package of currency.

Judge gasped audibly and started to splutter, when Henry jerked the sack closed, picked up both sacks and got to his feet.

"Take this sack," he whispered, shoving a sack into Judge's hands.

"But, Henry, will you listen?" pleaded Judge. "This isn't—"

"Take that sack!"

Henry blew out the lantern and shoved Judge toward the door.

"If you want my opinion—" spluttered Judge.

"I don't! Where on earth is that door?"

"Here is the door," grunted Judge. Henry had groped past it. As he turned around, Judge opened the door and stepped outside, with the sack in his two hands.

"What's—"

Smack! The sound of a sharp blow, cutting off Judge's exclamation, the thud of bodies, and Judge was forcibly thrown back into the stable, crashing into Henry, who went to his knees. The stable door slammed shut, and Henry heard the click of the padlock.

"Is that you, Judge?" asked Henry anxiously, but painfully.

"I doubt it," replied Judge in a choking whisper. "Oh, my head! What happened? Where are we, Henry?"

"We're where all jackasses should be, I suppose—in a stable. Are you hurt?"

"I—I—Something hit me on the head. Henry, where are you?"

"I'm right here, if that means anything to you, Judge."

"He—they got that sack," wailed Judge, pawing around in the dark.

"Well," said Henry, "we are locked in—unless there is a window."

Henry got to his feet, lighted a match and looked around. There was a small window, fastened from the inside, which Henry looked over appraisingly. He lighted the lantern, opened the window and turned to Judge.

"I'll help you through the window," he said.

"I'll never make it," sighed Judge. "Henry, my equator is too damn big around. And, anyway, if we stick our heads out, they'll knock 'em off, I suppose."

Henry secured a small box, stepped up on it and looked out. Nothing happened. With a sigh of resignation he began wriggling through it. It was a tight fit.

"You—uh—uh—might sh-shove a little," he panted.

Judge shoved. He gripped the seat of Henry's pants and heaved mightily. In fact, he shoved so mightily that the overbalanced Henry landed on the back of his neck in the dirt, while his heels described a perfect arc and thudded against the ground.

"Th—that window is bigger than I thought, Henry," observed Judge, peering over the sill.

"I—I never saw a lawyer in my life that didn't underestimate or overestimate," groaned Henry. "I believe you broke my neck."

While Henry was airing his opinions of the profession, Judge was crawling through the window. Gripping the sill with his hands under him, he lunged forward, tipping himself outside, and he came down with a crash on top of Henry.

"They got me, Judge!" yelped Henry. "Leggo my nose, you murderer!"

Judge fell off Henry, winded for the moment, while Henry made ineffectual attempts to strike him with both his fists.

"Oh, stop it!" wailed Judge, "I didn't know that you was under the window."

"Is that you, Judge?" asked the amazed Henry.

"The name is familiar," admitted Judge painfully, as he managed to get to his feet.

"But it doesn't make any difference who I am; I'm going away. Of all fool things! Sneaking into other people's stables! Henry, you are crazy."

"I'm not crazy," denied Henry, groaning as he stood up. "My idea was right. Come on, Legal Light; we are going now."

STUMBLING and limping in the dark, they started back for the main street of Tonto City. Judge was still mumbling, swearing, groaning.

Suddenly Henry stopped short, and Judge bumped into him. There was a flickering glow ahead, which brought out the Tonto Saloon building in sharp silhouette. Then they heard voices yelling:

"Fire! Fire! Fire!"

"Must be a fire," mumbled Judge foolishly.

"That is the first sensible opinion I've had from you since you became a lawyer," declared Henry. "Come on!"

It most surely was a fire. A blaze had broken out either in the Groves General Store, or in the vacant store-room, where the inquest had been held, as both buildings were in flames; and the high wind was driving the fire into the bank building.

Without any adequate fire fighting apparatus, and with the high wind blowing from the west, that whole side of the street seemed doomed. They were all weathered, frame structures, dry as match-sticks.

In a few moments all of Tonto City was in the street. There was a feeble attempt to form a bucket-brigade, but the sheriff ordered everybody to try and save as much stuff as possible from the buildings east of the bank.

Henry and Judge joined the crowd. Danny Regan was leading an attempt to move everything possible from the Harper store. Henry grabbed the sheriff and drew him aside.

"Smash in the bank windows!" he yelled in the officer's ear.

"No use!" yelled the sheriff. "Can't save it, Conroy!"

"We've got to get inside, I tell you! Come on!"

There was no time for explanation. Henry picked up a boulder beside the sidewalk and sent it crashing through a window. A gush of smoke came out through the broken pane; but Henry did not mind. Kicking the loose glass away, he went through the smashed pane, with the wondering sheriff close behind him.

Flames were already breaking through the wall, but not

enough yet to endanger them. However it illuminated the place well. The big safe was wide open, and lying in front of it was the body of a man, dressed in black. He was face down, his wrists wired together behind him.

"Quick!" panted Henry. "Got to get him out!"

"My God!" gasped the sheriff. "Must be Ed Walsh! Take his feet, Conroy."

Swiftly they carried the body to the window where Henry got out and they slid the body to the sidewalk. After the sheriff got out, others saw them, and came running. Willing hands carried the body over to the front of the Tonto Saloon.

The crowd was working feverishly to salvage valuables; too busy to ask questions. The sheriff turned the body over, looked at the face of the dead man, and jerked back.

"Tug Evans!" he yelled, looking up at Henry.

Judge staggered up and looked at the corpse. The sheriff got up and grasped Henry by the arm.

"You—you know this?" he spluttered.

"I guessed it," panted Henry. "This isn't all, Parton. Never mind the fire. Look! The wind is shifting. Come on—quick!"

"Where to?" asked the sheriff. "We've got to—"

"Never mind; this is a job."

It seemed a ridiculous thing to do, leaving the fire, with everyone else in the town trying frantically to save something from the flames. Henry led the way, with the sheriff behind him, and, straggling along in the rear was Judge, talking to himself. Henry was leading the way back to Walsh's house, which was still in darkness.

"Somebody's shore crazy as hell," said the sheriff.

"As far as that is concerned," replied Henry, "we're all more or less insane."

"You lean to the former," said Judge. "If anyone ever asks me for an opinion on your mental status—"

"I'll testify against him," panted the sheriff.

"Nuts!" snorted Henry inelegantly. "Here's the fence."

FOR NO apparent reason they crouched against the fence. They could hear the noise from the crowd in the street, the crackling of flames, an occasional yell. Then they heard a door slam shut at the front of Walsh's house. Henry gripped the sheriff's arm tightly. A man came off the porch and started toward the rear of the house. A moment later they saw a pencil of flame lick out in the darkness beside the house, and heard the thudding report of a big six-gun.

The sheriff started to get to his feet, but Henry pulled him down. Hurrying feet were going toward the stable, and they saw the dim figure of a man reach the doorway. They heard the rattle of the lock, and in a moment or two the door swung open.

"Your job, sheriff," whispered Henry. "The killer."

Softly the big sheriff squeezed through the fence and went nearly to the open door. A match flickered in the stable—went out. Another was lighted, and they heard the creak, as the lantern was opened. The light flared up, and the sheriff stepped inside.

Henry and Judge ducked, as two shots crashed out. The lantern jangled, as it fell to the floor. Then the sheriff's voice, a bit shaky, as he called: "Got him, Conroy!"

It was Ricky Dole, the handsome ex-foreman of the J Bar C, on the stable floor, his head and shoulders braced against the wall. He was hit hard, but was conscious. The left side of the sheriff's face was bathed in gore from a bullet-scrape across his cheek. The sheriff had Ricky's gun.

"Shot from his hip and almost spotted me," he said grimly. "Now will you tell me what the hell this is all about, Conroy?"

Henry rubbed his already red nose, squinted at the bleeding sheriff and then looked back toward the house.

"I suppose I better check up on things," he said, "I'll be back."

Henry trotted wearily toward the house, stumbled over the end of a wooden walk and fell sprawling. His hands touched a prostrate body, causing him to jerk back quickly. He managed to find a match, which he lighted, and looked at the remains of Banker Walsh. There was no question in Henry's mind—the banker was dead.

Limping and wheezing Henry got back to the stable.

"Well?" snapped the sheriff.

"Mr. Walsh," wheezed Henry softly, "is with his forefathers. In other words, he's as dead as the proverbial mackerel—and Mr. Dole is the man who murdered him."

"I hope to tell yuh I did," whispered Ricky. "That doublecrossin' coyote. He was pullin' out tonight with all the bank money."

"What the hell do you know about it?" groaned Ricky.

THE SHERIFF and Judge looked blankly at Henry.

"When you murdered Jim Conroy, you and Walsh stole all his money," said Henry. "Walsh fixed the books at the bank. You figured that eventually you would own the J Bar C. Then I came along and you tried to murder me, eh?"

"No," denied Ricky weakly. "I guess Walsh tried to. He tried to kill me, too. Wanted it all, the crooked polecat."

"You robbed and smashed the first bank," said Henry.

"I never got a damn cent—prove it," said Ricky defiantly.

"You won't live to know whether it was proved or not," said the sheriff. "Ricky, you might as well tell it all."

Ricky smiled grimly, painfully. "Think not?" he said.

"Even if yuh did, we've got yuh for murderin' Walsh, Ricky."

"Murder! Walsh was a killer. He framed that first robbery. Wanted to keep the money, until things was safe. He—he bought the bank, and then got the idea of robbin' Conroy; but Conroy got suspicious."

"What about those mortgages on the J Bar C?" asked Henry.

"One is all right, I guess; the other was forged. Never... recorded. Walsh got the money—all of it... somewhere. Belongs... to... ranch... and... Mrs. Harper... mostly...."

Ricky's shoulders sagged a little and his head dropped.

"Fainted," said the sheriff. "I'll get a doctor—he might last to sign a confession. Anyway, we've got three witnesses."

"Two," corrected Henry. "The estimable Judge hasn't done anything, except turn around and around and scratch his head."

"It isn't quite clear," faltered Judge.

"Quite clear?" snapped the sheriff. "There ain't nothin' clear about it. If this big-nosed—"

"Leave my nose out of it," interrupted Henry. "Ye gods! Can't I do anything, without giving my nose all the credit? All my life—But no matter now—we will go and get a doctor for our Exhibit A."

NEARLY one-half of Tonto City went up in flames. Except for what few things they had been able to salvage, there was nothing left of the Harper Millinery, except a pile of glowing embers. The Grove store was gone, as was the bank, when Henry and Judge stood at the Tonto bar, talking with the amazed crowd, while the doctor tried to save the life of Ricky Dole.

"I tell yuh, I don't know anythin' about it," declared the sheriff. "I don't know why Tug Evans' body was in the bank, with the hands and feet wired, and dressed in that black suit. Henry, you tell 'em."

HENRY HARRISON CONROY, disheveled, but still dramatic, lifted a glass of liquor and squinted through it at the light.

"You might call it intuition," he said slowly, "I call it brains. A man shot by mistake. An attempt to murder me. Why? Then a body stolen. Why would anyone desire a cadaver? Why would anyone desire to murder me? To prevent me from finding out certain things. Why would anyone try to assassinate Ricky Dole? To remove him.

"Gentlemen, I was satisfied that certain irregularities existed in our bank. In other words, the J Bar C was being robbed. When the attempt was made to murder Ricky Dole, it made me believe that Ricky was implicated. Tonight Mr. Groves, our estimable merchant, discovered that much of his kerosene was missing. A highly inflammable liquid, I believe.

"And then, gentlemen, I gave birth to an inspiration. A cadaver and a holocaust; a chance for Mr. Walsh to leave us in the lurch, with a burned bank, a wide-open safe, and what might be left of a body, burned beyond recognition, with hands and feet strongly wired. It would, no doubt, indicate that Mr. Walsh had been robbed and left to incinerate, while the dastardly perpetrators would never be apprehended. Is that clear, gentlemen?"

"Was it Walsh or Dole, who hit me at the stable door?" queried Judge.

"Mr. Dole, I believe," replied Henry.

"But he got that sack," protested Judge. "Why did he come back, and how did you know he would come back. He had the money."

"Pardon me, Judge," smiled Henry, "but he did not have the money. The sack I gave you contained food. He got his lunch-box, as you might say, and when you crashed back into me, I flung the money sack into a manger, I knew he would come back and try to get the money."

"Pretty smart for an actor," admitted Judge.

"Sherlock Holmes to you, sir," said Henry blandly. "And I am not an actor; I am a cattleman, sir—even if I don't dismount gracefully."

Henry fairly swaggered, as he walked through the crowd, and went outside, where Danny was trying to explain to Mrs. Harper and Leila that everything was all right; that they would get their money, and that he had been cleared of all charges.

Mrs. Harper met Henry, and in her excitement she grasped him by the bosom of his wrinkled, sagging shirt.

"Oh, isn't it grand!" she exclaimed. "Just to think! You are wonderful, Mr. Conroy!"

He looked at her in the light from the Tonto Saloon windows.

"Call me Hank," he drawled softly. "I've gone Arizony. What's yore first name, ma'am?"

"Why—Laura," faltered Mrs. Harper.

"All right, Laury; that's shore great. Danny, will yuh find some sort of a rig that we can all ride out to the ranch."

"I sure can," replied Danny.

Danny went hurrying down the sidewalk, and Henry looked at Leila and her mother.

"Yes," said Henry, "it is the proper ending—almost. The juvenile wins the fair maiden—and the hero—"

"You are the hero," said Leila.

"You certainly have been a hero tonight," said Mrs. Harper.

He reached over bashfully and put his arm around her shoulder.

"Thank yuh, Laury," he drawled softly. "When I took off my tight boots, and looked across the table at you tonight, I said to myself:

" 'Hank, you ain't young and you ain't pretty; so be a hero; that's all you can do.' "

"And I thought he was crazy," said Judge.

"Merely a disguise, my dear Judge; merely a disguise."

Danny was coming up the street with a livery team and a light wagon. Several of the boys crowded out on the sidewalk, and above the jangle of conversation came Oscar's voice:

"Vell, Ay will be dorned! Ay t'ought he was joost a funny man."

"Funny!" snorted Frijole. "He ain't funny—it's jist his nose."

II

WITH THE HELP OF HENRY

Henry claimed dead men tell no tales—yet see what happened when they wrote letters which mysteriously appeared as damning evidence.

CHAPTER I

THE NEW SHERIFF

HENRY HARRISON CONROY and Judge Van Treece sat on the veranda of the J Bar C ranch-house, in Wild Horse Valley. A description of these two men, and their actions, might serve to enlighten and enliven a commonplace statement of a commonplace scene.

Henry Harrison Conroy was about five feet, six inches in height, rotund and about fifty-five years of age. Born backstage in a theater, Henry had been an actor all his life, until he had inherited the J Bar C cattle-ranch, when his uncle, Jim Conroy, had been murdered, leaving him this inheritance.

Henry's face was moon-like, featuring a huge putty-like nose, which was forever red. For years this nose had been a feature in vaudeville, with Henry Harrison Conroy, as a background. Just now Henry was clad in a skin-tight blue shirt, overalls, which did not meet at the front by inches, and held together with a big, horse-blanket safety-pin, and high-heel boots, which he had never entirely mastered.

Judge Van Treece, christened Cornelius, was sixty years of age, six feet, four inches tall, and consistently slatlike from end to end. His face was long, lean, with pouchy eyes and a long, thin nose. He wore a wrinkled old cutaway coat, baggy pants, nondescript shoes, and on his lap he held an ancient derby hat.

Between them, on the floor of the veranda, was a two-gallon demijohn and two tin cups. The air in their immediate vicinity was redolent of corn liquor.

These two men were intently gazing at a cloth poster, which had been strung between two strands of barb-wire on the fence. The poster was about three feet long and two feet wide, and at that distance the old legible lettering was VOTE FOR HENRY H. CONROY FOR SHERIFF.

Slowly Judge Van Treece raised a Colt forty-five, cocked it, rested it over the veranda rail, while Henry closed his eyes, leaned back in his chair and gave every evidence of a man suffering from shell-shock, gun-shyness and danger of a physical breakdown.

The big gun roared and jumped. A tailless rooster, twenty feet away from the poster, went into the air with a squawk, and fairly flew to the stable. Henry's eyes blinked violently for several moments, before he tilted forward and reached for the jug.

*Henry and Judge
stared in amazement.*

"And still," he said ponderously, "there is no dot over the 'I' in sheriff. Judge, I—I hate to mention it—but you are drunk."

"There is a preponderance of evidence," agreed Judge. "In fact, we are both drunk, Henry. Your last shot hit a corner of the stable, which is fifty feet to the left of the I. Twice, I damn near killed Shakespeare, the rooster."

Henry closed one eye and squinted at the skyline.

" 'Tis nearly sundown," he said. "Only the tip remains."

"Queer," remarked Judge. "Very, very queer."

"Nothing queer about sundown, my dear Judge."

"You seeing the tip of the sun—that is queer—especially as you are looking toward the East. The sun, my dear Henry, sets in the West."

"So it does. How quaint of me. Let us drink to Mother Nature."

With great difficulty Henry poured the cups full of liquor.

Both men got to their feet, bowed low to each other, braced against the railing and drank deeply.

"The voting must be over," sighed Henry. "Soon they will be tabulating the votes."

"Henry," said the Judge thoughtfully, "suppose they elect you."

"Judge," replied Henry seriously, "if this county elected me sheriff, I would sell this ranch, gather together every cent I could beg, borrow or acquire dishonestly, and build an insane asylum large enough to incarcerate every voter in this county."

"You are a candidate, sir."

"Involuntarily, sir. My friends—if I may call them so—perpetrated a joke on me. I have never made a speech, given away a cigar, nor kissed a baby. I have grandly ignored my nomination. I haven't the nose of a peace officer. My Gawd, Judge! You don't suspect for a moment that they *might* elect me, do you?"

"I cast my vote against you, sir."

"So did I," replied Henry soberly. "We did our part. Oscar Johnson, that damnable Swede horse-wrangler, is the only man on the crew that I doubt. He doesn't understand. Frijole Bill swore he'd make that Swede vote against me, or bust his head. Ah, well, I worry unnecessarily. A drink to my defeat, Judge!"

"Yes, yes—a drink! But if you should be elected—"

"Verily, thou art a great hanger of crape, Judge. Nay, the world is not filled with fools. Sheriff!"

THEY DRANK, not omitting the bow to each other, and sat down again. And they were still sitting there, when the ranch buckboard came home, bringing Frijole Bill, the cook, and Oscar Johnson, the wrangler. Frijole was sixty years of age, five feet three inches tall, and would not weigh over a hundred pounds, in spite of the huge mustache, which decorated his skinny face.

Oscar was over six feet in height, with the frame of a Hercules. His head was huge and blocky, his face flat, with a button-like nose, and small, blue eyes. A mop of faded, blond hair stood up on his head, like the roach of an angry grizzly bear.

Frijole Bill was driving. He cramped the buckboard near the veranda and forcibly shoved the big Swede off the seat. Oscar managed to keep his balance, and stood there, blankly staring at Henry and Judge, while Frijole took the team down to the corral.

Oscar tried to take off the hat he did not have on, waved the invisible hat in the air and yelled huskily: "Hooray for Hanry for de shoriff."

"Frijole must have failed, Henry," said Judge sadly.

"One swallow does not make a summer," said Henry. "But, speaking of swallows, Judge——"

Judge tunked the demijohn with his toe. "As empty as—as Oscar's head," he sighed.

"Hooray for Hanry for de shoriff!" yelled Oscar, and sat down heavily.

"Drunk again," sighed Henry.

Frijole Bill came up from the stables. He stopped to look at Oscar, spat disgustedly, and came on up to the veranda. Frijole was not exactly sober. He had a penchant for prune whisky, which he distilled for his own use—a rather vile concoction, but with all the authority of a Supreme Court.

"I beg t' report the Tonto City vote," said Frijole. "Rollin' Stone, twen'y-sheven; Jack Nolan, thir'y-two; Hennery Harrishon Conroy, thir'y-three."

Henry and Judge looked at each other owlishly.

"You win by a scant nose in Tonto City, sir," said Judge.

"Scant?" whispered Henry. "A *scant* nose—me? There never was a scant nose in the Conroy family, sir."

"It was that damn Swede," sighed Frijole. "He campaigned all over Tonto City for yuh—until I caught him. But he'd already voted."

"The thirty-third vote," sighed Henry.

"But there are other precincts, Henry," reminded Judge. "When you only carry your own bailiwick by one vote—you should be swamped, sir."

"Hooray for Hanry for de shoriff!" cheered Oscar weakly.

IT WAS after midnight when Slim Pickins rode in at the ranch. He was singing a wild, range ballad, which has never been printed. He threw his saddle into the corral, tried to hang his horse on the fence, and weaved his erratic way up to the house, where he stood on the veranda and yelled like a Comanche.

"The drunken bum!" snorted Henry, crawling out of his comfortable bed. "I'll fix him."

"What aileth the idiot?" asked the Judge, sleepily. "And what time is it?"

"Time," grunted Henry, "is merely a figure of speech, as far as my young life is concerned. Watch the exit for Mr. Pickins."

Henry dragged an old double-barrel shotgun from behind the bed and sauntered, with murderous intent, through the dark living room, while Slim again gave the battle cry of a marauding savage.

Crash! went a piece of furniture, the thud of a falling body; and the ranch-house shook from the thunderous report of two twelve-gauge shotgun shells going off at the same time.

Slim Pickins cleared twenty-seven feet at the first leap, and a split-second later crashed against the corral fence, while Oscar and Frijole came stumbling out of the bunk-house, clad only in illfitting underwear and hats. With trembling hands, Judge lighted a lamp. In the middle of the floor sat Henry, an expression of dazed amazement on his red face.

"Who in the hell left that chair in the middle of the floor?" he demanded.

"You did, Henry," replied Judge mildly.

Henry gazed at the offending chair, nodded slowly and said:

"In my mental picture of the room, I forgot the chair. Isn't it queer what a trivial thing can do? For the moment I was a potential murderer. In my heart surged the blood-lust of a savage. In other words, my dear Judge, I went berserk. But I'm not berserk now. There is no blood-lust in my heart. I'm just a damned old fool, who fell over a chair and got kicked in the belly with both barrels of a shotgun."

Someone was knocking timidly on the door. "Who is it?" asked Henry.

"It's Frijole, sir; Frijole and Oscar. We caught Slim, before he could hurt himself. He—he has the full report of the election."

"Full report? Let us have it, man!" explained Judge.

"Nolan got sixty-two votes."

"Sixty-two for Nolan. Go ahead, Frijole."

"Sixty-three for Stone."

"Stone beats Nolan by one vote, eh? Very, very close."

"And Henry got sixty-four."

"Henry got—wait a minute, Frijole! Sixty-four, did you say?"

"Yeah, that's right—Henry's the next sheriff."

Henry got slowly to his feet, padded back to the bedroom in his bare feet, and came back quickly, with two shotgun cartridges in his hand. He picked up the offending shotgun, opened it and put in the two shells.

"Is Oscar out there yet?" he asked.

"He—he just went away," replied Frijole.

"Remember," said Judge soothingly, "there were sixty-four, Henry."

Henry nodded slowly, thoughtfully.

"Judge," he said softly, "I went out of vaudeville, because I believed that the world had lost its sense of humor. I was wrong—it was only the city people. Let's go to bed."

"I suppose we may as well, Henry. I wonder what Danny Regan will say. A great boy, that Danny Regan."

"Hauling poles," sighed Henry. "Hauling poles to remodel his little ranch-house—while the populace make me king—of

the sheriff's office. And
when the house is fin-
ished, he and Leila
Harper will be wed."

"A grand girl, Henry."

"Aye—a grand girl. A
grand couple, Judge. I—I
wanted 'em to live here,
with us—to run this
ranch. But Danny, the
red-headed, freckled,
young devil, is as inde-
pendent as a hog on ice.
He wants a home of his
own."

Henry Harrison Conroy

"Young birds," sighed Judge. "I—er—" he shot a sideways
glance at Henry, who was rubbing his already red nose. "Henry,
I had sort of an idea that you might be serious about Leila's
mother."

"Serious?" queried Henry.

"She's a mighty nice woman, Henry. It seems a shame that
she should be obliged to stay there in Tonto City and manu-
facture hats."

"Why in the devil don't you propose to her, Judge?"

"Me? My Gawd, man! Me? A broken-down old barrister,
with only a thirst remaining. You have this ranch, a position
with the county, and—and—"

"A very, very great thirst," finished Henry. "That is the rub."

"She doesn't like liquor, eh?"

"Devil's brew."

"Well," Judge cleared his throat raspingly, "this new responsibility may make a difference. You can not drink and be the
sheriff."

Henry gave his nose its final rub, sighed deeply, and said:

"I think I'll kill that Swede before breakfast, Judge."

CHAPTER II

TELLTALE FOOTPRINTS

DANNY REGAN WAS not Leila Harper's only suitor in the Wild Horse Valley country. Leila was not yet twenty-one years of age, tall and slender, with clean-cut features, dark, wavy hair, and large, dark eyes. She and her mother ran a millinery store in Tonto City.

Big Bill Parton, the present sheriff, admired Leila greatly. But Bill Parton was forty, a huge, gray-haired man, hard-faced, with a deep voice. Until a year ago, Bill Parton owned the Rafter P cattle outfit, eight miles east of Tonto City. It was a small outfit, but controlled a good range and good water. A youngish man named Joe Hall had purchased the Rafter P; and had apparently fallen head-over-heels in love with Leila. Hall was a good-looking, swarthy young cowboy; but Leila only had eyes for the red-headed, freckled, stub-nosed Danny Regan, who, in range parlance, was as salty as the sea, and as forked as a clothes-pin.

Judge Van Treece, a drunken old derelict, was picked up by Danny Regan, who took care of him, until Henry Harrison Conroy came along, made Judge legal adviser for the J Bar C, and made Danny foreman of the outfit. But Danny owned his own little outfit, and he wanted a home for he and Leila; so he worked for Henry, and put his wages into repairs and remodeling on his own place.

As far as Bill Parton was concerned, Danny only smiled at his efforts to attract Leila. But Joe Hall was a different matter. Hall had made disparaging remarks about Danny's looks, and Danny had slapped Joe Hall down in the Tonto Saloon, after daring Hall to use his gun. Bill Parton intervened, which did not help the situation. But nothing further in the way of trouble happened.

It was about noon the next day after the election, when Bill

Parton rode up to the J Bar C ranch-house. Henry and Judge were ready to go to Tonto City, and Oscar Johnson had the buckboard team hitched.

"Well," boomed the big sheriff, "I'm glad to congratulate you, Mr. Conroy, on your remarkable victory. You will make a great peace officer for Wild Horse Valley."

Henry looked at the sheriff.

"Mr. Parton," he replied, "I did not ask for victory. My brow is too tender for a wreath, because of the fact that all my life I have worn the cap of a fool. And I will not make a great peace officer for Wild Horse Valley, because of the fact that I am not going to qualify for the office."

"You mean—you are not going to accept?"

"That is exactly what I mean, sir."

"Well! I—I suppose you know best."

"Oscar sure campaigned for yuh, Conroy," he smiled.

"They say he was rather active," nodded Henry.

"I didn't see Danny in town yesterday. He didn't vote, did he?"

"Danny is working at his ranch," answered Judge. "He's rebuilding his ranch-house. You see, he's getting married soon."

"I see," nodded Parton, undisturbed. "Well, I'll be ridin' along, folks."

"Come out again," invited Henry.

"Thank yuh," said the sheriff shortly, and rode away.

"Ay don't like dis ha'r shoriff," said Oscar. "Ay t'ank he's hord horted."

"If he was a Swede, you'd like him."

Judge sniffed audibly and looked at Oscar.

"What the devil have you been drinking?" he asked.

"Yust a little prune yuice."

"Some of Frijole's brew?"

"Yah, sure. He call it whoop'n holler yuice. You like hear me sink? Joost like a mockin'-birt."

"Move over to the middle," ordered Judge. "I'll do the driving."

"With all due respect to you, sir," said Henry, quickly, "but I'd rather chance Oscar, even full of prune whisky. Proceed, Oscar."

Oscar leaned forward, slacked the lines, and emitted a Comanche war-whoop, which acted like an electric shock on those half-broken horses. The sudden jerk almost snapped the necks of Judge and Henry, and that buckboard went out through the ranch gateway, as though it were tied to the tail of a comet.

AND THEY were half-way to Tonto City before Henry and Judge had regained their equilibrium. Both men had lost their hats near the ranch-house. Oscar managed to slow down the team, but offered no excuses for his reckless driving, except to state: "Yust like that—and we are ha'r."

"Don't brag," said Henry huskily. "Just congratulate the team on sticking to the road."

"For deliberate and downright murder," said the Judge, "I can thoroughly recommend Frijole's prune whisky. I believe you could pour that on a man's tracks, after he has been gone a week, and bring him back, a corpse."

"You like hear me sink?" queried Oscar. "Ay know fine Svensky song. My grandfadder wars a Wiking."

"He was?" queried Henry. "One of those old boys, who had horns, like a cow, eh? Judge, it strikes me that evolution worked faster in Sweden than it did over here. In two generations, they bred out horns entirely. Look at Oscar—not a horn on his head."

"Not bred out, Henry," replied Judge. "Merely a hardening of the skull, which prevented the horns from emerging. If you were to open Oscar's skull, I'm sure you'd find them, rather twisted inside his cranium, taking the place of the brains, which he should have had."

"A point well taken," admitted Henry.

"Ay don't know what the hell dis is all about," said Oscar.

"Anyway," sighed Henry, "there is Tonto City ahead."

"Don't you ever have a craving for the lights of a city street?" asked Judge. "Don't you ever feel the urge of the grease-paint, the applause of the multitude, Henry? To be back there on the stage, listening to the thunder of clapping hands, the strumming of an orchestra."

Judge Van Treece

"I sometimes have a slight twitching in my nose," replied Henry. "And at times I feel a queer sensation at sight of a dog. No doubt my nose misses the old sights—and I followed dog acts for so many years—At times, they thought I was an encore for the dog act."

"You were on Broadway, Henry?"

"Twelve straight weeks—out of work. Twelve weeks of hot-cakes at Childs—once a day. Oscar, you better tie the team near the Tonto Saloon—I feel a break-down coming on."

"Yah, sure," replied Oscar. "Ay am broke, too."

As they dismounted from the buckboard they saw Leila Harper on the other side of the street, motioning to them.

"I suppose," remarked Henry, "the damsel wishes to congratulate me."

"Yah, sure," replied Oscar. "She is for Hanry for de shoriff."

"Prune juice!" snorted Henry, and walked across the street, where Leila met them at the edge of the sidewalk.

"I suppose congratulations are in order," she smiled.

"Peace, sister," whispered Henry, lifting his right hand. "I have no illusions—nor delusions. Was Danny in town yesterday?"

Leila's sensitive face clouded for a moment.

"He did not come in to vote," she replied, "but he came in last night."

Henry looked narrowly at her.

"And something went wrong?" he asked.

"Danny and Joe Hall had a fight," she said, "and Joe hit Danny over the head with a bottle."

"Was he badly hurt, Leila?"

"Badly enough—but he wouldn't go to a doctor. Joe Hall was saying things about you; and Danny resented it."

"I'm sorry about that," sighed Henry. "Awful sorry, Leila. Did Danny go back to his ranch?"

LEILA nodded slowly. "Mother bandaged his head. We wanted him to stay and see the doctor, too; but he wouldn't. I—I wanted to go down to see him—but I had no way to go."

"Was Joe Hall hurt in the fight?" asked Judge.

"I guess he was. They say that Danny beat him terribly. Danny had knocked him down, when Joe picked a bottle off the floor and flung it at Danny's head."

"I think we better go down and see him," said Henry. "You can drive, can't you, Leila?"

"Why, certainly."

"Well, I can't—and I'll admit it. Judge thinks he can, but I'll admit he can't. We'll leave Oscar here, until we return."

Leila was a better driver than Oscar. Henry sighed with satisfaction over the way she handled the team.

"Not exactly Oscar's technique," remarked Henry.

"Oscar does show a lack of finesse with horses," admitted Judge.

"Why did you two come bareheaded?" asked Leila.

Judge explained the manner in which they left the ranch, and just why they had no hats.

"If Ben Hur had been a Swede, I'd believe in reincarnation," said Henry. "Oscar should have been a charioteer."

"He campaigned strong for you," laughed Leila. "He stood in the middle of the street, waved his hat and yelled—"

"Hooray for Hanry for de shoriff," finished Henry. "Leila, I spent one whole week explaining to Oscar just why I didn't want the job. I even put the three names on a sheet of paper, and had Oscar mark X's after Stone's name. Day after day, I voted him. And look what he did to me. Got drunk, yelled my name to the four winds, and voted for me."

"True loyalty," smiled the girl.

The approach to Danny Regan's little ranch was along the edge of a low mesa, giving a clear view of the buildings below.

"Danny must be home," said Leila. "I can see his team and wagon at the corral fence."

She turned from the view to guide the team down a short grade, and Judge looked at Henry, a queer expression in his eyes. His lips drew tightly, as he turned his head for another view.

The team was there, tied to the corral fence, and the running-gears of the wagon were still loaded with poles.

They drove nearly up to the ranch-house, when Leila suddenly drew up the team. Between the house and the corral, sprawled flat on his face in the dirt, was a man. Leila was climbing over Henry's knees, trying to get out. Judge caught the lines from her hands, while Henry grasped Leila.

"Easy, girl," he said calmly. "Let me out first."

"Oh, Danny, Danny!" she was saying. "Danny, what have they done to you?"

Henry managed to get out, lifted Leila out, and she went running to the sprawled body, dropping on her knees. Henry hurried to join her, while Judge managed to tie the team to the porch.

BUT IT was not Danny Regan—it was Joe Hall. Near his outstretched right hand was a Colt forty-five, unfired. The three of them grouped around the body, staring at each other.

"Oh, where is Danny?" asked Leila hoarsely. No one could even guess.

Judge made a swift examination of the body, and got to his feet, brushing off his bony knees.

"Through the back," he said softly. "It's murder, Henry."

Leila looked at Judge and shook her head slowly.

"Danny didn't do it," she said. "Oh, God, he couldn't do murder!"

Henry turned away and walked to the house. It was unlocked. Not a thing had been disturbed in the house, but there was no sign of Danny Regan. He went to the little stable and found it empty. Danny's saddle was missing, too. He came back to Leila and Judge.

"His horse and saddle are gone," he told them.

"Let's sit down and talk this over," suggested Judge. They went up to the little porch and sat down on the steps.

"You don't think Danny did this, do you?" asked Leila.

"If we could only find Danny," said Henry, evading an answer.

"It looks bad," sighed Judge. "Especially since they fought last night. Joe Hall's face bears plenty evidence of that battle. But I can't believe Danny would shoot him in the back. And if Danny was on his way to notify the officers, we'd have met him. You say his horse and saddle are gone, Henry?"

Henry nodded slowly. "I think we better search the place."

They went all over the stable, corrals and out-buildings, but there was no sign of Danny Regan; so they came back to the body again.

"What's to be done?" asked Judge.

"Judge, the evidence is all against Danny Regan," said Henry. "Do you believe Danny killed him?"

"I can't believe it, Henry. Knowing Danny, as I do, I'd swear—"

"Don't swear in the presence of a lady. Get him by the legs, Judge."

"What do you mean to do?"

"Put him in the back of the buckboard."

"You mean—to take the body to town?"

"Do you want Danny Regan hung?"

"Certainly not! But why—"

"Grab his legs!"

It was not difficult for them to put the body in the back of the buckboard. Henry wiped the perspiration from his brow, and looked at Leila. "There is an old road, which leads to the main road near the J Bar C," he told her. "We are taking that road."

"But," protested Judge, "this is something for the proper—"

"Damn lawyers, anyway!" snorted Henry. "Arguments! You get in here, Judge; between Leila and me. We're going to hide this evidence."

"Hide it? My God, that would make us equally guilty, Henry!"

Henry turned and looked at Leila. Her face was white, but her lips were shut in a hard line.

"You don't mind being a little guilty, in a good cause, do you?" he asked.

"I'll drive," she said tensely.

"You ought to be ashamed, Judge," said Henry. "Leila is young—got everything to live for, while you—why, even the buzzards—" Henry hesitated, and his eyes softened.

"I don't want to hurt your feelings, Judge," he continued, "but I'm just the thickness of a cigarette paper from being disgusted with you."

"Compounding a felony," muttered Judge. "Accessory to— well, what are we waiting for, anyway? I owe everything to Danny Regan."

"I know where that road turns off," said Henry. "Danny showed it to me one day; a short-cut to the J Bar C."

"What about Oscar?" queried Judge. "He'll wonder where we are, and—"

"You didn't tell him where we were going, did you?"

"Fortunately not."

"Then don't worry about Oscar doing any wondering. By this time he's so full of corn juice he wouldn't miss us if we didn't come back for a week."

AT ABOUT the same time that they drove away from the ranch, Danny Regan was sitting in the sheriff's office at Tonto City. In the office were Bill Parton, the sheriff, and Rolling Stone, deputy, who had been an unsuccessful candidate for the sheriff's office in the recent election. Stone was a small, bandy-legged cowboy, with a huge sense of humor.

Danny was disheveled, his face bruised and there was a purple swelling above his left temple, where Joe Hall had hit him with the bottle. Danny's eyes were bloodshot, weary, as he looked at Bill Parton.

"I ain't disputin' yore story," said the sheriff, "but, Regan, you never could make a jury swaller that tale."

"I've told yuh the truth, Bill," declared Danny.

"Let's go over it again," suggested the deputy.

"I was cuttin' and haulin' poles this mornin', about eight o'clock," said Danny wearily. "I was comin' back with my first load, when I heard a shot. A few moments later I came out on the side of the hill, where I could see my place.

"There was a man in the yard, bending over what proved later to be Joe Hall. I reckon he heard me comin', 'cause he ran down past my stable. I didn't know what it was all about, but I whipped up fast. Just before I got to the corral, I seen this man cutting through the brush on a horse.

"I seen the dead man was Joe Hall. Then I saddled my horse, grabbed a 30-30 Winchester, and took after him. I've been tryin' to locate him ever since. That's my story, Bill."

"That was about eight o'clock this mornin', eh? And it's past noon, before yuh notify me."

"Why notify you—as long as there's a chance to catch him. You couldn't do anythin', Bill."

"That's what I've been tellin' him for two years," said Rolling Stone soberly. "Gee, you shore got a crack on the head last night."

"Joe Hall got several cracks from Regan," said Parton.

"I hit him with my hands," said Danny.

"Well, Bill," said Rolling, "you know the news now—so why don't yuh do somethin'? Or are yuh waitin' for the buzzards to gobble up the evidence."

Bill Parton got slowly to his feet and looked at Danny.

"I want to see the evidence before I do much," he said slowly. "I hope yuh ain't aimin' to duck out on me, Regan."

"Sometimes," replied Danny, "yo're as ignorant as yuh look, Parton."

"Check!" snorted Rolling Stone. "Let's go."

There was little conversation during the ride of seven miles down to Danny's ranch. The load of poles and the team were still at the corral fence, but there was no sign of the body. The three men dismounted and looked around. Danny pointed out the exact spot where the body had lain. Darkly moist ground proved this to be the spot, although none of them could swear that it was blood.

They went through the house and the stable, finally coming back to their horses. Bill Parton was mad; Rolling Stone merely amused. Danny was puzzled. The ground was packed so hard that the buckboard wheels left only faint tracks, too indefinite for anyone to notice.

"Well," said Parton, "it's gone."

"If I hadn't seen it myself, I'd say yuh was guessin', Bill," said the deputy. "It's the first time you've been right in two years."

Parton turned to Danny.

"Are you sure yuh wasn't dreamin', Regan?" he asked harshly.

"Come to think of it, mebbe I was," grinned Danny. "I do have a lot off queer dreams, Bill."

"Yuh ought to git one of them dream books, Danny," said

Rolling. "I've got one. If I think of it, I'll see what it means—seein' dead men, layin' on the ground, with a man standin' over him."

"I wish yuh would, Rollin'," said Danny.

"Aw, hell!" snorted the sheriff. "Comin' all the way down here to listen to a couple sagebrush comedians! Let's go back. If yuh have any more dreams, Regan—look up the answers for yourself."

DANNY watched them ride away, puzzled, but thankful that the body had disappeared. He was not going to question anyone's motives for removing the body. Finally, he went over to unload the poles.

It was Bill Parton who saw the fresh buckboard tracks, leading off on the old, abandoned road. He dismounted and looked closely at the marks of the horses. Then he mounted and motioned to his deputy.

"I want to see where that buckboard went, and why they took this road," he said. "The tracks are fresh."

"All right," grunted Rolling, "Are yuh sure them horse tracks point this way? I don't want to back-track no buckboard."

Bill Parton nodded grimly. "Sometimes I'm glad this here sheriff job is about over," he said.

"It's shore a strain on a feller like you," agreed Rolling. "When you took this job, you didn't have a line in your face, and now yore brow looks like a picture of the Japanese Current, flowin' into the Pacific Ocean. Yuh know what I mean—all them jiggly, little lines. Bein' sheriff has shore robbed you of yore youth."

"If you'd think more and talk less, you'd have lines."

"Mebbe. I was sort of a strong silent man, when I joined you, Bill. I hardly ever laughed. In fact, I never seen anythin' worth laughin' at, until I joined up with you. You've shore changed me."

"You've been a damned fool *all* yore life," grunted Parton.

"Another remark like that, Bill, and you can foller yore own danged buckboard tracks. Anyway, you ain't knowed me *all* my life. What was you like, and what did you do, before yuh came to Wild Horse Valley?"

"That's none of yore damn business!" snapped the sheriff. "You keep watchin' yore side of the road, in case that buckboard happened to turn off. I don't want to lose it."

"Yo're watchin' yore side, ain't yuh?" retorted the deputy. "Or is this the sort of buckboard that splits in two, the left side goin' off on its own most any time."

"That's a brainless remark."

"Couple idiots follerin' a buckboard track?"

"One, yuh mean!" snapped the sheriff.

"Yeah, I did, Bill. I merely included myself, so yuh wouldn't be sore. But you can take the honor; I'm merely ridin' with yuh."

"Wait a minute!" The sheriff drew up his horse. "Here's where they turned part out of the road. See them tracks?"

"Prob'ly turned out to pass a scorpion goin' west."

"No, they didn't; they stopped here. See where they cramped the buckboard? Here's where we investigate."

Fifty yards off the old road was the ruins of an ancient adobe shack, its walls nearly crumbled down; and here they found the body of Joe Hall. It was lying in the same position as it was when it was discovered at the Regan ranch, with the unfired Colt near the right hand. To all appearances, Joe Hall had been killed inside the old adobe.

BILL PARTON swore softly, as he walked around the corpse, while Rolling Stone sat down on the broken wall and rolled a smoke.

Suddenly the sheriff dropped on his knees beside the corpse and examined the ground carefully.

"C'mere," he ordered. "Look at this, will yuh?"

It was a clear imprint of a woman's shoe. Rolling Stone hunkered down and looked at it.

"A woman mixed up in it, eh?" he said.

Bill Parton shoved his hands deep in his chaps pockets and looked at Rolling.

"Answer that yourself," he said slowly. "There's her track. All we've got to do is find the woman to fill that track."

"I bet there'll be an awful rush down here," said Rolling. "Every woman in Wild Horse Valley will be anxious to fit up to that mark."

Bill Parton rubbed his stubbled chin, as he looked around for more tracks. He found more at the old doorway, and several more between there and the road; but he did not notice that Rolling Stone was following him closely, obliterating each footprint, as fast as the sheriff pointed them out and went hunting for more.

"We're follerin' that buckboard," declared the sheriff, as they mounted again.

"All right," replied the deputy. "There's only about twenty buckboards in this valley."

"I'll find the woman that fits them tracks, too," declared the sheriff. "She's as guilty as the man who shot Joe Hall."

They finally came to the intersection with the main road, which led to Antelope, the nearest railroad town to Wild Horse Valley. The heavy stage had obliterated the buckboard tracks; so they had no idea whether the buckboard had gone toward Antelope, or back to Tonto City. It was only about a mile from the intersection to the J Bar C ranch.

"I reckon we better go back to Tonto City," said the sheriff. "We've got to take the coroner down to look at that body; so we might as well do it now."

"And git somethin' to eat," added Rolling Stone. "I'm hongry."

About halfway between the intersection and Tonto City, they met the J Bar C buckboard. In fact, they were nearly run down by Oscar, who was driving.

The two officers merely caught a glimpse in the dust cloud of Henry Harrison Conroy and Judge Van Treece, clinging to each other, while Oscar did a fair imitation of Ben Hur, yelling at the top of his voice.

"There's a buckboard, but no lady," laughed Rolling Stone, as he spurred his horse back into the road.

"That damn Swede is goin' to kill them two old pelicans one of these days," said the sheriff. "I think I'll find out where that J Bar C buckboard has been today."

That was not difficult to do. There were a number of people in Tonto City, who had seen Leila Harper drive away with Henry and Judge. Several had seen them come back to town; and the bartender at the Tonto Saloon told the sheriff that Oscar had been left there, until the buckboard returned.

"And still," reminded Rolling Stone, "yuh don't *know* that it went down to Regan's ranch."

"I'm goin' to know," declared the sheriff.

He went to the court-house, where he explained things to the prosecuting attorney.

"We'll take some plaster of paris down there and make casts of those footprints," said the lawyer. "You get the coroner, and I'll meet you at your office, Bill."

"We've got to work smart," said the sheriff. "I figure that Danny Regan shot Joe Hall, got scared and pulled out. While he was makin' up his mind to come to me, Conroy, Van Treece and that girl went down there, stole the evidence and took it to that old adobe."

"We might have trouble in proving it," said the lawyer. "You say that no one positively seen them go to Regan's ranch; that no one, except Regan, saw the body at Regan's ranch; so there's no absolute proof that Hall was killed there. And, even if they did go to Regan's ranch, they could swear they never saw the body."

"Make it as tough as yuh can," growled the sheriff. "Get that plaster and meet me in ten minutes."

CHAPTER III

A DREAM AND A LETTER

JUDGE VAN TREECE stared moodily at his plate of bacon and eggs; sort of a hang-dog expression on his face. Henry Harrison Conroy flicked a drop of egg yolk off the front of his white shirt, and nodded approvingly, as Frijole Bill appeared with the pot of coffee.

"Little more Java, Judge?" queried Henry.

"No-o-o," mourned Judge. "I have no appetite."

"I noticed yuh was actin' kinda jumpy," said Frijole. "I used to bunk with a horse-thief that acted that way every mornin'."

"Huh?" blurted Judge. "Frijole, are you comparing me to a thief?"

"Calm down," soothed Henry. "Try the eggs."

"They're guilty as hell," sighed the Judge.

"I was readin' about them eggs they ship from China," offered Frijole. "Some of 'em are a hundred years old."

Judge shoved the plate out of his line of vision. Frijole went back to the kitchen, closing the door behind him.

"Worried?" asked Henry.

Judge nodded grimly.

"I moved dead men all night, in my sleep," he said wearily. "Why, I even shuffled 'em and played three-card Monte with them. I hid 'em, and we played button, button, who's got the button. Gawd, it was awful!"

"Pleasant dreams," mused Henry, sipping at his coffee.

"You don't seem to be worrying."

"Why worry?"

"Why? I'll tell you why. If Oscar—"

"Stop yelling. I know what you mean. Oscar has sworn to secrecy."

"Just like he was sworn to vote against you. Give him a skinful of prune whisky, and he'll shout the truth to the housetops. Henry, we've got to muzzle Oscar, or kill him."

"I prefer muzzles to murder, of course, my dear Judge. If—"

"Hey!" yelled Frijole, shoving open the door, "Miss Harper jist drove in. She's out in front."

"Gawd!" exploded Judge.

Leila was frightened and excited, when they met her at the front of the house.

"Oh, I'm frightened stiff!" she exclaimed. "The sheriff and Mr. Campbell, the prosecutor, tried to make me admit that we went down there and stole Joe Hall's body. They said they could prove it, and that they wouldn't do anything to me, if I'd admit it. They said they had a plaster cast of my footprints, which they found beside the body. But I didn't admit anything," she finished bravely.

"Well, well!" exclaimed Henry admiringly. "You are a very brave young lady. So they found your footprints, eh?"

"They—they made plaster casts of them."

"I see," mused Henry. "Clever, I'd say, Judge. Leila, have they brought the body to Tonto City yet?"

"Why, no, I—I guess not. No one has mentioned it, if they did. I saw the two officers and the coroner come back yesterday, without it."

"Perhaps they buried it down there."

"Why, they wouldn't do that!"

"Have you seen Danny?"

"He came last night," replied Leila. "He doesn't know we took that body away; doesn't know what became of it. Poor Danny is so muddled."

"He was born that way," said Judge dryly.

"No such a thing!" denied Leila. "Danny is smart."

"In some things," admitted Judge. "Such as picking you for a wife."

"I still have hopes," smiled Leila. "If we can both keep out of jail."

"**THEY** tell me that the modern jails are comfortable," said Henry. "I haven't been in one for years. I was suspected of poisoning a dog; a very intelligent pooch, it seems. They always are—after they are dead. An autopsy showed that the dog died from a combination of a hundred yards of wrapping twine, six dozen assorted pins and several razor blades. The Judge exonerated me."

"We are getting away from the case at hand," murmured Judge.

"The case at hand doesn't seem to be a case at all, Judge. In fact, from my position in the wings, it seems a first-class mystery."

"They tracked our buckboard," said Leila.

"I knew they would!" exclaimed Judge. "I knew they would."

"Well, I'm sure I don't know what to do," sighed Leila. "I just had to tell you. Mr. Bain, the blacksmith, loaned me his horse and buggy; so I could come out here. I suppose the sheriff knows I came here."

"Yes, I'd credit him with that much intuition," nodded Henry. "But that is all right, Leila."

"But what's to be done?" asked Judge anxiously.

"Nothing, my dear Judge. What is there to do?"

"I guess we have already done enough. Too much, in fact."

"He dreamed last night, Leila," chuckled Henry. "Spent the night trying to hide corpses."

"So did I," she replied. "And you kept digging them up. I had to tell mother what we did—and she had nightmares, too. It was awful."

"Here comes somebody!" exclaimed Judge. "Why, it is Rolling Stone."

The bandy-legged deputy rode up to them, trying to look

solemn, but was not successful. "Howdy, folks," he grinned. "How's everything?"

"That question covers quite a lot of territory, doesn't it?" asked Henry.

"I never thought about it thataway," laughed Rolling, "but I reckon it does. I—I wanted to git away from Bill Parton for a while; so I rode out here. Bill's fit to be tied, don'tcha know it? You've done heard about Joe Hall's demise, I suppose. Well, somebody swiped the body—unless Danny lied about seein' it in his yard—and me and Bill found it in that old adobe on the lower road.

"You men remember meetin' me and Bill yes'day afternoon, when you was comin' home in the buckboard, don'tcha?

"Well, we was comin' back from there, when we met yuh. Bill was trackin' a buckboard, but lost it, when we hit the main road.

"Then we went to town and got the coroner. Bill seen some female tracks around the remains; so him and Campbell took some plaster down there to make a cast of the print. That part would have been fine, except that we done forget to take any water along to mix the plaster.

"Anyway, it worked out all right, 'cause there wasn't any tracks left. Not a darn track left, in fact," said Rolling softly, "there wasn't no corpse either."

"No corpse!" exclaimed Leila, and suddenly put her hand over her mouth.

"No corpse?" parroted Judge. "No corpse. That's funny, Henry! No corpse!"

And Judge laughed chokingly, slapping Henry on the back.

"Nope, not a damn corpse," added Rolling Stone.

"What became of it?" asked Leila.

"QUIEN SABE?" replied the deputy. "It was gone—that's all I know. The coroner cursed the sheriff, the sheriff cursed me, and I got so mad that I flung the paper sack of plaster on the ground and busted it. Then I made some remarks about both of 'em, and we wasn't speakin' to each other all the way back.

"They acted as though I stole their danged corpse."

"And so," remarked Henry dryly, "you didn't find the corpse."

"Found it the first time," replied Rolling.

"You are sure he was dead?" queried Judge.

"He shore acted dead," nodded Rolling. " 'Course we didn't test him."

"How do you test dead men?" asked Henry curiously.

"This here talk is gettin' technical," laughed the deputy. "Bill and the coroner had the same argument. The coroner asked Bill if he was sure Joe Hall was dead, and Bill said he sure was dead. The coroner asked Bill how he knowed, and Bill got mad. He said—"

"Ha'lo, yents," interrupted Oscar, coming around the house.

Henry took one look at Oscar, and groaned aloud. It was evident that Oscar had been drinking some of Frijole's home-made liquor. Oscar had an air—and an odor.

"Hello, Oscar," smiled the deputy. "How are yuh?"

"Ay am yust as goot as anybody," declared Oscar.

"You've been drinking before breakfast," sighed Judge.

"Yah, su-u-ure. Last night Ay had a dream. Ay dreamed—"

"Stop it!" snorted Henry. "Never mind your dreams."

"But Ay like to ta'l about it."

Henry and Judge looked at each other in consternation. They couldn't let Oscar tell about his dream.

"You better go get some breakfast," said Henry.

"I'd like to hear a Swedish dream," said the deputy. "I've heard Irish, French, German, Dutch—"

"Das was goot dream," grinned Oscar, who stepped back.

"Nobody wants to hear your dream," declared Henry. "Go to breakfast!"

"Ay dreamed—"

"No! You didn't dream—"

"Ay ta'l you, Ay dreamed Ay vas—"

Henry fairly pounced on Oscar, clutching him by the throat, and they both went down under the impetus of Henry's attack. Leila screamed, as Oscar reached up, grasped Henry by the middle, and catapulted him six feet away, where Henry landed, sitting down, the breath knocked out of him. Oscar sat up, grinned widely and said:

"Ay dreamed Ay vas at a dance mit no pants on! Haw! Haw! Haw!"

"Aw, shucks!" snorted the deputy. "I've dreamed that a dozen times."

"That's funny," giggled Judge, almost in hysterics. "No pants on! Henry, he dreamed he was at a dance, with no pants on!"

"Oh!" exclaimed the dazed Henry. "He—he didn't have no pants—"

And Henry went into a paroxysm of mirthless laughter.

"Well, what's wrong with you gallinippers around here?" asked the deputy. "Have yuh all gone loco? Miss Leila, what ails 'em?"

Leila looked helplessly at everyone.

"No pants!" whispered Judge, inanely.

"At a dance," added Oscar. "Yeeminy, Ay vars ashamed! Haw, haw, haw!"

Henry got to his feet, panting a little, and brushed off his clothes.

"I—I hate dreams," he told Rolling Stone. "All my life I've been that way. It upsets me to have anyone tell me of a dream. If you have finished with your tale, Oscar, I'd advise some break-fast."

"Yah, su-u-ure," nodded Oscar. "You want me to drife bock-board today?"

"I hope not—but I'm not sure."

"Ay get breakfast now."

"Some day that Swede's goin' to kill both of you fellers in

that buckboard," declared the deputy, after Oscar disappeared. "Why don't both of yuh ride horses?"

"I suppose we shall have to take it up in self-defense," replied Henry.

"If yo're sheriff, you'll have to ride a horse."

HENRY nodded slowly. "I suppose I shall. I might make Judge my deputy, and both of us walk to and from the—er—corpses."

"Take my advice," said Rolling Stone seriously, "and when yuh find one—nail it down, and clinch the nails, or they'll walk out on yuh."

"I suppose it's the climate," said Henry. "The air of Arizona is very invigorating, you know."

"That's right. I was wonderin' if Frijole might—well, I forgot to eat any breakfast this mornin'."

"Sure!" exclaimed Judge. "I'll order him to cook some for you."

They walked into the house, leaving Leila and Henry together.

"That terrible Swede!" gasped Henry. "Leila, my heart was in my mouth, when he started about his dream."

"But what did Rolling Stone mean about losing the body again?"

"Sh-h-h-h!" cautioned Henry. "On the way back here yesterday, we met Parton and Stone. We knew they had been down to Danny's place, and that they had come back over the old road, trailing the buckboard. There was a strong possibility that they had discovered the body; so we drove back there, shifted the body to another spot, and came back. They had found the body. There were tracks of cowboy boots around it."

"That was why—oh, I see now! Oscar knows."

"Oscar knows," agreed Henry. "I've explained that if he don't keep still about it, he'll hang as high as the rest of us."

"Did he swear not to tell?"

"Oh, yes—he swore. He also swore not to vote for me."

"But this is serious, Mr. Conroy."

"Well, my dear, we will just have to wait and see how serious it is. I think we'll ride down and have a talk with Danny this afternoon. A few more buckboard tracks on that old road won't hurt anything."

"Well, I hope everything will turn out right, Mr. Conroy. I'll go back now."

"I'm glad you came out, Leila. Keep a stiff upper lip. Don't let the law bluff you. We know they lied about the plaster casts."

"Oh, I'm glad about that. It had me worried. I suppose mother is walking the floor, wondering why I don't come home. Come in and see us, won't you? Mother would be pleased."

"Sure about that, Leila?"

"Why, certainly. Mother thinks you are fine."

"When sober. I know, Leila. But this new job—if I take it—will require absolute sobriety. An entire new rôle for me; and I may be unsuited for the part. It will require a heroic figure—not a worthless old character actor. Henry Harrison Conroy, as the sheriff of Wild Horse Valley. A black mustache, piercing eyes, thundering voice. Can you imagine me—thundering? I'm a natural born nose polisher.

" 'Hands off that gal, Bert Nuttingall, or I'll shoot you in twain!' Can you imagine me? I squeak like a rusty hinge every time I try to raise my voice. Someone would soak me with an overripe egg, and at the next performance I'd be the mere voice, offstage, saying:

" 'No, sir; the afternoon stage don't git here in the mornin'.'"

"Anyway," laughed Leila, "come in and see us."

"Thank you, my dear—and my regards to your charming mother."

HE WATCHED her drive away. Judge and Rolling Stone were in the kitchen, talking with Frijole Bill; so Henry sauntered down to the buckboard, climbed into the seat and relaxed thoughtfully. Finally he took a blank envelope from his pocket, drew out the enclosure and looked it over carefully.

It was what was left of a letter, it seemed. Some of it had been torn away, while much of it was obliterated by a dark stain, which had left the paper stiff, completely blotting out the penciled scrawl. All that was readable was this:

> *Dear Chuck:*
> *Glad to hear from you again.*
> *I sure got a laugh out of your letter*
> *friend. So they elected him*
> *there. That sure is funny.*
> *made him part with his*
> *careful, Chuck.*
> *rat and he'd kill*
> *better make him give*
> *you'll be safe*
> *here as usual*

It was a letter Henry had taken off the body of Joe Hall, when they moved the body the last time. The bullet had torn through part of the letter, and the blood had blotted out nearly all that was left. There was enough of the date line left to show that it was from Carson City, Nevada, written on the tenth of August. And this was only the fourteenth. The envelope had been so nearly destroyed that they could not tell if the letter had been opened, or not. Judge attached no importance to the letter, but Henry was not so sure. There was no one at the Rafter P, who answered to the nickname of Chuck. Henry put the letter away carefully, when Judge and Rolling Stone came from the kitchen.

After talking with Judge for a few minutes, the deputy mounted and rode away. Judge came down and climbed up in the buckboard.

"I hope I never have to go through such agony again," said Judge.

"You mean Oscar's dream?"

"Yes. Did you tell Leila what we did about that body?"

Henry nodded. "Yes, I told her. Did Stone say anything about what the sheriff was doing?"

"Nothing important. He wants to find the body, of course."

"I've been thinking about that," remarked Henry. "We've got to let them find that body. It—it's something—well, Judge, you know yourself that in all this heat—"

"Exactly. But how will we do it?"

"I want to talk with Danny," replied Henry. "Suppose we go down the old road, pick up the body, and place it where it is bound to be discovered."

"Cautiously," nodded Judge.

"Certainly. By all means, with caution, Judge. And after that is done, we will wash our hands of the whole thing. Day after tomorrow, I am due to take my office?"

"Will you take it, Henry?"

"Who knows? It may be that they—er—will have to hand it through the bars to me."

CHAPTER IV

LOST CORPSE

LATER THAT DAY, three men, Bill Parton, Rolling Stone, and John Campbell, the prosecuting attorney, sat beside the crumbling wall of the old adobe. Near them was a white splash of plaster on the ground, covering what had been a woman's footprint, and which they fondly hoped would give them a fairly good cast of that woman's shoe. Near them was a large canteen, and a broken sack of plaster.

"Won't prove anythin', anyway," declared Rolling Stone: "There ain't no law that says a woman couldn't walk around here."

"True enough," admitted the lawyer. "But I believe we can

use this cast to frighten the Harper girl into a confession. If we can get her to confess that they moved that body, she will also admit that they found it on Regan's place. In this way we can build up a fairly good case against Regan for the murder."

Frijole

"If we had some ham, we could have some ham and eggs, if we had some eggs," said Rolling Stone. "But before yuh can charge a man with murder, you've got to have a corpse, Campbell. Instead of settin' here, pourin' plaster into footprints, we ought to be tryin' to find the remains of Joe Hall."

"If we can scare that girl—she'll tell where it is," said the sheriff.

"I thought you was stuck on her, Bill," said Rolling. "Yo're kind of a dog-in-the-manger, ain't yuh? If you can't have her— put her in jail."

Bill Parton's big face reddened with anger, but he kept his lips shut tightly.

"I think that cast is sufficiently set," said the lawyer, and gently pried it out. "There we are!"

"It don't look like anythin' to me," said the deputy. "If that's a copy of Leila Harper's foot, she better see a doctor."

"When we make the imprint in plaster," explained the lawyer. "It will show exactly as the print showed in the ground."

"All right," said the deputy. "If we ain't goin' to hunt for the corpse, I reckon we might as well go back to Tonto City."

The sheriff and lawyer had come down in a buggy, while Rolling Stone rode his horse; and they had left their transportation near the road. As the sheriff and prosecutor drove around a clump of mesquite, with the deputy close behind them, another vehicle came around a curve, the horses trotting swiftly, and were so close that the sheriff jerked up on his horses to prevent a collision.

It was the J Bar C buckboard, containing Henry, Judge and Oscar. At sight of the three officers from Tonto City, Oscar started to jerk up his team, changed his mind instantly, and slashed them with his whip. At the same time he half raised to his feet and emitted a yell that might well have been heard in Tonto City.

The effect on Oscar's team was electrical. In fact it was so dynamic that a line broke, and Oscar went backwards over the rear of the buckboard, landing on his shoulders in the road, almost in front of the sheriff's equipage. The horses whirled sideways, cramping the buggy so sharp that it upset, throwing its occupants sprawling, while the frightened team went up the road, dragging the wrecked buggy.

Henry and Judge grabbed each other, helpless so far as driving was concerned. There was another curve a hundred yards beyond where they had lost Oscar, and apparently the runaway team tried to straighten out this curve, with the result that the buckboard threshed over a washout, flipping high in the air.

In some unaccountable manner, both men managed to stay on the seat, but a large, blanket-covered bundle in the back of the buckboard, flew into the air and fell in the middle of the road.

Bill Parton was dancing up and down in the road, swearing like a mule-skinner, while Campbell sat there, dazed, wide-eyed. Rolling Stone slouched sideways in his saddle, an expression of amazement on his face.

"It's broke," wailed Campbell. "It's broke."

"Yore neck?" queried the deputy.

"No—our plaster cast. It's broke all to pieces."

"Oh, that damn Swede!" panted the sheriff. "Oh, that awful Swede!"

Oscar was sitting up in the road, trying to gather his breath.

"You done it!" puffed the sheriff. "Oscar Johnson, you done it!"

"Ay—didn't—do—it," panted Oscar. "Oll Ay done vars help hide it."

"You did, eh?" Campbell was on his feet, shaking a finger in Oscar's face. "You helped hide it, eh? Where is it now?"

"They done lost a big bundle out of their buckboard," said the deputy. "There she is, up there at the curve."

THE SHERIFF went limping up there and took a look at the bundle.

"Yeeminy!" breathed Oscar. "It yumped out!"

"This is Joe Hall's body!" yelled the sheriff.

"W'at de ha'l did you t'ink it vars?" asked Oscar.

The sheriff came back.

"You was goin' to take that body away and destroy it, eh?" he accused.

"No," replied Oscar sweetly, "ve vars only yust going to put it where it could be found. Yudge say ye got to give it up before it spoils."

Bill Parton turned to Campbell.

"That'll cinch 'em," he said harshly. "They'll either tell the truth, or we'll send 'em all to the penitentiary. Stone, why in hell don't yuh see if yuh can stop our team? Settin' there, like a damn wooden Injun! Do somethin', will yuh?"

In the meantime Judge and Henry were clinging to each other and watching that team eat up distance. Except for that first curve, they were staying on the road, but the buckboard was rocking and lurching wildly over the rough, rutty road. Judge risked a glance over his shoulder.

"We've lost it!" he yelled in Henry's ear. "The officers will find that body, Henry!"

"Yes—and a couple more, I'm afraid!" replied Henry. "Look out!"

The road made an almost right-angle turn; but the team did

not. They went straight across country, through mesquite and cat-claw, over cactus and rocks for possibly a hundred feet, where a front wheel hooked around a tough manzanita, slewed around, yanking the buckboard to a splintering stop.

But the horses kept going, leaving parts of harness scattered behind them. When the dust subsided, Judge appeared slowly from among some cat-claw, grasped a smoke-tree for support, and looked around.

"Hen-n-n-nry!" he called softly. "Oh, Hen-n-n-nry!"

There was no reply. Judge licked his lips.

"Henry's dead," he told the world. "Poor Henry is dead—and I'd give ten years of *my* life for a drink of whisky."

"If it isn't busted, there's a gallon jug of it, tied under the buckboard seat," stated Henry's voice.

Judge craned his neck. "You—you are not dead, Henry?"

"Find the whisky," said Henry. "In the meantime, I shall try to find out how in hell a man of my size ever came through a six-inch hole in a mesquite thicket."

"Can you get out, Henry?" asked Judge anxiously.

"If I do," replied Henry, "I shall go back into vaudeville, under the billing of Henry, the Houdini Hill-Billy. But not with these pants, Judge. If I lose one-eighth as much of them as I did coming in, I'll be as naked as the day I was born. Get the liquor."

It was no figure of speech with Henry. He managed to tear himself loose from the embraces of that natural barb-wire entanglement, minus ninety per cent of his pants, all of his shirt, except the neck-hand, and with a plentiful supply of scratches.

Judge had the jug, and they sat down in the shade of the smashed buckboard.

"All is lost," sighed Judge. "By this time the officers of the law have Oscar and the corpse."

Henry drank deeply and slowly closed his eyes.

"The way of the transgressor is hard," he said.

"There is a preponderance of corroborative evidence," sighed

Judge, accepting the jug. "Such damnable luck! To have the officers of the law meet us there—and us with the corpse."

"Dirty work at the crossroads," said Henry, recovering the jug. "I wonder how far it is to Danny's ranch. It can't be far."

"Possibly a mile and a half, Henry. But by going down there, we might possibly involve Danny."

"I am thinking of my pants," said Henry, surrendering the jug, "I might borrow some sort of raiment to cover my shame."

"You are, sir," declared Judge ponderously, "a hell of a looking wreck. It is really too bad that the voters of this county did not see you in this wise; you wouldn't have received a vote."

"Oh, yes, I would; you forget Oscar."

"Poor Oscar. The toe of his boot caught me under the chin, as he left us, Henry. Well, here is to Oscar—the son of a Viking."

"A son of something," agreed Henry, "but I wouldn't specify just what. Whew! I can still feel myself turning handsprings in the air. I take it that the team went on."

"Ah-h-h-h-h! Not bad liquor," said Judge. "A queer odor and a bit harsh—but not bad."

"Prune juice," said Henry, "I stole it from Frijole Bill. It must be at least three days old."

"Some daze," nodded Judge. "If I were asked for an opinion, I would say that we better start going somewhere—and keep the cork in that jug, Henry. No wonder Oscar thought he was a charioteer."

Henry corked the jug and placed it carefully on the ground. He looked at Judge, blinked several times and broke into a smile.

"Do you know any shongs?" he asked.

THE SUSPENSE was too much for Leila. She had seen the prosecuting attorney ride away with the two officers, and she was afraid they had gone to arrest Danny Regan; so she borrowed a horse and buggy from the blacksmith and induced her mother to close shop and go along.

Danny was alone at the ranch, nailing shingles on the kitchen roof; and he greeted them warmly. Leila told him why they came down.

"No, they didn't come down here," smiled Danny. "Have you seen Henry?"

"Not today," replied Leila. Danny looked at her closely.

"You're not worryin' about me, are yuh, Leila?"

"Suppose they can prove that the body was here?" she countered.

"It sure is a funny thing," he declared. "I can't make head nor tail out of it. Who on earth stole that body, and why did they steal it? It doesn't make sense."

"Under the circumstances, I think you should tell Danny the truth, Leila," said Mrs. Harper. "It can't make things any worse."

"The truth?" queried Danny. "What do you mean?"

"I suppose I may as well tell him, mother," agreed Leila.

Mrs. Harper nodded, and Leila proceeded to tell Danny all about how they found the body, took it away and hid it; and how Henry, Judge and Oscar took the body to another hiding place, after it had been found by the officers.

She told how they had tried to make her tell everything, after they had found her footprints near the body, and had told her they were going to make plaster casts of the marks.

"Well, God bless all of yuh!" exclaimed Danny. "It's wonderful of yuh to do all that for me—but I never shot Joe Hall."

"Henry wanted to be sure the evidence was away from here," sighed Leila.

"Bless his old heart—and nose," smiled Danny. "He's wonderful, and so is Judge; but, Leila, you're the most wonderful of them all. Just to think of you helpin' them take that—well, that's nerve. And Henry almost ready to step into office. Gee, I've sure got some great friends!"

"Our biggest worry is Oscar," said Leila. "Oscar is funny."

"In lots of ways," laughed Danny.

"I don't see why Henry Conroy keeps him," said Mrs. Harper.

"I asked Henry one day about why he kept Oscar, and he said he wouldn't part with him, until he had thoroughly made up his mind which of them—he or Oscar—was the bigger fool."

"They both drink," said Mrs. Harper seriously.

"And both sing, when they're drunk," added Danny, laughing.

"Terrible songs—and worse voices," said Leila. "But if you want to split your sides, listen when Judge Van Treece joins the chorus."

Danny, apparently unperturbed by what Leila had told him, took the two ladies and showed them what he was doing toward repairing the place.

"Stay down and have supper with me," he begged. "I get so lonesome around here. I'll do the cookin'."

"Young man," said Mrs. Harper severely, "if we stay, I shall do the cooking myself."

"I hoped you'd say that," grinned Danny. "I'm a terrible cook."

ABOUT an hour later, while Mrs. Harper was preparing supper, and Leila and Danny were sitting at the table, planning futures, someone outside the kitchen doorway said:

"Hoo-hoo-o-o-o! Hoo-hoo-o-o-o!"

The voice was not very strong. Mrs. Harper, skillet in hand, stepped to the doorway. For a moment she stood there, staring wildly, the smoking skillet held in front of her, like a weapon of defense. Then she dropped it and stepped back.

"Merciful Heavens!" she shrieked, and backed toward the table.

Standing near the kitchen doorway, hand in hand, was Henry and Judge. Henry was holding the jug in his right hand, and on the faces of the two old scarecrows were expressions of angelic innocence.

"H'lo, Danny," said Judge.

"Tha' wasn' Danny," said Henry. "Tha' was a woman."

"Im—impos'ble," declared Judge. "Thish ranch is not co-educa'nl."

Danny stepped from the kitchen, stopped short, staring at the two wrecks.

"What on earth happened to you?" exclaimed Danny.

"Young man," replied Henry expansively, "you are looking upon a couple losht shouls. Fug'tives from jushtish."

Danny came down to them, looking upon them with undisguised amazement.

"I never in my whole life—" began Danny, as Leila stepped out on the porch. She shrieked and darted back into the house.

"Goodn'ss gracious!" exclaimed Judge. "Is thish Regan's ranch, or Regan's sheminary?"

"Turn around," ordered Danny. "We're goin' to the stable, until I can get some clothes for you two. Forward march."

"Treated jus' like a horsh," complained Henry.

"My God, what a spectacle!" groaned Danny. "Leila and her mother are in the house, Henry. Don'tcha understand?"

"Perf'ly, Danny—perf'ly," and Henry started singing mournfully:

"Oh, a big, beer bottle, came drif'n in the shea. It drifted up to me—it drifted up to me-e-e. Inshide was a paper, with these lines written on, 'Whoever f'in's thish bottle, fin's the beer all gone.'"

Danny closed the stable door behind them.

"Danny," said Judge thickly, "the horshes ran away. We lost Oscar and the corpsh, right in front of the sheriff. We're shunk."

"Great lovely dove!" snorted the young cowboy. "The sheriff caught yuh with the corpse?"

"He ain't caught us yet, has he?" queried Henry. "But they got Oscar and the body."

"Perhapsh Oscar is dead, too," sighed Judge, and yawned widely.

"Oshcar," pronounced Henry, "is unhurt; he landed on his head."

"You stay right here, while I get yuh some clothes," ordered Danny.

"Henry," said Judge, after Danny had closed the door, "do you re'lize that there's two women at the housh?"

"In my pres'nt condition," replied Henry, "I can only re'lize my pres'nt condition. Sufficient for the day is the evil thereof—and we've cer'nly been evil."

CHAPTER V

ANOTHER CORPSE

THE COURT ROOM at Tonto City was crowded to capacity for the inquest over the body of Joe Hall. Leila, Danny, Henry, Judge, and Oscar were in the custody of the sheriff, who was first to testify. His testimony was at length, outlining as he did the trouble he had had in trying to get possession of Joe Hall's body.

He told of their first discovery, and that the body had been stolen the second time, during which time the woman's tracks had been obliterated. Then he told of the double-runway, in which the blanket-wrapped body had been thrown from the J Bar C buckboard, along with Oscar Johnson, who had confessed his part in the stealing of the body.

"You have the plaster cast of that footprint?" asked the coroner.

"No, I ain't," replied the sheriff. "When me and John Campbell was dumped out of that buggy, John sat on the cast and smashed it."

Danny Regan was called to the stand, and told the same story he had told the sheriff and deputy the day Hall had been murdered. He told them he knew nothing about the stealing of the body, until told about it, after the officers had possession of the remains.

"Who told you?" asked the coroner.

"Miss Harper."

Danny was dismissed, and Henry Harrison Conroy was called to the stand. Henry's appearance was impressive. He wore a checkered suit, brown shoes and brown spats, and carried a gold-headed cane. He was a showman now— not a cattleman. He beamed at the audience, and a

Oscar Johnson

chuckle swept the place. The coroner seemed confused.

"Mr. Conroy, will you please tell your story to the jury?"

"Gentlemen," said Henry softly, "I don't exactly know my status in this matter. I have heard rumors that I am a murderer, or a kidnaper—or just a plain fool. I firmly admit the latter, which, of course, is no alibi for the other charges. For any wrong-doing, which may be charged to Miss Harper, Judge Van Treece, or to Oscar Johnson, I insist that I, and I alone, am to blame. I stole that body from the yard of Danny Regan's ranch. Firmly believing that the officers had discovered the body, I went back and stole it again. Later, I decided to remove the body, in order to place it where it would be found. Circumstances over which I had no control, unmasked me. I sit before you, a disgraced old man, without a whole pair of overalls to my name."

It required some time to restore order in the court room.

"Mr. Conroy," said the coroner, "you stole that body in order to save Danny Regan?"

"I am no cadaver kleptomaniac, sir," replied Henry stiffly.

"You believed that Danny Regan had murdered Joe Hall, eh?"

"I believed that if the law discovered the body at that spot, they might be disposed to consider that Danny knew something about the demise of Joe Hall."

"But why did you steal it the second time, Mr. Conroy?"

"Well, sir, I happened to remember that Miss Harper was with us, and that none of us were careful about our footprints. So I took the body away and obliterated the prints. It seems that I overlooked one print—but that is immaterial now. I also neglected, the first time, to search the corpse."

"You searched it the second time?" asked the coroner quickly.

"Yes."

"What did you find?"

Henry shut his lips tightly, and his eyes narrowed perceptibly.

"Nothing at all," he said.

"Wait a minute!" snapped the sheriff. "What did you take off that corpse, Conroy?"

"You heard my reply to that same question—nothing."

"Why did you search?"

"Curiosity, sheriff."

"Yea-a-ah? All right"

The coroner made a short résumé of the evidence. He pointed out the fact that Joe Hall and Danny Regan had fought a battle the night before the murder, and that Joe Hall had been soundly whipped. The face of the corpse still bore witness to that fight.

"Why Joe Hall ever went down to Regan's ranch, we have no idea," he told them. "You have heard Regan's own story. It is your duty to decide this case on the evidence."

And those six men decided that Danny Regan must stand trial for the murder of Joe Hall. Apparently satisfied with a victim, the prosecuting attorney ignored the kidnapers.

BUT BILL PARTON was not satisfied. He went to the prosecutor, after Danny was in jail, and asked what about Henry Harrison Conroy and his three companions in crime.

"Drop it," advised Campbell. "It would only pile up expense

on the county, and no Wild Horse jury would ever convict them."

"I wish I knew what Conroy took off that body."

"He said he didn't find anything, Bill."

"He's a liar; he got somethin'."

Judge told Leila: "The county is too poor to feed us."

But Leila could see no humor in the situation; not with Danny in jail. Henry was diplomatic. He went down to the jail and talked with the sheriff, who asked him confidentially what he found on Joe Hall's body.

"I answered that question under oath," replied Henry.

"Are you goin' to qualify for this office?" asked the sheriff.

Henry shrugged his shoulders.

"If I don't—you'll stay in office, won't you?" he asked.

"Unless the board of supervisors decide to make an appointment."

"What will happen to Joe Hall's Rafter P ranch?"

"I'm takin' it back," replied the sheriff.

"Taking it back?"

"I shore am, Conroy. Joe Hall bought it on a shoe-string, and gave me his personal note for the balance—ten thousand dollars. He never had no deed to the place. It's still in my name. All I've got to do is move back there and take charge."

"He gave you a personal note, eh?"

The sheriff took an old bill-fold from his pocket and showed Henry Conroy the note, which was to run for three years, at seven per cent interest.

"And he never even paid the interest," declared the sheriff. "Damn it, he owes me over seven hundred dollars interest."

"Parton," said Henry seriously, "do you think Danny killed Hall?"

"If he didn't—who did, Conroy?"

"That is what I'm going to find out."

SLIM PICKINS and Oscar Johnson saddled horses for Henry and Judge next morning. One horse was a tall, bony roan, little less than twenty years of age, while the other was a shaggy, gray pony, weighing about seven hundred pounds, short-coupled, and many years past the age of discretion. Judge rode the pony, and his stirrups almost reached the ground, while Henry, on the tall roan, towered far above him, a huge sombrero on his head. Judge wore boots, but on his head was that time-honored derby.

Henry saw the expression in Slim's eyes, adjusted his hat to an exact balance, and said:

"Slim, I have no illusions. I know the age, disposition and general decrepitude of these steeds. I have a mental picture of us both, fore and aft; so go ahead and laugh."

"Well, yuh do look like hell," admitted Slim seriously. "But yuh wanted somethin' reliable."

"Thank yuh, Slim. You will observe that I use 'yuh,' instead of 'you.' Put me under a big hat, and I go entirely Arizona. I do not suppose you have ever seen William Faversham in 'The Squaw Man.'"

"No, I don't reckon I ever did, Mr. Conroy."

"Well, if you had, Slim, I'm sure you would see the vast difference in our appearance. Ready, Judge?"

"Speak to the horse," replied Judge.

"His name's Lightnin'," said Slim, internally convulsed.

"Das tall hurse is named Yhonny," informed Oscar.

"Thank yuh, Oscar," said Henry soberly, "just plain Johnny, eh?"

"Yah, su-u-u-ure. Ay yust named him."

"We really should have a bottle of something to christen him with," said Henry.

"Yuh might get a bottle of Frijole Bill's prune juice," suggested Slim. Henry shuddered and lifted a hand in protest.

"I'd be afraid to even break a bottle on his knees, Slim.

Knowing the power of that concoction, I'd shudder to say what might happen to me and Yhonny. Shall we proceed, Judge?"

"Proceed? What in the name of all seven devils do you think I have been doing since I mounted this moth-eaten wreck."

"Lift your feet a little, Judge," advised Slim, "You've been kicking your heels together."

AFTER all, the horses had some powers of locomotion left. Johnny had a swinging walk, which forced Lightning to trot, in order to keep up, and Judge was obliged to hold his derby with one hand, and the reins in the other.

"It cu-comes to my mind," said Judge, jiggling in his saddle, "that the Spaniards were responsible for introducing horses in this country."

"I have never heard of anyone introducing a horse," replied Henry. "But what has that to do with us?"

"Nothing mum-much," replied Judge. "I thought I only huh-hated Swedes—but I include Spaniards."

"Are you getting an impediment in your voice, Judge?"

"Impediment—hell! It's my upper plate shaking loose."

"False modesty," said Henry soberly.

"I'm dying for a drink."

"No drinks," replied Henry. "After the spectacle we made of ourselves? I'm blushing yet. If there was a pledge lying loose around here, I'd take it. All my life, as far back as I can remember, I have been able to carry my liquor like a gentleman—until I contacted Frijole Bill's prune juice. I'm cured, Judge; as cured as a picnic ham."

"Are you willing to swear on your honor as a gentleman that you will never drink whisky again, Henry?"

"That's the lawyer for you! Will you swear? Honor!"

"You are evasive, sir, damnably evasive."

"And my throat," said Henry, "is coated an inch thick with dust."

They stopped at Tonto City, but restricted themselves to six drinks, after which they mounted and rode on. It was Saturday, and many of the folks from the outlying districts were in town. But Henry and Judge were utterly oblivious to the mirthful glances.

They mounted, with difficulty, especially Henry, whose girth and short legs were a handicap in mounting a tall horse. There was a smattering of applause from across the street, but neither of them paid the slightest attention, as they rode away.

"I have been very patient," reminded Judge. "I have not been consulted in any way, nor do I know the slightest reason for this pilgrimage—if I may call it so. I am blindly following you, sir; like Sancho Panza following Don Quixote. But, damn it, sir, even they had a mission."

"Spearing windmills, if I recollect," nodded Henry. "A rather asinine occupation, it seems to me. Almost as bad as distilling the juice of a prune—or drinking it. As a matter of fact, we are going out to the Rafter P ranch."

"For any good reason, Henry?"

"Judge, I may answer in the negative. I say I *may*. As a matter of fact, I have started out to try and prevent the law from hanging Danny Regan."

"I do not believe there is sufficient evidence to hang him."

"With twelve jurors, selected in any way you can care to select them in Wild Horse Valley, they'd hang him, in spite of the evidence."

"I am afraid you are right, Henry."

"And," said Henry softly, "I love that damn fool, red-headed kid."

"So do I, Henry," admitted Judge. "If it were not for Danny Regan, I would be—God only knows. He made a man of me."

"Well," said Henry dryly, "I wouldn't give him any written recommendation for his ability in that respect; but I know what you mean."

"Thank you kindly. But why go to the Rafter P ranch? As I understand it, since Joe Hall's untimely demise, there is only

Juan Gomez, his mother, Mrs. Gomez, and one Poco, last name unknown, at the ranch."

"Your census is correct, Judge. Apparently Joe Hall preferred Mexican cowboys and a Mexican cook. A matter of personal choice, of course. A faithful trio, no doubt. I heard Joe Hall say that he would trust Juan Gomez further than he would any living American."

THEY TRAVELED slowly in the heat, Judge making spasmodic attempts to spur Lightning, and finally reached the Rafter P ranch-house; a rather large adobe structure. There was the usual out-buildings and corrals, and, as usual, in need of repair. Bill Parton had been fairly successful with the Rafter P; but Joe Hall had not startled the world with his ability to build up a herd.

There was no one in sight about the place, but the front door of the house was wide open. Henry and Judge dismounted at the front porch, stretched their cramped legs, and started for the front door, walking like a couple of sailors, who still had their sea-legs.

Just as they reached the bottom of the four steps, a gun thudded inside the house. It was so unexpected that Henry and Judge bumped against each other, both reeling aside. A man staggered into the doorway, as the gun blasted the silence again, and the man sprawled across the porch, and came falling down the steps, stopping just between Henry and Judge, who stared at him in amazement.

They heard a rear door crash shut, and dimly remembered, later, that they had heard the sound of someone running away.

"Damned unexpected—this!" exclaimed Henry.

"Why—why, the man has been shot!" snorted Judge. "Heavens above!"

Henry, acting in sort of a daze, stepped over, took the man by the shoulders and turned him over. It was Juan Gomez, whom Joe Hall had said he trusted beyond all men. There was no recognition in his eyes.

"Who shot you, Juan?" asked Henry. "Tell me who shot you?"

"He can't even hear you," said Judge softly. "He's nearly gone."

Juan's lips were moving, and they listened closely.

"I—never—tell—heem. Poco—knows—where—it—"

And Juan Gomez died, his statement unfinished. Henry looked at Judge thoughtfully.

"He never told who, I wonder? And what does Poco know?"

Judge shook his head, not having any ideas on the subject.

Henry got to his feet suddenly and walked into the house, followed cautiously by Judge. Off the big main-room was a fairly well furnished bedroom, which had been used by Joe Hall; and this room looked as though it had been through a cyclone.

The bedding had been flung around, the drawers of a dresser pulled out and emptied on the floor.

"Searching for something," said Henry.

They went all over the house, and came back to the bedroom again, where Henry searched carefully. Finally he found a letter, which Joe Hall had written the day before he was murdered, and had failed to post. It was addressed to a packing house in Chicago, asking for prices on different grades of cattle.

Henry pocketed the letter and they went back to their horses.

"We'll leave the body where it is," said Henry, "and notify the sheriff and coroner."

Judge was visibly shaken. No doubt the killer had seen them. He had been behind Juan, when he fired the second shot, and should have had a clear view of Henry and Judge.

"I believe we got off cheaply, Judge," stated Henry, as they rode back to town. "I have a feeling that someone was searching that place, when we showed up. It is my opinion that our arrival merely hastened the killing of Juan Gomez; because the man who was searching that house could not afford to have Juan tell who he was; so when he saw us coming, he killed Juan."

"I accept that, because I have no theories of my own," replied Judge. "I only know that my nerves are all twittering. The nerve of a man—to blast that poor inoffensive Mexican right into us! Why, he might have killed both of us! I'm jumpy, Henry."

"Jumpy? If somebody yelled boo at me, I'd go right over Yhonny's ears and establish a new record for a three mile run. I'm unused to murder, I tell you, sir. I hate it."

"I can see that," replied Judge. "Your voice squeaks on high notes. In fact, I wouldn't be surprised if, in your present condition, you could give a fair imitation of a novice, playing a flute. You positively do tootle, sir. And to complete the illusion, you might paint a number of imitation holes along your nose—and finger them, sir."

"In my time," replied Henry soberly, "I have used my nose for many things, but I have never used it for a flute. I detest flutes."

"Forgive me, Henry," said Judge sadly. "I—I'm rather hysterical. I can see poor Juan Gomez, staggering, falling and that damn gun, thundering into the house. I'll always see that; always. Damn it, Henry, I need a drink!"

"Don't we all?" queried Henry.

THEY FOUND Bill Parton and John Campbell, standing in front of the general store, and told them what had happened at the Rafter P.

"My God, what next?" exclaimed the prosecutor.

"You say—Juan Gomez is dead?" blurted the sheriff. "Wait! There is Mrs. Gomez and Poco, ready to leave town. I'll have to tell them."

Bill Parton went hurrying across the street.

"I wouldn't want that job," declared the lawyer. He looked closely at Henry and Judge.

"You two seem to run into trouble all the time," he said.

"You don't suppose it is habit-forming, do you?" asked Henry. "I would hate to go through life, finding one corpse after another."

"We might as well be undertakers," sighed Judge.

"I'll notify the coroner, John," called the sheriff. "You might as well go out there with us, if you're not busy."

The lawyer nodded and looked at Henry.

"I hope we find the corpse," he said.

"We don't guarantee anything," replied Henry, "except that it was there, when we left. You might take some plaster along, Mr. Camphell—someone might have left some tracks. Judge, I feel the deluge coming on."

Arm in arm they sauntered across the street to the Tonto Saloon. Mrs. Gomez, her mantilla covering her bowed head, sat in the seat of their ranch wagon, while Poco, an undersized Mexican sat very straight in the seat, holding the lines; but the team was still tied to the hitch-rack.

Henry halted at the entrance and looked at the couple in the wagon. When he turned, his eyes were suspiciously moist.

"That's Juan Gomez's mother," said Judge.

Henry nodded and turned to the doorway.

"And sometime," he said, "we think *we* have suffered."

The reaction from witnessing the murder was too much for Judge. He leaned against the Tonto bar, and refused to budge. He wanted to forget what he had seen. But Henry refused to make it a drinking bout. He took two drinks, left Judge in the capable hands of two cowboys, and went over to see Mrs. Harper and Leila.

They were anxious for news, and Henry had plenty to tell.

"I saw Mrs. Gomez today," said Leila. "She's a nice woman. And Juan was well liked. I know how his mother must feel about it. But who would murder an inoffensive person, like Juan Gomez?"

"*Quien sabe?*" replied Judge, and laughed shortly. "I'm getting good at talking Mexican."

"What can be done about Danny?" asked Leila. "The law won't even try to find the real murderer. By the time the trial is over—"

"I know," interrupted Henry, "All they want is a victim."

"I know how that is," said Leila. "I talked with Mr. Campbell today. He tried to be nice to me, of course; but he gave me to understand that he hoped to convict Danny."

"Well, that's his job," said Henry. "My job is to find the man who really did the shooting. I think I'll go out and have a talk with Bill Parton, as soon as they bring the body back."

"Do you think he will help you?" asked Mrs. Harper.

"I don't believe he will. In fact, he will likely resent my interest in his business. You see, I believe the man who shot Joe Hall is the same man who shot Juan Gomez."

Henry had the letter he had taken off the body of Joe Hall. He had put it in a plain envelope, and carried it in a hip-pocket of his overalls. He showed it to the women, but it meant nothing to them. They had lived in Wild Horse Valley for years, but neither of them had ever known anyone nicknamed Chuck.

CHAPTER VI

THE LETTER

IT WAS RATHER late in the afternoon, when they brought the body to town. Henry sat down with the sheriff and prosecutor, and went over what he had seen of the tragedy.

"Did you go into the house?" asked the lawyer.

"Naturally, we did. It looked as though burglars had been there."

"It kinda looks to me like somebody was lookin' for money," said the sheriff. "Mebbe Juan walked in and caught 'em at it."

"I don't believe they were looking for money," said Henry.

"Then what in the world were they looking for?" asked Campbell.

"I can't say, exactly. One solution occurs to me, but I'd hate to mention it, until I've gone into it a little further. But I will say this much: I'm on the trail of the man who killed both Joe Hall and Juan Gomez."

The sheriff laughed at him. "You better waste yore time, tryin' to find the man who killed the Mexican—we've got Joe's killer."

The prosecutor was a trifle amused, too.

"On their trail, eh?" he said.

"On *his* trail," corrected Henry. "One man pulled both jobs."

"All right," growled the sheriff testily. "You be here in town at ten o'clock in the morning, to testify at the inquest."

"I hope to be here," replied Henry. "I might have some news."

"And try to have that cock-eyed old pardner of yours here, too," ordered the sheriff. "We'll want him to swear to what you tell."

"That won't be difficult," smiled Henry. "We always rehearse, until he is letter-perfect."

"I can see that," said the sheriff.

Henry found Judge at the bar, enjoying himself greatly; but Henry steered away from him, and ate supper alone in a little Chinese café with only the clatter of dishes to interrupt his meditations. It was dark, when he finished, paid his bill and went back on the street, where he mounted the tall horse and rode out of town alone.

Nearly an hour later he reached the Rafter P, where he found Mrs. Gomez and Poco, sitting in the dark on the porch.

"*Que es?*" queried Poco.

"This is Henry Conroy. You know who I am, Poco?"

Mrs. Gomez went into the house, and Poco came to the railing.

"I know you," replied Poco. "Joe Hall ees talk 'bout you. Hees say to me and Juan, 'Theese fat fool from the J Bar C ees elect new sheriff; so theese law ees all shot from hell now.'"

"Yes," said Henry softly, "I'm sure you have recognized me. Poco, I want to talk with you."

"I am not fill like talk," replied the little Mexican. "Juan ees *muerto*. You *sabe?* He ees died."

"I saw him killed, Poco."

"You see heem keeled? Why—who keel heem?"

"I was right here—at the foot of the steps, Poco. Some man shot Juan, back there in the house. He staggered to the doorway, when the man shot again, and Juan fell all the way down the steps."

"*Madre de Dios!* You not see theese man?"

"No, I didn't see him."

"W'y you come back here now?"

"To talk with you, Poco. You liked Juan Gomez?"

Poco hesitated for quite a while. Then he replied:

"Theese Juan is like brother from me. Hees *mujer* fill awful bad."

"I know she feels bad. I feel bad for her, Poco."

"*Buena.* W'y you fill bad for her?"

"Her son is dead, Poco."

"Oh," said Poco. Perhaps the statement was a little beyond his powers of comprehension.

"W'at you wan' talk weeth me?" he asked.

"Did Joe Hall and Juan Gomez have some sort of a secret between them?" asked Henry.

"Cigarette?"

"No, no; a secret. Something that both of them knew, but no one else knew."

"*Secreto?*"

"That's it, Poco. Maybe Joe Hall gave Juan something to hide for him. Or he might have hidden it, and told Juan where it was."

"Juan ees died," replied Poco. "Joe Hall ees died, too."

"I know it—they're both dead. But before Juan died, he said, 'Poco knows.'"

"He say that?" asked Poco quickly. "He no say who keel heem?"

"He was badly hurt," replied Henry. "I think he was trying to tell us to have you find what was hidden."

Poco was silent for a space of time, but finally said:

"I'm fill too bad, Juan's *mujer* fill ver' bad. Not much *dinero* for *entierro*."

"*Dinero for entierro?*"

"Sure—for put heem een dirt."

"Oh, yes. Not much money for a funeral, eh? I see. Poco, would you like to see Juan have a fine funeral?"

"Sure. Ver' fine box, weeth seelver 'andles. Much seenging."

"All right, Poco; we'll make a trade. You show me what Joe Hall and Juan knew was hidden, and I'll pay for Juan's funeral."

"I'm not know w'at theese theeng ees, *Señor* Conroy."

"Perhaps it is a letter, Poco. Do you know of a letter—hidden?"

"*Por Dios*—yes!" exclaimed Poco excitedly. "Juan tell me, 'Theese *carta* ees for somebody, after Joe Hall ees died from keeling.' He say for me kip damn face shut. Sure, I know."

"Did Juan give it to anybody?" asked Henry.

"I'm don' theenk so."

"Show me that letter, and I'll give Juan the best funeral you ever seen."

"*Buena!* I get lantern."

POCO WAS back in a moment, with a lighted lantern, and led the way down to the stable. In the opposite corner from the doorway was a large, hinged-top grain bin. Poco lifted the cover, while Henry held the lantern. There was not over a bushel of oats in the bin, and Poco scooped them aside. He lifted up a loose board and took out an envelope of regular letter size, sealed.

He handed it to Henry, who fairly grabbed at it. But he did not stop to even read what was written on the envelope. He shoved it deep in his pocket, and as he turned away from the bin, something hit him on the head, with stunning force. As his consciousness faded out, he dimly heard someone yelling; but it meant nothing to Henry.

He awoke in the ranch-house of the Rafter P, dazed and sick, but fully conscious. He was on the floor, with Mrs. Gomez bathing his head in cold water. Seated, humped over in a chair, nursing a closed left eye and a lumpy temple, was Poco.

"*Buena!*" exclaimed Mrs. Gomez, as Henry struggled to sit up. On the left side of his head was a sizeable lump, and he was bleeding a little from a gashed scalp.

Mrs. Gomez hunched over a wash-pan of water, holding the dripping towel in both hands. Henry stared at her and at Poco, wondering what it was all about. Gradually he remembered being at the stable—and the letter. Painfully he reached to his hip-pocket—and found it empty. The important letter was gone.

"What happened, Poco?" he asked weakly.

"A man heet us," replied Poco painfully. "I'm not see heem, biffore he heet you. I'm yell like hell and start to ron—but he heet me, too."

"What did he look like?"

"I'm don' know; I'm scare like hell."

"He got that letter, Poco."

"*Por Dios*, that ees bad! Juan never 'ave fine funeral now."

"Yes, he will," declared Henry. "I'll give Juan a good funeral, even if we did lose the letter."

"*Gracias, Señor,*" said Mrs. Gomez. "Juan was good boy."

She wiped her eyes with the wet towel, and Henry turned away. He grasped the side of a chair and got slowly to his feet. He was dizzy for several moments, but it passed, leaving only a dull ache.

"How long ago did we get hit?" asked Henry.

"Mebbe one hour," replied Poco.

"Oh, not that long!"

Mrs. Gomez nodded. "I'm theenk you never wake up, *Señor*."

"I don't usually sleep that sound," said Henry. "I—I hope he didn't hit my horse, too."

"Thees 'orse ees all right," stated Poco.

Henry took a deep breath and caressed his sore head.

"I suppose I may as well go back home," he said. "I'll give the coroner a hundred dollars for the funeral, Mrs. Gomez. He'll handle everything for you."

"*Gracias, Señor* Conroy; you mak' me ver''appy. But that ees too much money. Feefteen dollar be plenty."

"Not weeth seelver 'andles, *Mujer*," interposed Poco.

"No," agreed Henry, "it woudn't be enough. When I plant—I plant. Well, *buenas noches.*"

"*Buenas noches, amigo. Vaya con Dios.*"

Henry managed to mount the tall horse and start for Tonto City. He had lost his hat, but did not mind, because the cool night air felt good on his feverish head. His hopes were almost as low as his physical condition now. He felt sure that the letter would have told him some of the things he wanted to know; but the letter was now in the hands of the enemy.

THE ROAD seemed endless that night, and it hurt his head to have the horse trot; so they merely went shuffling along. The road led down through a narrow arroya, before it opened out, a mile or so from Tonto City. The starlight was very bright, and as he rode down through the arroya, something made a swishing sound above him, like the swift flight of a night bird; and the next moment a rope yanked tightly around his body, jerking him bodily out of the saddle.

Henry merely had time to realize that someone had roped him, before he crashed down in the hard roadway, knocked unconscious again. It seemed to him that the unconsciousness was only momentary, but when he awoke there was no rope around him, his shirt had been almost ripped off, and every pocket had been turned inside-out.

He sat there in the road, after this discovery, blinking at the stars. Finally he said aloud:

"My God; an encore!"

He got unsteadily to his feet, carefully tested himself for broken bones, decided that he was still intact, and began walking to Tonto City. It was only about a mile to town, but it tested his powers of endurance.

At the doorway of the Tonto Saloon he halted. A reedy tenor, a cracked baritone and a harsh bass were singing:

"...a wild sort of devil, but dead on the level was my ga-a-al, Sa-a-a-al."

Henry stumbled into the place and looked around. Judge, Oscar and Slim Pickins were at the bar, lifting glasses to each other's health.

"Vell Ay vill be a damn liar, if here ain't Hanry!" exploded Oscar.

"My old colleague!" exclaimed Judge. "Why, where have you—Henry, you are a mess, sir! I repeat, sir; you are—"

"Do I get a drink?" asked Henry weakly. "Or—well, do not stare! Don't you realize that it is bad form to stare?"

"If you could see yourself, you wouldn't blame us," interrupted Slim. "Henry Conroy, I—I'll be danged! Look at the welt on his head! And his shirt all tore up thataway!"

"Make mine whisky," said Henry painfully. "And don't ask questions."

After three drinks, Henry turned to Slim.

"Did you come in the buckboard?" he asked. Slim nodded.

"We will let Oscar ride Lightning, while you drive the buckboard team," said Henry. "And we shall go home now."

"Sure," agreed Slim. "I'm ready."

"Ay am to ride das Lightnin' hurse?" asked Oscar.

"Sure," grinned Slim. "We'll leave a light burnin' for yuh."

"Das all right; Ay had good sleep last night. But where is das Yhonny hurse?"

"Das Yhonny hurse," replied Henry soberly, "is old enough to take care of himself. Ready, gentlemen?"

The murder of Juan Gomez, following so closely, as it did,

the murder of Joe Hall, attracted nearly everyone in Wild Horse Valley to the inquest. The inquest was scheduled for ten o'clock, but it was nearly noon, before the court room was called to order.

Because of the fact that Henry Conroy and Judge Van Treece were the only witnesses to the killing, the sheriff had persuaded the coroner not to allow Judge inside the room, until after Henry had given his testimony. Judge was indignant, and he told them so, in no uncertain terms.

HENRY was very stiff and sore. Judge told Leila and her mother:

"I am not allowed to divulge what happened to Henry last night, but I will tell you that he is one mass of bruises. When we got to the ranch last night, he laid on the bed, while Frijole Bill put cold compresses on his head. He kept Frijole busy for an hour, refused even to get up and remove his clothes; and slept in them all night. This morning he put on a clean shirt, and came to town."

Leila and her mother went to the inquest. John Campbell, the prosecutor, spoke aside to the coroner:

"Did you notice that Henry Conroy is carrying a six-shooter in the waistband of his pants? I've never seen him carry one before. And I noticed a decided bulge about the hip line of Judge Van Treece."

The coroner was grimly thoughtful for a few moments.

"I'll speak to the sheriff about it," he said, and walked away.

The jury was finally selected, and the six men tried to appear intelligent, watching the coroner closely. After a short, preliminary speech by the coroner, explaining the reasons for the inquest, he said:

"Henry Conroy, please take the stand, and be sworn."

But before the coroner could start his inquiry, Bill Parton, the sheriff, said:

"Conroy, why are you wearin' a gun?"

Henry smiled slowly and caressed his nose.

"I am getting to a point where I do not even trust people in a court of law," he replied.

"Das is good!" snorted Oscar. "You can't fool Hanry, by Yimminy!"

"Another remark from you, Johnson, and out you go," declared the sheriff angrily. "What do you think this is?"

"Don't you know?" asked Slim Pickins innocently.

"This bickering must cease!" roared the coroner. "Another remark, and the sheriff will clear the room."

The room was silent again, and the coroner turned to Henry.

"Mr. Conroy, you will please tell your story to the jury."

In a few words Henry told them all he knew about it.

"You did not see the man who did the shooting?"

"I did not. We heard him slam a back door and go running away, but we were too stunned by the tragedy to even think of trying to see the murderer."

"Any questions, sheriff?" asked the coroner.

"Just one," replied the sheriff. "What was you two doin' out there at the Rafter P ranch, Conroy?"

Henry looked at him curiously, smiled and said:

"I don't remember."

"You were both drunk," declared the sheriff harshly. "Neither of yuh was sober enough to see or hear things straight."

"I bow to superior judgment," said Henry. "But I may point to the fact that several persons saw me mount that tall horse—which is quite some acrobatic feat for a man of my dimensions—cold sober."

The crowd laughed, and the sheriff scowled at them.

"Finished with the witness, sheriff?" asked the coroner.

"I may recall him, after we have heard Van Treece," growled the sheriff, and sat down, scowling around.

The coroner motioned to Rolling Stone and told him to call Judge Van Treece, who was waiting in the hallway. He came in, tall and dignified, his face set in grim lines. He looked neither to the right nor left, as he came down the aisle, and went straight to the witness chair, where he lifted his right hand and took the oath.

"Mr. Van Treece," said the coroner, "will you please tell the jury exactly what you saw happen yesterday at the Rafter P ranch."

"And," added the sheriff, "try to tell the same story that Henry Conroy told."

JUDGE VAN TREECE'S eyes glanced slowly around the room. The old man seemed hard and grim, and his bony hands were clenched tightly.

"Gentlemen of the jury," he said slowly, "I believe things have gone far enough. A coroner's jury decided to have Danny Regan held for trial for the murder of Joe Hall. It was a—"

"Wait a minute, Van Treece," interrupted the sheriff. "That inquest is over. This inquest is over the body of Juan Gomez. All you have been asked to do is to tell what you saw, and what you know about the shootin' of Juan Gomez."

Judge turned his head slowly and looked at the coroner.

"Are you conducting this inquest, or is the sheriff doing it?"

"Well, I—I—" faltered the coroner, not sure of himself.

"Make up your mind," urged Slim.

"I—I believe Van Treece should be allowed to tell his story in his own way," said the coroner.

"Thank you," said Judge softly. "Perhaps I started wrong."

Judge got to his feet and faced the jury.

"Gentlemen!" His voice rang sharp, "Joe Hall was afraid he might be murdered. He knew a man who would kill him in a minute, if that man wasn't afraid that a certain document would—"

Judge reached in his pocket and drew out an envelope.

"This document would convict him. In some way he found that Juan Gomez knew—"

Big Bill Parton was on his feet, head hunched forward, his jaw sagging. He was like that for a moment, swaying—and then his right hand flashed to his gun.

"Damn you to hell!" he screamed. "Back! I'll kill every damn man that—"

A big gun thundered in the close-packed room. Men were ducking wildly, sliding out of their chairs; anything to get below, or out of the line of fire.

Bill Parton was still standing there, gripping his gun, but his right arm was sagging slowly. The gun fell to the floor, clattering on the wood; and Bill Parton sank down across it.

Henry Harrison Conroy sat there near the witness chair, a smoking Colt across his lap.

"That one was for Juan Gomez," he said calmly.

The shocked crowd were on their feet now, crowding in. The coroner, badly dazed by the tragedy, but with the true instinct of a trained physician, was the first to Bill Parton. The big sheriff was not dead, however.

"Bad, Doc," he whispered.

"It didn't pay," said Parton, his voice audible in the stilled room. "I was safe, until Joe Hall came here. Van Treece has the letter that Hall wrote. It'll tell all about it. I—I tried twice last night to take that letter away from Conroy, but I must have missed it. He figured it out some way."

"You killed Joe Hall?" queried the coroner.

"Yeah, I got him. I figured Juan Gomez had that letter, and that I could get it. Hall forced me to give him my ranch—blackmailed me. I killed Juan Gomez."

"Went out like a match," said Rolling Stone, and the doctor nodded.

"I guess that settles it, folks," said the coroner. "The inquest is ended. Mr. Campbell, I suppose we shall have to turn Danny Regan loose."

"We could hardly hold him, after this confession," said the

prosecutor, white faced. "I have never been so shocked in my life. Van Treece, may I see that letter you have?"

JUDGE handed him the envelope, and Campbell drew out a folded sheet of blank paper.

"Why—why—" he stammered. "This isn't any letter!"

"It was the best we had," said Henry. "Needs must, when the devil drives, Campbell. Parton didn't know."

"You lost the letter—and bluffed?"

"What else to do. He knocked me down in the Rafter P stable, after I put the letter in my pocket. I already had a letter in that pocket, and he must have taken that one. After I recovered, and was on my way to town, he roped me off my horse and searched me again. I knew he did not have the letter, on the second search, or he wouldn't have made the search; so I bluffed."

"But what on earth made you suspect Bill Parton?"

"A letter I took off Joe Hall's body. It was almost blotted out with blood and bullet, but there was enough left to make me believe that Joe Hall was up to something. Then Parton told me about having Joe Hall's note for ten thousand dollars. I saw the note; so I went to the Rafter P, saw Juan Gomez killed, and got a sample of Joe Hall's writing, with his signature. Joe Hall never signed that note—it was a forgery."

John Campbell shook his head slowly.

"And some misguided, blamed fool said you wouldn't make a sheriff. Henry Conroy, you would damn near make a United States Marshal."

"With a little more experience," nodded Henry soberly. "One never knows, does one? Ah, there's Danny!"

He was with Leila and her mother, and they all hugged Henry. Suddenly Henry drew aside, wiggling his right boot, a queer expression on his face. Then he reached down, jerked his pant-leg from the boot-top, shook it violently, and a crumpled letter fell to the floor.

It was the letter Poco had taken from the grain bin. Henry stared at it for a moment, and a broad grin spread across his face. He turned to the prosecutor and handed him the envelope.

"There it is!" he exploded. "No wonder Parton didn't find it. In my excitement I shoved it inside my pants, instead of in a pocket! He tore off my shirt, when he should have torn off my pants."

Henry whooped, grasped Danny by the shoulders, and did a war-dance around him. Campbell was reading swiftly.

"It's all here, Conroy," he said. "Parton and Hall robbed a bank in Nevada twelve years ago, and shot a cashier. In a gun battle, Hall was wounded, while Parton got away with the money. Hall went up for ten years. Then Hall located him and began blackmailing Parton. The whole thing is here in detail. He signs his name Charles F. Holton, alias Chuck Holt, alias Joe Hall. Why—"

Campbell looked around. "Where's Conroy?" he asked.

"They're out on the street by this time," replied the coroner.

Which was true. None of them were interested in Joe Hall's letter now. Judge Van Treece was crossing the street, heading directly for the Tonto Saloon, his old derby hat clutched in one hand.

Mrs. Harper, Leila, Danny and Henry stopped and watched him.

"A wonderful character," said Henry. "The stage lost a great actor, when Van Treece studied law."

"Wouldn't you like to join him, Henry?" asked Mrs. Harper.

Henry turned his head.

"Laura," he said huskily, "I would not lie to you—I would. But I am not going to do it. I'm going down to your house for supper. I know you hate liquor, and could never care for a drinking man. But I'd never swear off for the love of a woman, because I'd never stay sworn off; and I hate a hypocrite. I like my liquor."

"Well, Henry," she replied softly, "it doesn't seem to have hurt you any."

Leila looked at her mother in amazement, grasped Danny by the arm, and hurried down the street.

"It is great to be in love, Laura," smiled Henry.

From across the street came Oscar's voice:

"Hooray for Hanry for de detective!"

III

THE SHERLOCK OF SAGELAND

"You're no good as sheriff, Henry. You're the
laughingstock of Wild Horse Valley"—but
Henry turned his cheek—and the tables.

CHAPTER I

THE VALLEY LAUGHS

HENRY HARRISON CONROY, sheriff of Wild Horse Valley, made three distinct attempts to hook his spurred heels over the edge of his desk, failed in every attempt, and sighed deeply. Only once had he succeeded in doing this, and that time the chair went over backwards with him, nullifying his triumph.

Henry was about five feet, six inches in height, very rotund, and fifty-five years of age. Henry had been born in a dressing room of a theater, and had been an actor all his life, until Jim Conroy, his aged uncle, died and left him the big J Bar C cattle ranch.

Henry's face was moon-like, with a huge, putty-like nose, which was forever red; a nose known from coast to coast, with Henry as a background. Henry's eyes were squinty, and he was rapidly approaching the bald stage. As sheriff of the county, Henry wore a robin's-egg blue shirt, which fit as tightly as the skin on a sausage. The tops of Henry's overalls were girded together with a six-inch horse-blanket pin. On his rather small feet he wore high-heel boots with huge silver spurs.

The sheriff's office was a rough, unfinished room, about fifteen feet square. The front door opened directly to the sidewalk of the main street of Tonto City. There was one small, unwashed window. The furnishings consisted of four chairs, whittled until they were liable to collapse at any time, the sheriff's desk, a battered safe and an army cot. A state map and

137

"Reach for the sky!"

numerous reward notices, together with a well-filled gun-rack, completed the wall decorations.

At the rear of the office was a heavy door, which opened to the corridor of the small jail. There were no prisoners in the jail. In fact, there had not been any prisoners of late.

Seated in three of the rickety chairs were William Grey, Richard Herrick and Martin Archer. William Grey was a tall, lean, sour-faced individual. Herrick was heavy-set, with a huge mustache, and bow-legs. Archer was slight, a faded blonde in coloring, and slightly dyspeptic. These three men comprised the Board of Commissioners of Wild Horse Valley.

They sat there and watched Henry Harrison Conroy fail to hook his spurs over the edge of the desk. Henry lighted a cigarette, and looked gloomy.

Herrick started to speak, the preliminary being a nervous up and down motion of the mustache; a sort of flitting-wing action. Henry's eyes opened wide for the moment, and his nose twitched.

"Gentlemen," said Henry, slowly and distinctly, "I would gather from what you have said that my régime as sheriff is, as we would say on the stage, a flop."

"We came to talk with you about it," nodded Herrick.

"As a matter of fact," added Grey, "you ain't done a damn thing, Conroy—except git drunk—you and yore deputy and jailer. Tonto City and the county feel that—"

"Have you," interrupted Henry heavily, "been feeling of Tonto City and Wild Horse county, Mr. Grey?"

"You know what I mean, Conroy."

"There was that Silver City hold-up," said Archer.

"Aye," nodded Henry, "and the stage robbery at Red Bluff. Let me see-e-e. The total spoils amounted to—hm-m-m—I've forgotten."

"Twenty-seven thousand dollars!" snapped Grey.

"And there ain't never been an arrest," added Herrick. "That's what we came here—"

Henry made another attempt to hook his heels over the desk, but failed, as usual.

"Either the chair is too low, the desk is too high, or I'm too damned fat," said Henry. "Go ahead, Mr. Herrick. You were saying that—"

"What was I saying?" queried Herrick, his mind off the subject.

"Something laudatory to the sheriff, I believe," suggested Henry. "As a matter of fact, these crimes were committed during the régime of Bill Parton. These were his dirty clothes—and I'm expected to wash them. Gentlemen, I deplore crime. It irks me. Do any of you august trio know what an irk is? Well, it is a qualm, gone to seed. Surely you know what a qualm is. Most surely would I incarcerate the perpetrators of afore-mentioned crimes. I would deem it my duty. But, as the simple directions for the Frenchman's flea-powder stated—first catch the flea."

WILLIAM GREY got heavily to his feet. "I don't know what in hell you are talkin' about," he admitted. "But I do know that we've got to have action in this valley. You are not worth a damn as an officer of the law, Conroy. Yore deputy, Judge Van Treece, and yore jailer, Oscar Johnson—well, the whole damn valley are laughin' at yuh."

"Laughing?" Henry seemed quite amazed. "Already? At us, you said? Well, perhaps. At first glance—but no matter. Proceed, Mr. Grey."

"We've taken the bull by the horns," declared Grey. "In a few days we'll have a professional detective in here to solve all these crimes. And don't you hamper him in any way, Conroy."

"That, sir," said Henry, "is an insult to my intelligence. Who steals my purse, steals trash, as the poet says. But he who steals from me the right to apprehend—well, it doesn't matter."

"I'll tell yuh what I think," said Herrick disgustedly. "I think that—"

"Just a moment," interrupted Henry. "*You* think? Ah, that reminds me of a line from Hamlet, in which Hamlet says: 'There is nothing either good or bad, but thinking makes it so.'"

"Hamlet ain't got a damn thing to do with it!" snorted Herrick. "A lot of damn fools elected you to—"

"Oh, but I agree!" exclaimed Henry heartily. "Fools filled with humor. And ye say they are already laughing? Good!"

"Ah, what's the use?" blurted Archer, getting to his feet. "We ain't gittin' no place, gents."

Crash! The office shook from the force of an explosion, and a section of the doorway to the jail splintered out, showering the three men with fragments of wood.

A fraction of a second later, and the room was cleared, with the exception of Henry, who went over backwards in his chair.

Untangling his feet, he was peering around the desk, as Judge Van Treece and Oscar Johnson cautiously opened the damaged door. Oscar had a sawed-off, double-barreled shotgun in his hands, and an expression of amazement on his face.

"Anybody dead around ha'r?" he asked huskily.

Henry got slowly to his feet and leaned on the desk. He reached up and dug a piece of wood from inside his collar.

Judge Van Treece was sixty years of age, six feet four in height, and of the physical proportions of a two-by-four. His face was long and lean, with pouchy eyes and a long, thin nose. His usual garb was an old cutaway coat, baggy pants, nondescript shoes and an ancient derby hat. Just now, as befitting his office, he wore high-heel boots and a huge, black sombrero, a size too large.

Oscar Johnson, known as "the Terrible Swede," was well over six feet tall, and with the frame of a Hercules. He had faded, blond hair, which stood up like a roach on a grizzly, a button-like nose and small, innocent-looking blue eyes.

"Just what was the salvo for?" asked Henry.

"Das ha'r gon," explained Oscar, "vent off."

"Yes, it did," corroborated Judge.

"There is not one dissenting voice," said Henry slowly. "Oscar, didn't I tell you to let the guns alone?"

"Yah, sure," admitted Oscar.

"It needed cleaning," said Judge. "The bore was in terrible state, and the workings were all gummed up with ancient grease. We have been out on the back steps, giving the gun a cleaning. We did a good job, I'm sure. As we came into the corridor Oscar replaced the two cartridges, closed the gun—and both barrels went off. Henry, I'm of the opinion that the gun is dangerous."

HENRY eyed the door reflectively, and sat down again. "There is something in the last statement that rings true," he said. "I should hate to think about any man, what those three commissioners are thinking about me right now."

"Were they still in here, Henry?" gasped Judge.

"They were. In my time I have seen speed, gentlemen. One matinee, a professional baseball player—a lefthander—threw an egg at me from the second gallery. But, no! It had the pace of a broken-legged turtle, compared with the speed with which those three commissioners left this office. That door, as I see it, is just slightly choke-bored, as you might say, but they went out together. They may have scattered, after they got out, but I swear to you that they were side-by-side on their exit. Oscar, if you don't put down that gun—"

"Ay am not goin' shood," protested Oscar.

Judge took the gun and put it on the rack, wiped his tall brow, and sat down.

"And what, if I may ask, sir, was the occasion of a visit from the high-and-mighty delegation?" he asked.

Henry dug another splinter from inside his collar, his nose twitching, as he squinted at the luckless Oscar.

"Oh, the delegation! Pardon me, Judge; my mind was on how to perpetrate a perfect murder. Well, they came to sort of confer with me as to the best methods of combating crime. A very fine trio of men. I might say, bright-minded, unassuming, kindly. Adjectives fail me, Judge."

"I can imagine the rest, Henry," replied Judge. A scraping noise caused him to turn toward Oscar, who was dragging an old violin case from under the cot. Slowly Henry drew his gun, cocked it and laid it on the desk. The click of the lock caused Oscar to look up, and he saw the cocked gun. With a deep sigh, he hooked his heel against the case, and shoved it out of sight.

"I am a man of few words," said Henry meaningly.

"Das is oll right," said Oscar. "Von streeng is bruk, anyway."

"You broke it last night, serenading Josephine, the waitress at the Tonto hotel," said Judge.

"So that was it, eh?" mused Henry. "Tom Rickey, the owner of the hotel, asked me this morning what the penalty was for shooting a Swede; and I didn't know what he meant. Is she pretty, Oscar?"

"Who?"

"Is Josephine pretty?"

"Yosephine is yust right."

"But the commissioners, my dear Henry," said "Judge. "We digress."

"Aye," sighed Henry, "the commissioners. Well, Judge, they are hiring a professional detective to solve all crime. I fear they seek to humiliate us."

"The devil!" snorted Judge.

"A fitting job for him, were it he," nodded Henry. "But what is there for even his Satanic Majesty to work on, Judge? For instance, the Silver City bank robbery. Description, two masked men, well over six feet tall; huge creatures, carrying cannons.

"**THEN** there is the stage robbery at Red Bluff. One man, tall and thin. Height varies from six feet to seven feet, eight inches. Companion not over five feet tall. Last, but not least, the bank at Scorpion, which was robbed by two short men. Judging from these descriptions, we have at least three tall men and three short ones, all capable of holding a cannon in each fist."

"Ay am going to Silver City to a dance with Yosephine," announced Oscar blandly. "Ay vant to borrow hurse and buggy from de ranch."

"Of all the inane remarks," snorted Judge.

"Oscar," said Henry seriously, "are you not interested in crime?"

"Crime?"

"Yes—crime. Robbery and murder and—"

"Shooting?" queried Oscar, glancing at the ruined door.

Henry sighed and shook his head. He tried again to hook his spurs over the edge of the desk, and nearly upset his chair.

"Oh, let's go and get a drink, Judge. I sit here and try to concentrate on the solution to three crimes—and all the while I have homicide on my mind. Oscar, you tend to the office, while we're gone—*and let them guns alone.*"

"Yah, sure," agreed Oscar. "Ay vill play de fiddle."

"Well—all right. Don't break a string and put out one of your eyes."

Perhaps Henry and Judge showed undue haste in getting over to the Ton-to Saloon, where they leaned on the bar and looked blissfully at their reflections in the back-bar mirror.

"What was the shootin' down in yore office?" queried the bartender, as he produced glasses and a bottle of rye.

"A Swedish uprising," replied Henry, pouring carefully.

"I didn't know there was enough Swedes in this country to start an uprisin'."

"It only takes one," sighed Henry. "Your very good health, Mr. Van Treece."

"To you, Mr. Conroy," responded Judge. They were always formal in these drinking matters.

"I reckon somethin' uprose," said the bartender. "I seen Bill Grey, Dick Herrick and Mart Archer come out of yore office, like three coyotes, huntin' for a hole to dive into."

"Coyotes," said Henry seriously. "Ah-h-h-h!"

"I said 'like three coyotes,'" said the bartender.

"We don't," said the Judge seriously, "have to like 'em if we don't want to. That whisky really has a tang, Henry."

"It has. I believe Webster's definition—one of them—says: a projecting shank, prong or fang. It most certainly has a tang. If you have no objection, Mr. Van Treece, let us be shanked, pronged, or fanged once more. I like the sensation."

"How's crime these days?" asked the bartender.

"Crime in Wild Horse Valley is in its infancy," replied Henry. "Were you to question Mr. Grey, Mr. Herrick and Mr. Archer, they would tell you that murder and robbery were our predominating pastimes. But that is merely because they have had cold facts brought to their immediate attention.

"For instance, Mr. Herrick is the banker at Silver City. He was robbed of a sizeable sum. Not a king's ransom, it is true; but enough to rise the ire of Mr. Herrick. Mr. Grey happened to be a passenger on the Red Bluff stage, when the driver was killed and the treasure stolen. It was not Mr. Grey's money, but he feels the outrage keenly. Last, but not least, Mr. Archer was cashier of the Scorpion bank, when two men walked in and removed the money. Is it any wonder that their minds run to violent robbery?"

"Permit *me*," said Judge, placing a quarter on the bar.

"Permission granted, Mr. Van Treece. Another tang to the tonsils."

AS THEY bowed and drank, Danny Regan came in. Danny was in full charge of Henry's J Bar C ranch, since Henry became sheriff. Danny was twenty-four years of age, a lithe, well-built cowboy, with a mop of red hair, freckles and a wide grin. His eyes were very blue, under the brim of his big hat.

"At it again, eh?" he said, grinning.

"Yes," corrected Judge solemnly. "Have a snifter, Danny?"

"No, thank yuh kindly."

"Love does that," said Henry. "Could he go across the street, with a reek of whisky on his breath? Love's funny. Oscar says he's not going to drink again; and I happen to know that Frijole Bill brought him a gallon of prune whisky last night."

Frijole Bill was the cook at the J Bar C.

"That stuff is rank poison," said Judge. "But if Oscar really means it—well, in moderation it is not so bad. Did you note where it was placed?"

"Locked up in one of the cells," replied Henry.

"Stay away from it," advised Danny. "You two are hereby invited to eat supper over at Harper's house—and yuh can't go there drunk."

"My dear boy," said Henry loftily, "we have no idea of getting drunk. To supper with the estimable Harper family, did you say? It is a privilege and a pleasure. The world is one vast bed of flowers."

"Well, stop irrigatin' 'em," grinned Danny. "Shall I tell the folks that you both accept the invitation?"

"From the depth of our hearts," said the Judge grandly.

Just before supper-time Frijole Bill came to Tonto City. The J Bar C cook was sixty years of age, five feet, three inches tall, and would weigh about one hundred pounds. He had a skinny, little face, bushy eyebrows, and a huge mustache.

Frijole found Oscar at the sheriff's office, sitting on the cot, half dreaming.

"Hallo, Free-holey," said Oscar sadly. "No supper at the ranch?"

"Danny's in town, and Slim and the rest are down to Silver City. Whereat is the boss and his lawin' pardner?"

"Eatin' supper at Harper's house. How are you, Free-holey?"

"Listen," said Frijole, "that old sway-back gray horse got into the shed where I stored my prune whisky, and busted both jugs. How are yuh fixed?"

"Ay am fixed fine. You want drink?"

"You didn't think I was askin' 'bout yore liver, didja? Trot out that jug. I'm as dry as a smoke-tree leaf in Death Valley."

"We better set on back step," suggested Oscar. "Ay tol' Hanry that Ay am no longer drinking man; but Ay do like that prune-yuice."

"She shore brings on the whoop 'n holler," agreed Frijole, as they sat down on the back steps of the jail and opened the jug. "Yuh know, this stuff is pretty old, too. Uh-huh. Last Wednesday, I made this batch, and I cut up half a plug of chawin' tobacco in it. That's what makes her taste so good.

"Don'tcha think I'm improvin' the flavor, Oscar?"

"Yah, sure," agreed Oscar sadly.

"What's eatin' yuh, Swede?" asked Frijole.

"My hort is joost about bruk."

"Yore heart? Aw-w-w, yuh can't bust a heart. You can cut one, but yuh can't break it. Hell, you ain't got no bone in yore heart."

"My hort is very sad, Free-holey."

"Love? Yuh don't mean—yo're in love, do yuh?"

Oscar tried to explain about Josephine Swensen, the big waitress at the Tonto hotel.

"Yeah, I know what yuh mean," admitted Frijole. Oscar went further into the subject.

"Yuh mean to say," said Frijole, "that the boss of the hotel told Josephine to tell you to keep to hell away from there with yore fiddle?"

"Yah, sure. He say Ay wake oop everybody."

"Well, the particular son-of-a-gun! And no ear for music!"

"My hort is very sad, Free-holey."

Frijole wiped the prune whisky off his mustache, gave quite an audible "Ah-h-h-h!" and settled back against the door.

"What can yuh play?" he asked.

"Va'l, Ay can play 'Stor Strangled Banner.'"

"No wonder they all got up! Hell, that's no love song tune."

"Ay don't know love tunes, Free-holey."

"Yuh don't? Well, it's time yuh did. Git yore fiddle, and I'll learn yuh one. And yuh might bring a couple tin-cups; too much of this whisky runs down the inside of yore collar."

Henry and Judge, as nearly sober as either of them ever were,

were enjoying the hospitality of the Harper home, an apartment behind their millinery store. Leila Harper and Danny Regan had been engaged for several months. Leila was twenty, tall, slender, with clean-cut features, dark, wavy hair and big, dark eyes. In her youth, Mrs. Harper had been a beautiful girl—and she was still handsome.

Judge Van Treece, christened Cornelius, was a broken-down lawyer, bumming drinks in the mining district of Gold Valley, when Danny Regan first saw him. The place was infested with high-graders, stealing rich ore, and for some reason they believed Van Treece was a detective.

Danny Regan wasn't interested in the detective angle, but he was interested in protecting a defenseless man; so he shot a way out for himself and Van Treece, brought the old man to Wild Horse Valley, where, later, Van Treece's ability as a criminal lawyer saved Danny from a murder conviction.

CHAPTER II

THREE SHOTS

WHEN HENRY HARRISON Conroy came to Tonto City he saw in Judge a kindred spirit, and made him attorney for the J Bar C. Much liquor had passed down their throats since that day, but they were still going well. Henry came to Tonto City, immaculate in black clothes, white linen, fancy waistcoat, and spats; and jauntily swinging a gold-headed cane. Arizona had changed his garb, but his face had not changed at all.

"My dear Mrs. Harper," he said, as he shoved slightly back from the table, "I have no illusions of western grandeur. Never in my wildest flights of fancy have I pictured myself galloping a swift steed over the Arizona landscape, gathering up bandits with both hands.

"I do believe that my name will go down in history, as the worst specimen of Arizona sheriff that ever existed. No doubt, if the state legislature ever offers a booby prize, I shall get it, even if I have retired from office. My election was a joke. When I was officially notified of my election, I lifted both hands in supplication, and said 'My God, what have the people of this valley done?' And ever since then, I have been waiting for an answer."

"I believe," said Judge, "that the answer does not exist."

"Time will tell, Judge."

"Henry, what was this I heard about the commissioners being in to see you today?" asked Danny.

"Aye. They came, they spoke—but they really didn't conquer. You see, Oscar cleaned a shotgun today. In coming back to the office, he inserted the two cartridges, closed the gun—and both barrels went off. Luckily, the gun was pointed a few inches above the commissioners, and only showered them with splinters from the door."

"He'll kill somebody before he gets through," declared Leila. "I heard Mr. Rickey complaining that Oscar came late last night to serenade Josephine Swensen with a fiddle, and woke up everybody in the hotel."

"That adorable Swede!" choked Henry. "Woke up everybody. Well, I've heard him play that fiddle. He only plays one tune, a discordant, Swedish version of our National Anthem. No, I am wrong, he has one more, which defies translation. He thinks he is playing 'Annie Laurie,' but I'll defy any other fiddler to play 'Annie Laurie' to the tune of 'Sweet Bunch of Daisies,' and make it sound like 'The Campbells Are Coming!'"

"Why, that would be impossible, Henry," replied Mrs. Harper seriously.

"My dear Mrs. Harper, to one of Oscar's ability, nothing is impossible. In my years before the footlights, I have met and studied many queer characters—but there is only one Oscar. To me he is Oscar The First, Second and Last. The whole valley wept when I became sheriff. They stiffened with a jerk when I appointed Judge as my deputy—but they fainted when I made Oscar my jailer."

"But I think you are doing fine," said Mrs. Harper warmly.

"Excellent, my dear—excellent! We are still alive—and haven't accidentally killed anyone—yet."

"Was that the opinion of the commissioners?" asked Danny.

"The commissioners, my boy, were unanimous. They condemned me most heartily. In fact, from them I learned that my ancestors did not come over in the Mayflower, that my grandfather spat on the sidewalk, and that my own father was either a milk-sop or a collector of knickknacks, when he didn't strangle me at birth. Like many other people, they saw the point of the joke, but did not appreciate it."

"What was the point of the joke?" asked Mrs. Harper.

"Me—my dear. Ah, well, such is life."

TONTO CITY was not an all-night town. As a usual thing, all the town was in darkness, except the saloons, at midnight. It was within an hour of midnight, and Oscar and Frijole were still behind the jail. Very little was left in that gallon jug, but the violin lesson was apparently pleasing to both Frijole and Oscar.

"You've got'r, feller," applauded Frijole. "Swedes ain't dumb. You c'n saw cat-gut with anybody. Jist remember where to start and where to end—and the middle c'n take care of itshelf."

"Free-holey, you are great faller," declared Oscar thickly. "Have you ever been in love?"

"Lizzen," replied Frijole owlishly, "I'm what you'd call a inter—internashunal lover. Three times in Spanish, once in Dutch, twice in Eye-talian and once in the Apache Reservation. I'm cured. I'll help—but I won't make eyes."

"Ay tank you are great faller, Free-holey."

"Tha's all ri', Oshcar. F'rgit it. S'all we forw'rd marsh?"

"Yah, sure."

Their forward march was not without difficulties. They decided to walk not on the street, but to keep to the back of the buildings. In order to do this, they had to cross a street, pass behind Harper's place, the post office, a general store, and the Tonto City Bank.

Between the bank and the hotel was a twelve foot alley, and Oscar knew that Josephine's room was on this side.

Woodpiles, piles of discarded boxes, and all sorts of impedimenta blocked their way. Twice Oscar lost his fiddle, and they were obliged to search for it. Then Frijole lost the six-shooter from inside the waist-band of his overalls, and this necessitated a search.

"Tha's all ri'," assured Frijole. "The path 'f true love never is sus-smooth. Jus' don't f'rgit the tune. Af'er all I've gone through with you thish evenin'—don' f'rgit that tune, Oshcar."

In some unaccountable way, they reached the alley between the bank and the hotel, where they sat down to recuperate. Oscar clutched the fiddle in one hand and the jug in the other, until they sat down.

Tung! went a string.

"Whazzamatter?" asked Frijole. "Fiddle blowin' up on yuh?"

"Ay vars mishtooken," explained Oscar heavily. "Ay t'ought de key from the fiddle vars a curk."

"A curk? Whaz a curk?"

"A stopper in de chug."

"Oh! Well, let's have 'nother drink, and then shing."

They finished the last of the prune whisky, rolled the jug aside and prepared for the serenade. Oscar made a preliminary search for the right note, clamped his finger down on the string and got a death grip on the bow.

"Ready?" asked Frijole.

"Yah, sure. Ha'ar ve go!"

With a mighty swipe of the bow, Oscar sent a wailing note into the night, and from Frijole's throat burst forth: "Just a shong at twi-i-i-i-ilight, when the li-i-i-ights—whoa!"

The "whoa!" was for Oscar, who was playing madly, wildly, but it did not stop Oscar. Frijole lifted his head, opened his mouth and just as he took a deep breath, resolved to at least add his part of the serenade; regardless of the accompaniment, he was hit in the face with a deluge of water.

A moment later a heavy object came whizzing down, crashing through the bank window, and a voice yelled from above: "If you bums are there, when I come down—"

Frijole spat out a pint of water and went staggering around the rear corner of the bank, with Oscar stumbling behind him. Someone lunged into Frijole, sending him headlong. A gun was fired almost in Oscar's face, and he went flat on the ground.

FRIJOLE struggled to a sitting position, sober enough to draw his gun, and took a shot at a shadowy figure. A bullet whined off the back steps of the jail, and Frijole shot at the flash. That is, he thought he did.

"Oshcar, are you killed?" he asked.

"Ay tank Ay am going to get out of *here*," replied Oscar.

Oscar got to his feet, and started traveling like a runaway horse, ignoring all obstacles, while Frijole did a staggering gallop in his wake. They were two houses away, when a last shot was fired. Then they galloped across the street, entered the back door of the jail and sat down on a cot.

"My goo'ness!" exclaimed Frijole owlishly, his mustache still dripping water, "I knowed it was bad, but I didn' think they'd shoot at's, Oshcar."

"Oh, Ay los' my fiddle," wailed Oscar.

"Yuh did? Well, I'll tell yuh, feller; lookin' at it from my schtandpoint, it's a godshend. That fiddle will be the death of you."

Henry and Judge were just leaving the Harper place, when the shooting started, but they had no idea of the location of the shots. They echoed back from across the street, making it rather confusing. Several men were running across the street from the Tonto Saloon; so Henry and Judge followed them to the front of the bank.

"It was over here," declared one of the men, peering into the front window of the bank.

Tom Rickey, owner of the hotel, put in an appearance, bareheaded, and wearing carpet-slippers.

"Did you hear the shooting, Mr. Rickey?" asked Henry.

"Yes. I heard the shots. I was in bed, when that damnable fiddle—"

"Oscar!" exclaimed Henry.

"Yes, Oscar," replied Rickey. "I threw a pitcher of water, and then I threw the pitcher. Of all the damned music I ever heard!"

They moved around into the alley, where Judge stepped on the fiddle. It was too dark to observe the damage wrought by the pitcher. They circled the bank, but found nobody. Henry tried the back door of the bank, and found it partly open.

He called to the others, and they crowded in with him. Lighting matches, they discovered Claude Adams, the cashier, bound and gagged, lying half under a desk. There was broken glass all over the floor, and Henry stooped to pick up the handle of a porcelain water pitcher. Quickly they unbound Adams and removed the gag. He was unhurt, but a little groggy. The safe was intact.

"Two masked men jumped me outside my house tonight," he told them. "They gagged me and forced me to come up here, where I had to open the back door for them. In here, they tied me up, and tried to force me to tell the combination of the safe. I wouldn't tell; so they were going to burn my feet with a candle, to make me tell. One of them started to take off my shoes, when we heard the darnedest music I ever heard. Then something smashed through the window, sending glass all over the place—and the men ran out."

"Your pitcher, Mr. Rickey," said Henry. "I've heard of pitchers busting up ball games—but never busting up bank robberies."

"But what was the shooting about?" queried Rickey. "There were at least four or five shots fired."

THEY went outside, locking the door behind them, and made a search of the premises. It was Judge who made the discovery. Flat on his back near the rear porch of the hotel was Martin Archer, commissioner, and cashier of the Scorpion bank—dead. He was wearing a dark suit of clothes, dark shirt, brown hat and black shoes.

Doctor Clemens was quickly summoned, and made an examination by lantern-light.

"Shot twice," he told them. "One shot, I believe, broke his leg near the hip, while the other went through his heart,"

They secured a cot and carried the body down to Clemens' house, where the doctor, who was also the coroner, completed his examination, while Henry and Judge went to the office. Oscar and Frijole were both asleep on the small cot, fully dressed.

"Frijole Bill, too, eh?" muttered Henry. He went out to a cell, where the prune whisky had been left, but the jug was gone.

Frijole still had his gun. Henry opened it, disclosing two empty shells, recently fired, three loaded cartridges, and one empty chamber in the cylinder. He and Judge looked it over gravely.

Henry deftly poked a handkerchief through the barrel with a pencil, wiped it out thoroughly, loaded the two forty-five cartridges from his own stock, and put the empties in his pocket. Then he replaced Frijole's gun, and sat down at his desk.

"Compounding a felony," said Judge solemnly.

"Confine yourself to being a good deputy," advised Henry. "Use a little horse sense, and forget the legal aspect for the moment. Frijole appears to have fired twice. Unless I am badly mistaken, each of these men have imbibed two quarts of prune whisky. Knowing the potency of that whoop 'n holler juice, I defy any man on earth to drink two quarts, and still shoot straight enough to hit a man twice—in the dark."

"Frijole is a good shot," sighed Judge.

"We shall forget that Frijole fired a shot," said Henry. Just at that moment Frijole snored, snorted and awoke. He sat up, goggling at the light, rubbed his nose violently with a clenched fist, and looked at Henry and Judge. Then he looked at the snoring Oscar.

"No brains," he said hoarsely. "For three hours I tried to learn him a tune on his fiddle, but it's no use. All he'll ever be is a cat-gut sawyer. There ain't no music in his soul."

"Frijole," said Henry, severely, "did you know you killed a man tonight?"

"Me?" Frijole's eyes snapped wide. "I killed a man? Hell—no!"

"You fired two shots out there behind the bank."

"I—uh—" Frijole pulled out his gun and examined the cylinder.

"No, I—wait a minute! Why, I thought I dreamed it. That's right, I remember. Somebody was shootin' at me and Oscar."

"Wait a minute now," said Henry. "Get it straight. You fired two shots."

"Yeah, I reckon I did."

"Where were you, and which way did you shoot?"

"Lemme see-e-e. I'd be on the northeast corner of the bank. Yeah, that's right. I shot once in this direction. That'd be south. Then I fired the next shot kinda north. Yeah, that's the way it was."

"You didn't fire both shots in the same direction?"

"I shore didn't."

"How many shots were fired at you—two?"

"Lemme think, will yuh? One—two—three. Yeah, there were three. One shot was fired when we was runnin' down this way. I 'member that, 'cause I caught up with Oscar and passed him jist after that shot went off."

"You knew Martin Archer, didn't you, Frijole?"

"That bank feller from Scorpion? Yeah, I know who he is."

"He's dead—shot twice. We found him near the back steps of the hotel."

Frijole blinked and licked his lips. "Twice, yuh say? Well, mebbe I hit him once, but it's a cinch I didn't hit him twice. But what was the shootin' about?"

Henry explained about the attempted bank robbery, and how it had been frustrated. Frijole blinked foolishly at him.

"Get on your horse and go home," ordered Henry. "Don't talk to anybody about the robbery. You were too drunk to remember—and you didn't fire any shots."

"Henry," said Judge, after Frijole had gone, "you seem to be throwing monkey-wrenches into the wheels of justice."

"And of you, sir, may I ask," replied Henry, "if your soul has become so that you no longer realize that there is a sharp line between law and justice? Wheels of justice? You mean the maw of the law. Rather good, eh? Maw of the law. Sounds like a maternal parent for a lot of damnable mistakes."

"The evidence," replied Judge stiffly, "points to Frijole."

"The evidence? What evidence? Who can prove that Frijole fired one single shot? I'll bet you one dollar, even money, that Oscar won't remember who fired the shots. If he does, it's the first time in his life he ever remembered anything. Let's go to bed."

CHAPTER III

INQUEST

THE KILLING OF Martin Archer created a furore, especially in Scorpion, where he was a prominent citizen. Henry was down at the doctor's office early that morning.

"It seems to me," said Doctor Clemens, "that Archer must have been hit twice in rapid succession. The shot through the hip would have knocked him down, almost instantly. But, judging from the direction taken by the bullets, the man was upright when the two shots struck him. I extracted the bullet from his hip. It is a forty-five. But the other bullet went through him."

"I see," nodded Henry thoughtfully.

"Has anyone advanced any theory as to why Martin Archer was out there behind the hotel at that time of night?" asked the doctor.

"Yes, they have," nodded Henry. "Archer was staying at the hotel. About ten or fifteen minutes previous to the shooting, Archer was in the lobby of the hotel. He said he couldn't sleep, and was going out to walk around a while."

"He never seemed very robust," said the doctor. "Well, it is too bad. Luckily he has neither wife nor family. I don't know what relatives he has, except William Grey, who is his uncle."

"I suppose Grey will take charge of the body," said Henry.

Grey and Herrick had gone to Scorpion, but were among the first contingent to arrive that morning. Henry groaned aloud and walked out the back door, leaving Judge to entertain the remaining two-thirds of the commission. He walked along behind the buildings, following the same route taken by Oscar and Frijole, and reached the rear of the hotel, where he sat down on the steps, a picture of utter dejection.

He studied the exact spot where Archer's body had laid. He could picture the exact angle. He studied it in relation to where Frijole said he had been, when he fired the shots.

"One shot north and one shot south," he muttered. "And still, Mart Archer was shot twice."

Henry got carefully down on his knees, grimacing a little. Here was the exact spot where Archer laid. The ground was still damp with blood. With the point of his pocket-knife Henry began digging carefully. The ground was sandy. Suddenly the knife lifted an object out of the sand. Voices were coming from the alley. Henry had pocketed the object, just as William Grey, Richard Herrick and Judge Van Treece came around the corner.

Slowly Henry got to his feet, grimacing a little from the stiffness of his knees.

"Oh, here you are!" exclaimed Judge. "Mr. Grey and Mr. Herrick wanted to see where Archer fell; so I—"

"That's all right," interrupted Grey. He walked up and looked at the spot where Henry had been digging.

"What in the hell were you diggin' for?" asked Grey.

"Gentlemen," smiled Henry, "I must admit that you have caught me. When I saw you come to town, I decided to dig a hole and bury myself."

Herrick came up and glanced at the ground.

"Where did yuh find Mart's body?" asked Grey.

"Right here," said Henry blandly. Grey glanced at the spot, and turned to glare at Henry.

"And what are you doin' about it?" he demanded. "You are the sheriff of this county. Where's the murderer of my nephew?"

"My dear sir!" protested Henry. "Things are not done that way—not even in books nor on the stage. Were I able to accomplish results with such speed and acumen, murder would be the most unpopular thing in this world. Murder would cease to exist. What you need is a seer."

"Seer! I want results."

"Do you," propounded Henry seriously, "know any bank robbers who are frightened of thrown water-pitchers? I ask this, because I believe Martin Archer was killed by the bank robbers. It is my theory that he wandered in to their path, as they were making a get-away, and paid for his insomnia with his life."

"**WHAT** about that drunken Swede who was here?" asked Herrick.

"Oscar? My dear sir, neither of those fatal bullets came from a fiddle. In fact, I doubt if that fiddle has ever been loaded. Oscar does not carry arms."

Grey grasped Herrick by the arm. "C'mon, Dick," he urged. "Let's get away from here, before I poke that idiot in the nose."

"Either way suits me fine," replied Herrick, and they went back through the alley.

"What in the devil *were* you digging for?" queried Judge.

"Curiosity," replied Henry. "I wanted to see how deep human blood would sink in sand; so I tested out my own theory."

"Were you right, Henry?"

"Judge, since you have known me, how many times have I been wrong?"

"Practically a perfect score, Henry."

"Right?"

"No—wrong."

Henry sighed and shook his head. "How true are the words, 'Consistency, thou art a virtue.' Has our Terrible Swede emerged from behind the veil of prune yuice?"

"The Swede is a teetotaler," replied Judge. "He says he hopes to be struck dead, if he ever gets drunk again."

"That's really too bad," sighed Henry. "I don't know where I can get a man to take his place."

They went back to the office, where they found Oscar on the cot.

"So you have quit drinking, eh?" said Henry.

"Ay have quit everyt'ing, including love. My fiddle is bruk."

"Well, things look a little better," said Henry. "We are holding the inquest about one o'clock, but before that I want to have a talk with you, Oscar. You are the chief witness."

"Ay don't remember much," sighed Oscar.

"I hope," retorted Henry, "to fix it so you won't remember anything."

The inquest, held in a vacant storeroom, attracted a large crowd. The jury was quickly sworn, and Doctor Clemens was the first to give testimony, which was purely technical. Tom Rickey caused quite a bit of amusement, when he testified to dumping water into the alley, and then throwing the pitcher, which went through the bank window.

"Was there any conversation between you and the serenader?" asked the coroner.

"Well," laughed Rickey, "after I threw the pitcher, I yelled: 'If you bums are there when I come down—'"

"Just a moment. How many men were down there, Mr. Rickey?"

"I don't know—it was too dark. Might have only been one. Night before last, Oscar Johnson played his fiddle out there, and made enough noise for a whole orchestra."

Henry and Judge breathed more freely, as Rickey left the stand.

Oscar Johnson was called, took the oath and sat down. "Your name, please," said the coroner.

"Oscar Yohnson."

"You are the jailer?"

"Ay am—Ay hope."

"Oscar Johnson, you were behind the Tonto City bank last night, between eleven and twelve o'clock, were you not?"

"Ay yust can bar'ly remember."

"Answer yes or no."

"Yas or no."

"All right; we'll pass that. Tell the jury what happened."

OSCAR cleared his throat and looked around, a silly grin on his face.

"Val, Ay vars drinking prune yuice and played some tunes with my fiddle."

"You mean," corrected the coroner, "you had your fiddle and was drinking prune whisky, don't you?"

"Oh!" grunted Oscar. "Did you see me, Doc?"

"Well, go ahead and tell it in your own way."

"Val, Ay vars drinking prune yuice with my fiddle," said Oscar triumphantly.

"Who was with you?" snapped the coroner.

"My fiddle."

"I see. Well, what happened?"

"Ay don't know," replied Oscar blandly.

"You don't know? Why don't you know? You were there."

"Doc," asked Oscar confidentially, "did you ever drink a gallon of prune yuice?"

"Certainly not!"

"Val, if you never have, you have missed something."

"Now listen to me!" snapped the exasperated coroner, "you must remember the shooting."

"Val, of coorse."

"That's good! Who fired the shots?"

"Ay don't know."

"You don't, eh? What did you do when the shots were fired?"

"Val," grinned Oscar, "Ay fall down, and den Ay get oop. And den Ay say, 'Oscar Yohnson, you get to ha'l out of ha'ar.'"

"And you did, eh?"

"Ay am a man of my vord, Doc."

When the laughing had subsided, the coroner asked:

"When did you hear that Martin Archer was dead?"

"Dis morning."

"You didn't know it last night?"

"Last night? Yumping Yiminee, last night Ay didn't even know my fiddle was bruk."

"You are excused," sighed the coroner.

Back at the office, Henry looked upon Oscar with admiration. The jury had brought in the usual verdict—killed by a party or parties, unknown.

"Oscar," said Henry, "there are times when I love every bone in your thick head."

"Yah, sure," nodded Oscar. "Ay t'ink Ay will ride out to de ranch to see de boys."

"Prune yuice!" snorted Judge.

"Ay hope," said Oscar, "you will excoose me. Ay have been under terrible strain."

"Go ahead," said Henry dryly. "Go out to the ranch and have your physical and mental breakdown. You've earned it."

After Oscar left, Danny Regan came to the office. The young, red-headed cowboy seemed very grave.

"You ain't been quarreling with Leila, have you?" asked Henry.

"No." Danny shook his head quickly. "I just came from the Tonto Saloon. There's a lot of fellers from Scorpion over there, and they ain't satisfied with the inquest."

"You mean," said Henry slowly, "they are not satisfied with me."

"Oh, well, that's to be expected. Archer was one of 'em, down there. Grey and Herrick are as bad as the rest. They talk about runnin' you and Judge both out of the county. Tar and feathers, and all that."

"They say," remarked Judge, "it is very hard to remove."

"Oh, don't make a joke of it!" exclaimed Danny. "It's serious, I tell yuh."

"Today?" queried Henry.

"Mebbe not today—but soon—unless you can do something to find the men who have been doin' all this devilment. They say you haven't done a thing, except sit here and draw a salary."

"**THEY** forget that this is our first crime," said Henry. "Bill Parton was unable to apprehend the men who committed three of our major crimes—and they didn't tar and feather him."

"Bill Parton was the biggest crook we had. Perhaps he was in with this gang. Mebbe he was their leader."

"It's rather confusing," sighed Henry. "Adams says the two masked men who attacked him were of medium height. That gives us three tall men, three short men, and two medium men. Another robbery, or two, and the whole valley will be under suspicion."

"Lock up and come out to the ranch," suggested Danny. "It will give them time to cool off. That Scorpion bunch are the agitators. If you leave town, they'll soon go back home."

"Danny," replied Henry kindly, "I appreciate your feelings. But would *you* run away and hide from trouble?"

"Oh, I know, but this is different."

"The difference lies in the fact that you might shoot your way out of trouble, while Judge and myself would have to resort to oratory. Are you weakening, Judge?"

"I?" snorted Judge indignantly. "Weaken? When the foliage of our glorious trees wither and die forever; when the glorious rivers flow no more, and the lakes are but forgotten drifts of dry sand; when the tops of our mighty mountains crumble, and when the—er—"

"We won't be here to care," finished Henry.

"Very true," agreed Judge meekly.

"Ain't you two *ever* goin' to be serious?" asked Danny.

"I don't know," sighed Henry. "But why be serious—in this life? Perhaps I shall be serious when I walk up to the last box-office and ask Saint Peter if he has two on the aisle, about midway in the house."

"I can see the old Saint," murmured Judge. "He stands there in his golden robes, looking at Henry for a long time. Then he speaks."

"Saying?" prompted Henry.

"Go to hell, Henry; this is a drama—not comedy."

Henry nodded slowly, thoughtfully.

"The picture is not alluring, Judge. I'm just wondering—do they have the tar hot or cold—and where do they get feathers?"

"I reckon I'm wastin' my time," said Danny. He walked to the doorway, and stopped. "I'll bring Slim in with me this evenin', just in case they start heatin' tar. Oscar's out at the ranch, too, ain't he?"

"Don't enlist Oscar," said Judge quickly. "That man is so dumb that he would probably furnish the feathers."

"Yeah, I reckon you're right," agreed Danny. "I'll be back."

THE STAGE from Red Bluff came in about four o'clock.

William Grey and Richard Herrick were at the stage depot to welcome a stranger, with whom they talked for fifteen minutes in a hotel room, after which they took him down to the sheriff's office. Henry and Judge were there.

"Conroy," said Grey grimly, "this is John Swayne, a private detective, of San Francisco. I told you we were hirin' him."

"Oh, yes!" exclaimed Henry.

Swayne tossed his card on the desk and looked around the office. Swayne was a big man, hard-faced, with greenish-gray eyes. He wore a dark blue suit, soft shirt, red necktie and black shoes. His hat was a medium-size black Stetson sombrero. Henry squinted at the card, and looked up at Swayne.

"From Frisco, eh? That's my old stamping-ground. You must know my old friend Roscoe Britton, head of the Britton Agency."

"Well, I'll say I do!" exclaimed Swayne warmly.

"And Abe Cullison, that famous Chinatown detective?"

"Known him for years," replied Swayne.

"Well, that's great!" beamed Henry. "We're going to get along fine, Mr. Swayne. Meet Judge Van Treece, my deputy."

Judge shook hands with the detective and bowed low.

"A pleasure, I assure you, Mr. Swayne," he said. "And a right hearty welcome to Tonto City."

"We'll leave you fellers to talk it over," said Grey.

"All right, Bill," replied Swayne. "See yuh later."

Grey and Herrick left the office, and the three men sat down.

"So this is crime country, eh?" smiled Swayne.

"Terrible," admitted Henry. "It comes in bunches, like bananas. Is this your first trip to Arizona?"

"To this part of the state."

"The county hired yuh, eh?"

"Yeah, that's the arrangement. Mr. Grey wired me several days ago."

"He knew your reputation, eh?"

"Well, not my personal reputation."

"Oh, I see. He didn't know you personally."

"No," replied Swayne. "I reckon we might as well get down to business, Conroy. What's the dope on this murder of Archer?"

Henry rubbed his nose thoughtfully.

"Didn't Grey explain the details?"

"Oh, yeah, he told all *he* knew. What I want to know is this: what have you doped out?"

"Pardon me," said Judge meekly, "but didn't you come here to—er—dope the thing out for yourself?"

"Certainly!" snapped Swayne. "I merely thought that you might have some sort of a lead for me to start on."

"Well, there's the murder, itself," said Henry. "If Grey told you all about it, you know as much as we do. No one saw it. Go right ahead and solve the mystery. If we can be of any assistance, call on us."

"Thank you," replied Swayne dryly. "Grey told me that you wouldn't be of any assistance to me."

"Well, I wouldn't go so far as to say that," said Henry soberly. "When you have the guilty parties apprehended, our guns might come in handy—as sort of a climax."

Swayne tried hard to suppress a smile.

"The gunmen of Arizona are famous," he said. His eyes strayed to the splintered door, where Oscar's two loads of duck-shot had torn a gaping hole.

"**A WILD** Swede, with a double-barreled shotgun," explained Henry. "He fired both barrels through the door, and then came charging in."

"Then what happened?" queried Shayne seriously.

"I just took one look at him," replied Henry grimly, thrusting out his chin, "and he put down that gun."

Swayne's eyes were a bit credulous.

"You jailed him, eh?" he said.

"Jailed him? For what? My dear Mr. Swayne, we do not jail 'em in this country for missing."

Swayne snorted softly and got to his feet.

"Well, I'll see you later, gents," he said. "If I need you, I'll call."

"Do," replied Henry. "We are here to serve."

Judge got to his feet and bowed, as Swayne walked out. Then he sat down and looked quizzically at Henry, who tried twice to hook his spurred heels over the edge of the desk, but failed.

"So San Francisco is your old stamping-ground, eh?" commented Judge.

"Well, I—I laid that on a little thick, I'll admit, Judge. I've been in San Francisco—but did very little stamping, as I remember."

"But Mr. Swayne knew those two detective friends of yours, Henry."

"You know, Judge, that is rather remarkable," mused Henry.

"What is so damnably remarkable about it?" asked Judge.

"Why, the fact that we both know two men, who, as far as I know, never existed."

"What? You mean—you made 'em up out of whole cloth, Henry?"

"I'm sorry if I have increased the census, illegally; but your surmise is perfectly right, Judge."

"But—but, damn it, Henry—why, the man lied!"

"No, Judge," denied Henry quietly. "I lied—and he swore to it."

"Hm-m-m-m!"

"Quite a character, this Mr. Swayne," observed Henry. "Gets very familiar on short acquaintance, it seems."

"I didn't notice that characteristic, Henry."

"No? Possibly it was a slip of the tongue. However, you remember that he did not know Mr. Grey; and yet he called him 'Bill,' when Grey and Herrick left the office."

"Nearly everybody calls him Bill Grey."

"But Mr. Swayne is a newcomer, Judge; and doesn't know everyone."

"Well, Henry, what is your honest opinion of Mr. Swayne?"

"My opinion, my dear Judge, would need to be snap judgment on short notice; but I hope to Heaven that no one ever has the same opinion of me."

CHAPTER IV

A BOTTLE AND OSCAR

THE TAR-AND-FEATHER PARTY did not materialize. Most of the Scorpion contingent went home, giving Henry and Judge a chance to breathe more freely. At least the danger was past for a while. Henry and Judge ate supper together at the Tonto hotel. Grey, Herrick and Swayne came in and ate supper together.

Dug Wheeler, long, lean driver of the stage to Red Bluff, ate at a table near Henry and Judge. The stage was scheduled to leave at eight o'clock that evening.

Imbued with a sudden inspiration, Henry produced paper and pencil, and wrote a telegram to the Police Department of San Francisco. It read:

> WIRE ME ALL THE INFORMATION YOU HAVE ON JOHN SWAYNE PRIVATE DETECTIVE ADDRESS FIVE HUNDRED AND TWO SILVERTON BUILDING ON MISSION STREET YOUR CITY.

When Wheeler finished his meal, Henry called him over, gave him the telegram, and money to send it from Red Bluff.

Danny Regan and Slim Pickins arrived from the ranch, and met Henry and Judge in front of the restaurant. They all walked down to the office, where Henry lighted the lamp on his desk

"Let's drop in at the Harper place," suggested Danny. "Leila was goin' to make some candy this afternoon. And while we're up there, Slim can go over to the Tonto Saloon and see what information he can pick up."

John Swayne

They left the lamp burning, and went up to see how the candy-making came out, while Slim went on a still-hunt for information. They were making inroads on the candy, when Slim came back.

"Bill Grey and Dick Herrick left for Silver City," said Slim. "I reckon most of the Scorpion bunch have gone home; so there's nothin' to worry about."

"My gracious, I don't know what this country is coming to," declared Mrs. Harper. "Bringing in a detective, who doesn't even know the country. What can he do?"

"Answer the question, Judge," said Henry. "I am entirely absorbed in taffy. My dear Leila, this is delicious."

"I know very little about detectives, except what I have read," replied Judge. "Sherlock Holmes, for instance."

"I'd hate to be this John Swayne," said Slim. "If he ever does git on the right track, they'll fill him full of bullets."

"A big price for a little glory," smiled Henry, reaching for more candy. "At least, that is my theory."

"They're goin' to take Archer's body to Scorpion for burial," said Slim. "I heard that much tonight."

They finished up the candy. Henry relaxed in his chair, a picture of perfect contentment. They heard the stage pull out for Red Bluff.

"Don't forget we left the lamp burning," said Judge.

"The county pays for the oil," laughed Danny.

Suddenly they all jerked to attention. From somewhere on the street came the unmistakable report of a gun. Henry got to his feet and went to the front door of the shop, while the others crowded in behind him. There were several people on the street, looking for the source of the shot. Tom Rickey, the hotel man, walked down to them. He had heard the shot, but had no idea where it had been fired.

"A drunken cowboy wouldn't stop on one shot," he said.

Men were standing in front of the Tonto Saloon, talking about it. A horse and rider came slowly down the street, and as he passed through the illumination from the Tonto Saloon windows, Henry groaned aloud:

"The Terrible Swede, saturated to the gills!"

"It is indeed," replied Judge. "Prune yuice wins again."

Oscar's horse stopped in front of the office, and they saw Oscar go staggering into the place.

"He's heading for the cot," said Henry.

"Frijole spent the whole mornin' makin' prune liquor," said Slim. "It's a wonder it don't kill both of 'em. I never drank a worse mixture in my life."

"And it has all the authority of the Supreme Court," added Judge.

"Is that the stuff that induces Oscar to serenade Josephine?" asked Rickey.

"That—and love," laughed Henry. "What a mixture! But the fiddle is busted—and I fear that love grows cold, Mr. Rickey."

"Maybe I was wrong in throwing that water-pitcher—I dunno."

"Here comes Oscar!" exclaimed Leila.

"Tryin' to run!" blurted Danny. "There he goes—off the side-walk!"

OSCAR'S sense of direction was very faulty. He fell down in the street, but got right up and fell back on the sidewalk.

"Were de ha'l is everybody?" he yelped. "Halp! Halp! Halp!"

The men hurried down to Oscar, where he was pawing around in the dark, and dragged him to his feet.

"Too much prune yuice, eh?" said Henry. "And you swore off."

"Ay am oll right," declared Oscar. "Ay ta'l you. Ay am oll right."

"Then what in the devil are yuh runnin' around for, yellin' for help?" asked Danny.

"By yiminy, Ay forgot!" blurted Oscar. "A dead man in de office!"

"A dead man?" snorted Danny.

"Yah, sure! Ay ta'l you—"

But they didn't wait to be told; they let loose of Oscar and ran to the office, where the lamp was still burning.

Sitting in Henry's chair, his head and shoulders on the desk, was Doctor Clemens. Behind him, a bullet-smashed window attested to the fact that he had been shot by somebody on the sidewalk. Henry's examination was brief.

"Right in the back of the head," he said huskily. He turned helplessly to Slim.

"Will you go to Silver City and get a doctor, Slim? It's no use, as far as saving Clemens is concerned—but we've got to have—well, go get him, Slim."

Men were crowding in, questioning, looking at the body of the elderly doctor, whom everybody liked.

"It don't make sense," declared Rickey. "Why, Doc Clemens was everybody's friend. Who on earth would kill him?"

Someone mentioned the private detective, and a man hurried up to the hotel, returning in a few minutes with John Swayne.

"Another one, eh?" he remarked to Henry, who made no reply.

Swayne made a perfunctory examination of the body, went outside and looked through the bullet-hole in the window pane. Many had heard the shot, and several had recognized Oscar, when he rode into town. Swayne turned to Henry.

"Where were you?" he asked bluntly.

"Up at the Harper place. Judge, Danny, Slim and myself were there. We heard the shot."

"Well, what about this drunken Swede?"

"He came into town after the shot was fired. It was he who discovered the body."

"Uh-huh. Did Doctor Clemens have any enemies? Think hard, now. Even a doctor makes enemies, yuh know."

"This one didn't," replied Henry.

"And that's the truth," added Rickey. "I've known him for years."

"What was he doing, setting in yore chair?" asked Swayne.

"You ask and answer the same question, Mr. Swayne. At least, it is the only possible answer now. He was sitting in my chair."

"Was he in the habit of occupyin' yore chair, Conroy?"

"To my knowledge, this is the first time, Swayne."

Seldom did Henry leave off the prefix on a man's name.

"Married?" asked Swayne.

"His wife is dead," replied Rickey. "An old lady keeps house for him. Doctor Clemens was the coroner of this county."

"I reckon we'll move the body down to his house," said Henry. "We can use that cot to carry him on."

THERE were plenty of volunteers. Only Henry and Swayne were left in the office, as Judge went along to break the news to the housekeeper. With the removal of the body, the crowd outside broke up and drifted away.

"We've got to find a motive for this murder," said Swayne.

"A motive, eh?" said Henry softly. "Swayne, there was no motive to murder Doctor Clemens."

"What do you mean, Conroy? There always is a motive."

Henry's eyes squinted thoughtfully at Swayne for a long time.

"Well, out with it!" snapped Swayne.

"You're a hell of a detective, if you don't know what I mean. Didn't you notice that Doctor Clemens is about my build? Our hair, what there is left of it, is nearly the same color. Looking through that window he could easily have been mistaken for me. That's my theory."

Swayne laughed shortly.

"Why would anybody want to kill you, Conroy?" he asked.

"Reasons make no difference," replied Henry. "But if you think you can develop a better theory, I'd certainly be relieved to hear it."

"I'll do the best I can," said Swayne, and left the office. Henry saw him go over to the Tonto Saloon, where a crowd were talking over the murder. Henry blew out the light, and went out to find Judge. He had made up his mind to spend the night at the ranch.

The four o'clock stage from Red Bluff brought the Red Bluff *Bugle*, a weekly, which carried the following story on the front page:

> As we go to press no new developments have been reported on the crime situation at Tonto City. William Grey, chairman of the Commission, reports that a private detective has been engaged by the county in an effort to put the criminals behind bars.
>
> "We feel that the local peace officers are incompetent," said Mr. Grey, as he was leaving for the southern part of the county. "It becomes our duty to engage a private investigator to take over the work, which should have been done by the sheriff's office.
>
> "Since the death of Martin Archer, Mr. Herrick and myself have been bending every effort to clean up this deplorable situation. The voters of this county made a great mistake at

the last election, of which they are well aware by this time. Both Mr. Herrick and myself feel that if the sheriff's office will only remain as inactive as usual, and not interfere with the work of an investigator, we shall soon be able to clear out the criminals of Wild Horse Valley."

Henry and Judge were reading this, when Jim Moody, in charge of the stage stations, came into the office.

"Here's a hell of a tale," he said huskily. "Last night's stage to Red Bluff never got there!"

"Wait a minute!" snapped Henry. "Say that again, Mr. Moody."

"It never got there, I tell yuh. Red Bluff thought it was a break-down that stopped it. But today's stage never even seen hide nor hair of the other stage."

"It—it sounds ridiculous," faltered Judge.

"But it ain't! That stage, four horses and the driver are gone!"

Henry got to his feet and buckled on his gun.

"How much money was on that stage, Moody?" he asked.

"Not a red cent! There wasn't even a money-box. If it was a hold-up—they never got a cent."

"Rather unusual, isn't it?"

"Not under the circumstances. Banks are sending money privately, instead of taking chances on a stage hold-up."

"I see. Buckle on your gun, Judge; we're riding."

"My poor legs," sighed Judge, getting to his feet.

As they walked out and locked the door, Danny and Slim came riding in from the ranch. Henry quickly explained what had happened, and the two cowboys volunteered to go along. The posse was augmented by Moody and several others, including the driver of the other stage.

ABOUT ten miles from Tonto City the road wound along Rocky Horse Cañon for at least a mile. It was a narrow road, and in some places the cañon side was precipitous. About midway of the cañon grade, and at a sharp turn around a jutting spire of granite, they found the spot where the stage went over the edge. The wheel marks were very plain. The cañon wall was about a forty-five degree angle, all solid rock for a hundred feet, from where it pitched straight off. There were scarred places, where the shod hoofs and iron-shod wheels struck and slid.

The men stood at the edge, staring down into the cañon, saying nothing. Finally Danny Regan said: "Back there about a mile, there's a trail down into the cañon. It's the nearest place I know."

Danny led the way back to the trail, where they all went into the depths of Rocky Horse. Henry and Judge rode most of the way down with their eyes closed, trusting to their horses entirely. It was slow traveling, even after they reached the bottom, but they finally reached the spot.

The stage was only a piled mass of wreckage, the four horses all dead. They found Dug Wheeler, the driver, about twenty feet from the stage, wedged in among some rocks.

"Dug was drinkin' quite a bit yesterday," offered one of the men. "He must have went to sleep and drove off the edge."

"We'll never know," sighed Moody.

Wheeler's clothes were not badly torn. Henry searched his pockets, finding a little money, a watch, knife and a few keys. Nothing of any value was found on the stage, except the sack of mail, which was intact. Moody took charge of that. Danny Regan volunteered to take the body back on his horse, while he doubled-up with Slim. In this way they took the body back to Tonto City, where they found the doctor from Silver City, acting as an emergency coroner.

But Henry and Judge were not interested. Saddle-sore and weary of body and mind, they sat in the office and looked at each other.

"I have a feeling," said Judge wearily, "that the time is ripe for a wholesale resignation. Oscar won't mind, Henry; he doesn't know what it is all about, anyway—and neither do we."

"I feel," replied Henry thoughtfully, "that our act has been miscast. We are trying to do a mystery drama, when we should be doing a farce. Not that we haven't been doing a farce, Judge."

"I don't quite agree, Henry. You have done as well as any man could, under the circumstances."

"But I, my dear Judge, do not look the part. There is the rub. My face is an open book. I have nothing to conceal. They look at me and say to themselves, 'Nothing worth while would lurk behind such a nose.'"

"You have the soul of an artist, Henry."

"And the actions of a fool. Unfortunately, our souls do not show. I'll admit that right now I am the most serious-minded man on earth. Laughter is as far from me as the Poles. If you could take away my nose, I could pose for a tableau of Napoleon on his way to Saint Helena, looking back at France "

"What we need," declared Judge, "is a lot of good whisky."

Henry blinked at Judge for several moments. Gradually he smiled.

"Judge," he said quietly, "I believe you have touched the hidden spring. We haven't had a drink for at least twenty-four hours. This crime wave almost washed away my thirst. But not in Tonto City. We shall make our purchase, and go out to the ranch."

MORE TROUBLE in Tonto City brought William Grey and Richard Herrick back to town. They were not concerned over the wrecked stage and the death of Dug Wheeler, because that had been decided an accident, but over the murder of Doctor Clemens.

They met Swayne at the Tonto Saloon, and the detective was obliged to admit that he had not been able to discover a single clue.

"What did that fat-headed sheriff have to offer?" asked Grey.

Swayne snorted disgustedly. "What could *he* offer?"

"That's true," agreed Herrick. "But you investigated, Swayne?"

"Oh, sure. I investigated a dead man and a hole in a window.

They swear that the doctor had no enemies; so what can I do? That fat-headed sheriff, as you call him, said he believed the killer had mistaken the doctor for him. They're about the same size, yuh see. And he admits that this is the first time he had even known of the doctor sitting at his desk."

"Well," said Grey grimly, "that's a possibility. I'll buy a drink."

Danny Regan and Slim Pickins came in for a drink, and Grey nodded to them. "Where's our estimable sheriff today, Regan?" he asked.

"He just came in from the ranch with us," replied Danny.

"Hidin' out?" grinned Swayne. Danny looked keenly at him.

"Hidin' out from what?" he asked curiously.

"Well, he said he believed that shot was meant for him, instead of the doctor," replied Swayne.

"I see," nodded Danny soberly. "Mebbe he's right; but I don't think he's hidin' out, as you call it."

"Might as well, for all the good he is," growled Herrick.

"Has yore detective found out anythin' yet?" queried Danny.

"Yuh don't expect him to find it all out in a day, do yuh?"

"You expected Henry to solve crime problems that happened long before he went into office. You wasn't willin' to give *him* time."

"The whole valley can't be wrong," said Grey.

"The whole valley! It's you and Herrick. You don't like Henry, and you're doin' yore damnedest to stir up sentiment against him. If you want my honest opinion, I think you and Herrick are a pair of meddlin' polecats."

"You've got a lot of gall to make cracks like that," said Herrick.

"I've got gall—and I've got guts," declared Danny. "Now, if yuh don't like my talk—try to stop me."

"Nobody's tryin' to stop yuh," said Grey. "A man's entitled to his own opinion—until he gets too personal."

"I don't know how much further I can go," said Danny,

"unless I punch yuh in the nose. Henry Conroy is my friend. He's as square as a die, and a whiter man never lived."

"Are you fightin' his battles?" asked Grey.

"He don't need me to fight his battles, Grey. But if I happen to be around durin' one of his fights, I might mix in a little."

"We should have elected you sheriff," said Herrick. "At least, we would have had action."

Danny and Slim finished their drink and went out.

"Tough hombre, eh?" mused Swayne. "Talks a lot."

"Just a word to the wise," said Grey, picking up his glass. "That tough hombre is just that, Swayne. He'd shoot at the drop of a hat, and drop it himself. That kid's got chilled steel nerves. And don't choose him for a fist fight—unless you're plenty good with yore hands. He's *hombre mucho malo*, if yuh know what that means."

Swayne smiled, as he drank.

"I didn't come here to fight," he said.

Danny and Slim went over to the office, where Henry sat, tilted back in his chair, his spurred heels hooked over his desk, an expression of satisfaction on his face.

"How did yuh make it?" asked Danny curiously, looking at Henry's feet.

"I've solved it!" exclaimed Henry. "I put them up, one at a time!"

"Yeah, I reckon that's the way to do it. Bill Grey and Dick Herrick are back again."

"The two buzzards!" snorted Henry. "They always show up after the kill has been made. They'll be over to see me, I suppose."

"Why don't you resign?" asked Danny. "Come back to the ranch and be a cowman once more. Let somebody else worry about crime. They'll eventually force yuh to quit."

"I'll think it over, Danny," replied Henry soberly. "I'd hate to admit defeat—since I can hook my spurs over the desk. At least, I have worked out one solution; and you'd be surprised how much better I can think. By the way, Danny, I wonder if you can fix that shotgun, so it will stay cocked."

DANNY took the gun from the rack, removed the side-plates, and examined the works. A small file and some careful work fixed it temporarily.

"It's all right for a while," said Danny, "but I wouldn't depend on it too long. Better turn it over to a gunsmith."

"Thank you, Danny. I believe that will do nicely."

"Just what are you goin' to do with that shotgun, Henry?"

"Shoot it—I hope."

Danny looked at Henry curiously, wondering if the sheriff of Wild Horse Valley had a theory of some kind. Henry took an old canvas case off a rifle and fitted it over the shotgun. Then he put the gun back on the rack.

"Listen to me," said Danny earnestly. "If there's any shootin' to be done, let me and Slim in on it. We'll back yore play; and you know it."

"I appreciate that offer, Danny. I realize the sincerity of the thing. But I hope there won't be any shooting, my boy. However, if there is, I shall feel much safer behind the butt of a shotgun than the grip of a six-shooter. I have no delusions regarding my ability with a Colt. This 'shut-eye and jerk quick' method of mine is all wrong. But with a scatter-gun, I still have possibilities."

Dug Wheeler's body was shipped back to Red Bluff on the night stage, where it was to be buried. Henry and Judge were at the stage, when the box was roped to the top. William Grey, Richard Herrick and John Swayne were also there.

Grey walked back to the office with Henry. Judging from his remarks, he was not so sure that Swayne was going to be able to clear up the situation.

"In a case like this," said Henry, "it is my opinion that a detective loses ninety per cent of his value by being known."

"Mebbe you're right, Conroy. But Swayne has a big reputation."

"I haven't noted anything particularly clever about the man. He is a good two-fisted drinker, and he seems to play a fair game of poker. That about covers his case, Mr. Grey. My honest opinion, and it is not professional jealousy, is that Mr. Swayne could not follow the track of a wagon-load of loose hay across a snow-covered field."

Dug Wheeler

Grey flushed quickly. "You dislike the man, and that's—"

"Pardon me," interrupted Henry. "I have neither like nor dislike for the man. If he can run down the criminals in Wild Horse Valley, I shall be the first to take off my hat to him."

"Well, we'll just have to wait and see what he can do."

"Give him a fair chance," said Henry. "It's a big job, Mr. Grey."

"We realize that more every day. Conroy, were you sincere in the belief that someone mistook Doctor Clemens for you?"

"I am. In fact, I've been covered with goose-pimples ever since."

"But why would anyone want to kill you?"

"I'm not quite ready to answer that question, Mr. Grey. I only hope that the driver of that last stage don't run off the grade. I'm depending on him to bring me an answer to a telegram tomorrow. When I read that reply, I might suggest a reason for an attempt on my life."

"I'll be interested to hear the reason," said Grey soberly.

Judge and Oscar came in from supper, and Grey talked with them for a few minutes, after which he went up the street.

"Judge," said Henry seriously, "I shall be away for the night, and I'm taking Oscar with me. No, don't ask questions. Go out to the ranch, lock up the office, and if anyone asks for me, I've gone out to the ranch to spend the night."

"Out for the night—with Oscar? Why and where, Henry? And taking a shotgun with you? Why, I don't understand!"

"As I said before, don't ask questions, Judge. Are you willing to go with me, Oscar?"

"Yah, sure," nodded Oscar, looking askance at the shotgun.

"You take that damn t'ing?"

"Danny fixed it for me," smiled Henry, as he took some cartridges from a desk drawer. "We'll be back tomorrow, Judge. Follow me, Oscar."

"Of all the crazy things!" exploded Judge. "Well—all right."

Oscar followed Henry out to their little stable, where they threw the saddles on two of the horses. Oscar dug a bottle of prune whisky out of a manger, and took a big drink. As an afterthought, he handed the bottle to Henry, who examined it by lantern-light.

"I don't see how in the devil you drink this stuff," he said.

"Yust goolp and swaller," explained Oscar.

CHAPTER V

UNMASKED

THE SOUTHBOUND STAGE from Red Bluff reached the grades above Rocky Horse Cañon about two-thirty in the afternoon. The big driver sat stiffly, one booted foot on the brake, as he eased the four horses around the narrow grades.

Apparently there was a full load, because several bed-rolls had been stacked on the top, making a sizeable pile behind the driver. Carefully the driver swung his leaders around the hairpin curves, braking at the right moment, speaking softly to the team.

They passed the place where the stage had gone over the edge, traveled along a straightaway for a hundred yards, swung to the right, where the road sloped down to another hairpin turn to the left.

The leaders swung far out to the right, almost to the very edge, where they shifted to the left again, and as the front of the stage twisted around the corner, two masked men stepped into the road, forcing the lead horses to shy in against the inside of the grade. Both men covered the driver with their guns.

"Reach for the sky!" ordered one of the men. The driver caught the lines between his knees, and started to lift his hands, when from behind that pile of bed-rolls came the smashing report of a shotgun.

The masked man, standing nearest the heads of the lead horses, was literally blasted off his feet. He flung out both hands and fell into the horses, which were already rearing with fright, and the next moment the four-horse team was lunging along the grade, with the driver trying frantically to recover the lines.

The other masked man was nearly knocked off the grade, in trying to dodge the hub of the right front wheel. Things had happened so quickly that he had no chance to do more than save his own life. By the time he picked himself up, the stage was around the next curve, and going fast.

From among the bouncing bed-rolls appeared the head and shoulders of Henry Harrison Conroy. He glanced around, grabbed hold of a rope with both hands and yelled at the driver: "Stop them, Oscar!"

But Oscar Johnson was unable to do this little thing. The brake-rod had parted at a connection, and Oscar's sole hope was to keep the equipage out of Rock Horse Cañon.

"Oscar!" yelled Henry. "Oscar, can't you hear me?"

"Ay can't hear damn t'ing!" howled Oscar. "Das damn shotgun go off in my ear."

"Stop 'em, Oscar!" howled Henry, hanging on for dear life. "Stop 'em, I tell you!"

"T'al de hurses!" yelped Oscar. "Ay am yust de driver."

A sudden lurch almost threw Henry off the top; so he let Oscar do the driving, while he hooked one elbow under a rope, and offered up a prayer that they could keep out of the cañon.

A long straight up-hill stretch gave Oscar his needed chance, and he managed to pull the team down to a reasonable pace.

"Ay can't stop on hill!" he yelled at Henry. "De damn brake is bruk."

"It don't matter—now," sighed Henry. "Keep going, you re-incarnation of Ben Hur."

"Ay can't hear a t'ing," declared Oscar, shaking his head. "Das shotgun go off in my ear. But by yimminy, you get one faller!"

"Both barrels went off," said Henry. "I—I'm glad we didn't stay there. Hold them, while I get into the seat."

Puffing and blowing, his face very red, Henry managed to slide over the back of the seat and sit upright again. He reached back and secured the shotgun, which he opened and removed the two empty cartridges.

"That shotgun is not reliable," he told Oscar.

"Yah, sure," nodded Oscar. "Ay bet you one dollar that one masquerade faller won't dance no more. Ay am yust beginning to hear."

"Were you frightened?" asked Henry.

"Yah, sure. Ay am always scare of shotgun."

"Oh!" exclaimed Henry softly.

THE USUAL crowd waited for the stage at Tonto City, and they voiced their surprise at seeing Oscar Johnson driving, while Henry sat beside him, a shotgun across his lap.

"Must be a load of money," said a bystander, as Oscar drew up at the bank to deliver the treasure box, before continuing down to the stage office, where the crowd waited.

But Henry offered no explanation. He got off the seat, looked at the crowd, and went swaggering down to his office, the shotgun over his shoulder. The stage clerk questioned Oscar, but the Terrible Swede swore he couldn't hear a word he said.

Judge was in the office, writing a letter, when Henry came in and placed the shotgun on the gun-rack. Judge sat up very straight and looked at Henry, who closed the door and sank into a chair.

"Well?" queried Judge severely.

"Well enough," admitted Henry, "except that when I pulled one trigger, both barrels went off, and I wasted that extra charge on the same man."

"My God, Henry, do you mean—you killed a man?"

"As Slim would say, I hope to tell yuh, I did."

"Wh-why—who?"

"Ah! Now you have me, Judge; I don't know. Quit opening and shutting your mouth, like a fish out of water, while I explain."

Without going into detail, Henry told Judge what happened on the Rocky Horse grades, while Judge sat there, an expression of amazement on his long face. At the conclusion, he said:

"Henry, if I may ask, what in hell were you and Oscar doing on that stage—and why? It doesn't make sense. Am I to infer that you anticipated a hold-up today?"

"I had a devil of a job, persuading the stage company at Red Bluff that I am not crazy, Judge. They balked on Oscar, too. Still, I proved no mean orator, as you may see "

"Are you sure you killed the man?"

"At twenty paces, with both loads. And that means two and one-half ounces of coyote-shot. Yes, I am fairly sure."

"But, damn it, Henry, we'll never know who he was!"

"Of course, that is a possibility."

A horse and buggy went past, and they looked out to see John Swayne, driving to the livery-stable. Judge smiled and shook his head.

"The eminent detective will brand me as a liar," he said. "An hour ago he asked me where you were, and I said you went out to the J Bar C. Apparently he hired a horse and buggy, in order to prove me a disciple of Ananias."

Henry smiled slowly. "I wonder if Mr. Grey and Mr. Herrick are still in town."

"They went back to Silver City this morning. It is too bad you couldn't have brought in a dead bandit for their edification."

"It would have been satisfying, nodded Henry. "But, at least, we have the satisfaction of knowing that the criminal population is shrinking. One at a time, Judge."

Henry laughed softly and pointed a finger at Judge.

"That's it, Judge—one at a time. Why, that's how I discovered the system of putting my feet on the desk."

"One at a time is satisfactory," nodded Judge. "But can you keep it up, Henry?"

"At times, my friend, you show the impatience of a commissioner. I just happened to think—I'm hungry. Hast thou nourished this afternoon?"

"Nor drank," replied Judge. "I believe it is fitting that we offer a libation to the—to the aim of a Conroy."

"We really should wait for Oscar. Judge, the man is priceless. With an empty gun in my hands, and a loaded gun in the hand of a masked bandit, Oscar the Peerless Swede, allowed the team to run away. You will say it was an accident on his part. Granted. But it was done."

"He might have killed you both, Henry."

"He might. But, except for his carelessness, I'm sure that bandit would have shot us both off the stage. It was might against a dead certainty—and might won. Yes, we shall wait for Oscar; he is worth waiting for."

Oscar arrived in a few minutes, but declined to join them in a drink.

"Ay have some prune yuice left in stable," he told them. "Ay like it better.

"Das common whisky is oll right for veaklings. It taste oll right. But das prune yuice tak' right hold."

"No wonder they wore horns and sailed the north seas," said Judge, as they crossed the street to the Tonto Saloon.

OSCAR drank up all his prune juice. Then he remembered a little saloon at the end of the street where they sold a particularly vile whisky, which suited Oscar just right. He found the bartender, seated in a chair, attempting to play an accordion.

"Can you play one of these things?" he asked Oscar.

"Ay can play anyt'ing," declared Oscar. "But first, we have drink."

"If yuh can play it, I'll sell it cheap."

"Yah, sure. How mooch?"

"Five dollars, Oscar."

"Val, of course, five dollar is a lot of money. But my fiddle is bruk. Ay must have moosic."

John Swayne and Tom Rickey sat at the lobby window of the hotel, and saw Henry and Judge go over to the Tonto Saloon.

"I can't quite figure out why Conroy and Johnson were on the stage today," said Rickey. "Johnson driving, while Conroy sat beside him, holding a big shotgun."

Swayne's eyes were grimly speculative.

"Unless there was a big money shipment," added Rickey.

"Might have been," murmured Swayne. He was wondering why Judge lied about Henry being at the ranch.

"The Tonto City Bank does quite a big business," offered Rickey. "It was sure a lucky thing them two fellers failed to get the safe open."

"A newfangled safe, eh?"

"Oh, not so awful new; but the best in the county, I suppose. You heard how they got scared away, didn't you?"

Swayne nodded.

"You ain't makin' much headway on the case, are yuh?" asked the inquisitive hotel keeper.

"No," replied Swayne. "And I don't believe anyone else could."

It was nearly dark when Richard Herrick came in from the south. John Swayne was sitting in front of the hotel, and Herrick stopped to talk with him. Their conversation lasted about five minutes, and Herrick rode on.

Henry and Judge saw him come and go, and then sauntered over from the saloon. Swayne had gone upstairs, but Tom Rickey was in the doorway. He grinned at Henry and drew him aside.

"Dick Herrick just rode in from Silver City," he said. "He's on his way to Scorpion. I heard what he told that detective, as he was leavin'."

"What was it?" asked Henry.

"Herrick told him he'd better be showin' results, or they'd tie a can on him and send him back home."

"That's interestin'," agreed Henry.

"I guess they had it hot and heavy," said Rickey.

"A Parthian shot," smiled Henry.

He and Judge went back to the office, where Henry shaved carefully in a cracked mirror. Rarely did he miss his daily shave. He was nearly finished, when the door opened and John Swayne came in, carrying a suitcase.

"I just dropped in to tell yuh good-by and good-luck," said the big detective.

"You're not leaving us?" exclaimed Henry.

"I am."

"Rather sudden, isn't it?" queried Judge.

"It may seem that way," replied Swayne. "I came here in good faith to work on this case. I was told that I could handle things in my own way, and without interference. Well, there's no use cryin' about it—I'm through."

"I believe I know what you mean," said Henry. "The commission would have built Rome in a day."

"That's right, Conroy. Well, I'm through."

"Going north on the stage?"

"I am not. One trip on that stage was enough. No, I have hired a horse and buggy from the livery-stable—and the county will pay for it. Then I'll take a train from Red Bluff. Well, good-luck, Sheriff."

"Thank you kindly, Mr. Swayne," replied Henry. "And when you get back to San Francisco, give my best regards to Roscoe Britton and Abe Cullison."

"I'll be glad to do that," nodded Swayne. "If you ever come to San Francisco, look me up."

Swayne went down to the livery-stable, and a few minutes later they saw him driving out of Tonto City.

"And thus," said Judge, "endeth the chapter, in which the famous detective appeared in the story. I suppose he resented having Richard Herrick tell him how to detect."

"Any good detective would," nodded Henry. "I even resent having them tell *me*."

"I know you do, Henry. But Mr. Swayne has more brains than you have."

"My dear Judge! On what do you base that assertion?"

"He has resigned, Henry."

"I see. But, on the other hand, Mr. Swayne might be what is known as thin-skinned. Forty years on the stage had hardened my epidermis, until the barbs of criticism slide off me, like water off the back of a well-oiled duck."

"I suppose," sighed Judge. "But isn't there times, Henry, when you would like to forget Wild Horse Valley, don the grease-paint and face the world across the footlights again?"

Henry's eyes were a little wistful, as he nodded thought-fully.

"I sometimes dream of it, Judge, it was the only life I knew, until I came down here. But I was through—my contract can-celed—when the letter came, telling me of my inheritance. But I can still dream."

"I think I understand," said Judge. "The beams of the spot-light, the applause of thousands."

"Yes," whispered Henry. "Only last night, in my dreams, I dodged an egg—and hit my head on a bed-post."

"You *would* jest, Henry. I wonder where the Terrible Swede went."

"I'm afraid Oscar is *hors de combat* by this time. There was nearly a full bottle of prune juice in the stable."

"Very likely he is still in the stable."

"I said bottle—not barrel, Judge. Oscar's capacity is far beyond the contents of a mere bottle."

"I suppose that is true. No doubt he has even forgotten to feed the horses. I sha'll see to that."

But Oscar had fed the horses, and when Judge came back the office was in darkness, and Henry had gone. Judge sauntered up to Harper's shop, where he expected to find Henry, but he had not been there. A visit to the general store, hotel lobby, and post office failed to locate the sheriff.

Taking it for granted that Henry was searching for Oscar, Judge went to the Tonto Saloon. Several of the gambling layouts were busy, and Judge noticed that quite a number of men were there from the upper end of the valley. Slim Pickins was among them, and when he went outside, Judge followed him.

"Where's Henry?" asked Slim.

"He must be around town somewhere," replied Judge.

"We better find him," said Slim. "There's a bunch in from Scorpion, and more to come."

"With the tar-and-feather complex?" queried Judge anxiously.

"Yeah. I listened to enough talk to know they're here for no good."

"Where is Danny?"

"He'll be here in a little while. But we've got to git Henry out of town, Judge. If that dang fool would only resign."

"He won't, Slim. Henry is not lacking in nerve."

"Ignorance!" snapped Slim.

"Which amounts to the same thing—in most instances. I wonder where Oscar is tonight?"

"He's down at the White Hawk Saloon, stewed to the gills. Him and the bartender are both pickled. When I was down there, they was settin' at a table, playin' some cock-eyed game, and sayin', 'Simon says, thumbs up! Thumbs down! Wiggle-waggle.' And then Oscar slaps the bartender on the top of the head, and almost knocked him out."

"I'm afraid that this is the end of the régime of Conroy and company," sighed Judge.

"I dunno what a ree-geeme is," replied Slim, "but I seen a feller once what had been covered with tar and feathers. I think that's Danny ridin' in now. Yeah, it is; he's stoppin' at Harper's place."

Danny had gone inside when they arrived; so they followed him in, hoping to find Henry there, too. Danny was talking with Leila and her mother.

THEY WERE all greatly concerned, when Slim told about the men from Scorpion. Judge said he had only been away a few minutes, when Henry had disappeared.

"I'm afraid they've already got him," said Danny. "They might have sneaked in and grabbed him, and took him away, holdin' him until they all got to town. Let's go down to the office and see if there is any sign of a battle."

But the office was all in order. They went through the jail, and out to the stable, where the three horses munched their hay. Then they separated and looked into every lighted building on the street, making discreet inquiries. But Henry Harrison Conroy seemed to have disappeared completely.

"Well, what's to be done?" queried Slim, when they all met at the office, following the search.

"We can't do a thing—now," replied Danny grimly. "They've

got him in a safe place. We'll just wait, and watch. When that Scorpion gang starts driftin', we'll drift along. And if they ever try to tar and feather Henry, there'll be plenty food for coyotes in the mornin'."

"We shall be badly outnumbered," sighed Judge.

"It'll be fun—while it lasts," said Slim.

Leila and her mother became so worried that they walked down to the office. The town was quiet, but more men were drifting in, a few at a time. Danny went over to the Tonto Saloon and circulated about the place, trying to pick up some information. Neither Grey nor Herrick were there, but Danny heard a man tell another that the two commissioners were due there at any time.

"Herrick won't be here," declared Judge, when Danny came back with his report. "Herrick is on his way to Red Bluff."

"Wait a minute," said Danny. "You say he's on his way?"

"He went through here at dusk. I know he did, because of the fact that he stopped to argue with Swayne. That was the principal reason Swayne resigned, I believe."

"All right, Judge. If that is true, Herrick must have met the men from Scorpion, somewhere between here and Red Bluff."

"Yes, that is true enough. Well, possibly he came back and—"

"I believe I've got it!" exclaimed Danny. "The reason Herrick is not in evidence is because he's helpin' hold Henry some place. He came back and helped them capture Henry. Bill Grey would probably come from Silver City."

"But isn't there something that can be done?" asked Mrs. Harper.

"Not a thing," replied Danny grimly, "until *they* start out to really do somethin'."

"Why don't you all come up to our place?" suggested Leila. "You can watch the Tonto from there."

"Might be a good idea," agreed Danny. "This office don't need any protection. Have you got a gun, Judge?"

"No, I haven't, Danny. Anyway, I'm not—"

"Get that shotgun. You can at least make a loud noise."

"Yes, I suppose I—"

Judge looked at the gun-rack closely, and glanced around the room.

"That shotgun," he said, "is not here."

"A smart flock of pelicans," said Danny. "They took the shotgun, too. Well, it can't be helped. Take that thirty-thirty along, Judge."

"That dang gun will shoot a mile," said Slim.

"Yes, I believe that is true," agreed Judge, handling the rifle gingerly. "I—I only hope I shall have to shoot it that far."

It was about ten o'clock, before the crowd in the Tonto showed any signs of restlessness. They began to saunter around. Two men went down to the sheriff's office, which was in darkness, and found the door locked. Two more went over to the hotel, while others began moving from place to place.

"I don't savvy things," declared Danny, "unless they're tryin' to locate us, in case we might try to interrupt proceeding."

"What's botherin' me is the fact that the main gang might sneak out the rear of the Tonto and pull off their job, while we watch these few drifters," said Slim.

"We'll wait a few minutes more," replied Danny.

About fifty feet behind the rear of the Tonto City Bank, two men crouched in the darkness beside a pile of old boxes. One of them glided like a shadow to the rear door of the bank, where he hunched down. After possibly five minutes he gave a low, hissing whistle, and the other man left his concealment to join him. A moment later they were both inside the bank, with the door closed.

Except for an occasional sound on the street, the town was very quiet. Then, far down at the rear of a building, came a splintering crash as though someone had deliberately wrecked a wooden box. There was a period of complete silence. Then a shadowy figure, weaving an erratic course, came along behind the buildings.

It was a huge figure of a man, traveling with all the steadiness of a rudderless boat in a typhoon. He tacked across the alley between the store and the bank, going rather swiftly, when his cargo seemed, to shift, causing him to head directly for the unrailed steps at the rear bank door.

Apparently in trying to catch his balance, he went swiftly, tripped on the steps and went down with a crash against the door. Following his crash came the screaming wail of an accordion, and the bank door banged open.

From inside the bank came a fusillade of revolver shots, directed through the doorway, followed by a man, who sprang high, clearing the obstruction. But the man behind him was not so fortunate. He encountered the rising form of the man who had inadvertently sounded the alarm, and turned a complete somersault into the yard. The first man went to his knees, sprang to his feet and started to run, when, from behind the pile of boxes, a shotgun flamed in the darkness, and the smashing report followed.

Badly jarred by the double load of that shotgun, his eyes blinded by the flash, Henry Harrison Conroy threw the boxes aside and went staggering out, where two figures were threshing and flailing about in the dirt.

"Yump on my skveese oorgan, vill you?" yelped Oscar. "Ay can't have damn t'ing 'round h'ar, eh? If you bruk my oorgan, Ay break your neck."

Men were pouring through the alley, seeking the sounds of conflict. Someone brought a lantern, holding it high. Danny, Judge and Slim were in the front ranks, looking down at Oscar, who had a strangle hold on Richard Herrick, whose nose was bloody, one eye almost closed.

"That is sufficient, Oscar," said Henry calmly.

"My leg is broken," whined Herrick. "I never—"

"Well, I'll be damned if this ain't the detective!" snorted the man with the lantern, looking at the man Henry had shot.

QUESTIONS were coming thick and fast; Henry merely stood there, looking down at Herrick.

"So it was Bill Grey I killed on Rocky Horse grade, eh?" said Henry. "I tricked you, Herrick. You and Grey and Archer were all in on those other robberies, and each gave a different description of the robbers. Frijole Bill accidentally shot Archer. He called to you, didn't he, Herrick? And you saw he was badly hurt; so you shot him through the heart, so he wouldn't talk. I dug the bullet out of the ground."

"No!" panted Herrick. "It was Bill Grey, I tell yuh. He shot Archer. I—damn yuh, I need a doctor. I never done anything. Yuh can't touch me."

"What were you and Swayne doing in the bank?" asked Henry. "You see, I watched you pick the lock on the back door."

"Swayne picked the lock."

"Gentlemen," said Henry triumphantly, "I firmly believe we have overcome the crime wave of Wild Horse Valley."

"I hope to tell yuh!" snorted Slim. "But what in the devil ever gave yuh the hunch to watch the bank, Henry?"

"Their lack of time to do anything else, Slim. Grey was dead. I killed him, when he and Herrick attempted to hold up the stage and get the important telegram, which was supposed to be on that stage. My belief is that Mr. Swayne was a professional safe-breaker, masquerading as a detective, brought here as a sop to the people of the valley, and to crack the Tonto City Bank safe. Mr. Swayne resigned this evening, and hired a livery rig to drive to Red Bluff. Ahead of him was Mr. Herrick, presumably going to Red Bluff, too.

"Our friend Mr. Herrick killed Doctor Clemens, thinking—"

"No, no!" panted Herrick. "Not me. Swayne shot him."

"I just wanted to be sure," said Henry dryly. "And another thing, Dug Wheeler never got drunk and drove off that grade. He was killed and his stage destroyed, in order to secure a telegram I sent to Red Bluff.

"Gentlemen, no doubt you would like to lynch Mr. Herrick.

It is your inclination to use the rope or a barrel of tar, I understand. But I am taking Mr. Herrick to jail, where he will get
medical attention, and later be tried for his many and varied
sins. Danny, will you and Slim attend the patient?"

Putting the shotgun over his shoulder, and with measured
steps, Henry walked through the crowd, followed by Judge,
who was a few paces to the rear. Leila and her mother were out
in front of their shop. Henry stopped and grounded his shotgun.
Oscar Johnson, with several men, was crossing the street.

"Ay t'al you, he busted the hinches on my skveese oorgan!"
complained Oscar. "Das h'ar town makes me sick. Every time
Ay try play moosic for Yosephine, some damn bank robber ruin
de tune."

One of them made an inaudible remark, and Oscar replied:
"Yah, sure; that's my yob."

"What's that?" asked one of the men.

"Val, Ay scare 'em and Hanry shoots 'em."

"You see, my dear," said Henry to Mrs. Harper, "when all is
said and done, being a sheriff, with such assistance, is a simple
matter."

"Do not make a hero of yourself, Henry," said Judge dryly.
"As a matter of fact, weren't you hiding behind those boxes,
fearful of tar and feathers?"

"Why, Judge!" exclaimed Mrs. Harper. "That is terrible! How
can you imagine that of Henry?"

"It even amazes *me*," admitted Henry. "I did not think that
Judge had such powers of deduction. However, I have covered
ourselves with glory—thanks to the Glorious Swede."

From over in front of the Tonto Saloon came Oscar's voice:
"Val, of coorse Ay vars! You don't t'ink Ay vars dere from accident, do you? You yust let me and Hanry run dis yob, and ve
do oll right. Yah, sure t'ing."

"I believe that answers your question, Judge," said Henry
dryly.

THE DIPLOMACY OF HENRY

*Whenever Sheriff Henry follows his nose, he is
usually led into more trouble than he can handle—
unless Judge and Oscar manage to help him.*

CHAPTER I

TROUBLE IN THE VALLEY

HENRY HARRISON CONROY, sheriff of Wild Horse Valley, opened one eye and looked indifferently at the telegram, which Judge Van Treece handed him. Reluctantly he reached out a pudgy hand and took the telegram, while Judge sighed, sat down in a rickety chair and mopped his brow with a huge handkerchief.

"If hell is any hotter than Arizona," said Judge seriously, "there is a good and sufficient reason for repentance of sin."

"Or even as hot," added Henry. "In such anticipation, I have sat here and examined my conscience, Judge."

"And, no doubt, discovered many reasons for reformation?"

"On the contrary, sir, I find that I am nearly pure. My conscience is as white as the driven snow."

"It must be the heat," sighed Judge.

Henry looked malevolently at Judge and proceeded to open the telegram. Henry was five feet six inches in height—and fat. He was fifty-five years of age; and fifty-four years and a few months had been spent in and around theaters. Born in a dressing room, of theatrical parents, an actor almost before he could walk, he had only left the profession to accept the J Bar C cattle ranch, left to him by a deceased uncle.

Henry's face was like a full moon, with a huge nose, small squinty eyes, and an almost bald head. The nose was very red; a featured organ of vaudeville for years. Henry was merely the background of that nose.

Henry and Oscar
hurried off, with
Judge at their heels.

Coming into a country and a life of which he knew nothing, and taking charge of a cattle ranch of which he knew less, the voters of the county had played a practical joke, in electing him sheriff; a practical joke upon themselves, it seemed.

And Henry Harrison Conroy dressed the part. Just now he wore a pink shirt, so tight that it threatened to burst asunder at any moment. His overalls, tight of leg, and tighter of waist, were held around his middle with a six-inch safety-pin. His rather small feet were encased in a very tight pair of fancy-top, high-heel cowboy boots, surmounted with a pair of fancy, silver-mounted spurs. On the desk was a heavy belt, studded with cartridges, a holster, and a big, pearl-handled Colt .45.

Henry was tilted in an old and rather rickety swivel chair,

"Show how fast yuh can run!"

his knees drawn up almost to his chin, his heels hooked under the top edge of his desk. Judge Van Treece eyed him closely, as he started to read the telegram.

Judge was as much a character as Henry. He was six feet four inches in height, very thin and loose-jointed. Sixty years of age, with a long, lean face, pouchy eyes and a long, thin nose, he could drink whisky by the quart and quote Blackstone by the page. Whisky had long since driven him from practising law. In Judge, Henry had found a kindred soul, and after his election, he had made Judge his deputy, much to the amazement of the people.

With great dignity, Judge wore high-heel boots, a Stetson sombrero, a size or two too large, and abandoned suspenders in favor of a silver-studded belt. Prior to becoming a peace officer, Judge wore an ancient cutaway coat, baggy pants and a once-green derby hat.

As Henry read that telegram his face grew red. In fact, as he finished, he was apoplectic. He turned baleful eyes upon Judge, as though Judge were to blame.

"By golly, sir!" he roared. "I'll have you know, sir!"

Shoving back with his feet, as though attempting to give himself room, the old swivel snapped loose, and Henry Harrison Conroy went over backwards, landing with a crash against the wall. The back of his head struck rather solidly against the baseboard, and he sat up, goggling at Judge, who looked upon him unperturbed.

"I've expected that for weeks," stated Judge. "Screws loose."

"Who's got screws loose?" asked Henry.

"I meant the chair, sir; but in this case—well, no matter."

Slowly the sheriff got to his feet, rubbing his head. He put a hand on the desk, and looked blankly around.

"Now—uh—just where was I?" he asked.

"Your last line was, 'I'll have you know, sir,'" replied Judge.

"Oh, yes. I must have fallen. Oh, yes, I remember."

HENRY picked up the offending telegram, rubbed the back of his head and sighed deeply.

"I am afraid, sir," he said to Judge, "that I let my angry passions rise. If, in that atrophied old brain of yours, you ever feel the urge to rend something limb from limb—stop and consider. Why," Henry became very serious, "you might cause yourself untold injury. At your age, Judge, you might even burst a blood vessel. Be calm under all conditions."

"Just who in hell fell over backwards—you or me?" queried Judge. "I was under the impression that it was you, sir. I may be wrong; but I am very sure that you are not rubbing my head."

"Do not be facetious, Judge: I know my own head. It—it was this damnable telegram, signed by a man who was my agent for years. A very, very estimable blood-sucker, if I may malign all blood-suckers. A likeable Shylock, who took twenty-five per cent, and sent all telegrams collect. Listen to this:

" 'If you have new, snappy monologue, can book you for five a day in Northwest at seventy-five and short jumps in picture houses Stop Try out new act in Seattle soon as possible Stop Must have new and original stuff as red noses not funny since nineteen hundred Stop Kindest personal regards.' "

Henry glared at Judge, who nodded solemnly.

"I hardly understand all that gibberish," said Judge. "The reference to red noses is perfectly understandable, of course. I doubt if you are in any physical shape to even do short jumps, Henry. That would be funny, in itself, of course. Stop glaring at me, sir."

"Glaring! Five shows a day—at seventy-five measly dollars a week—in picture houses! By gad, he doesn't know who I am."

"However," reminded Judge mildly, "he sent you his kindest personal regards, Henry. Perhaps he only remembers you as you were. And Seattle is a very nice city, as I remember it."

"Quite," agreed Henry. "And he sent it collect—as usual."

Judge started to remark, but from the corridor of the jail came the sound of very heavy footsteps.

"The Terrible Swede is back," sighed Judge.

The Terrible Swede was Oscar Johnson, erstwhile horse wrangler at the J Bar C, but now jailer for the sheriff's office. Oscar had the figure of a Hercules, faded blond hair, a button-like nose and small, innocent blue eyes. He flung the door open and surged into the office.

"Ha'l is busted loose, Ay skal ta'l you!" he blurted. "Oll dem ships—"

"Whoa!" interrupted Henry. "Keep on dry land, Oscar."

"Ay yust said dem ships—"

"Easy, Oscar!" snapped Judge. Oscar blinked angrily, as Judge turned to Henry.

"Ay ta'l you, dis is serious," insisted Oscar. "T'ousands of ships! Ships oil over ha'ar."

"Must be the navy and the merchant marine combined," said Henry.

"Yust a lot of damn fools," sighed Oscar.

"Wait a minute," said Henry seriously. "Oscar, can it be, by any chance, that you mean sheep?"

"Yah, su-u-ure! Ay say ships, yust as plain as anybody."

"Check it with the scenery!" snorted Henry. "Where are the sheep, Oscar?"

"Over on das odder side of Vild Hurse River. De Saxty Seven outfit are yumpin' high, Ay ta'l you. Yorge Bellew say to me:

" 'You better ta'l das damn fool shoriff he's goin' have to bury lots of ship-horders.' "

"**SWEET,** sweet music," sighed Judge. "Well, Wild Horse Valley has always been afraid of sheep. They've sworn that no sheep could ever have a mouthful of Wild Horse grass. Henry, I'm very much afraid that hell is going to bust loose."

Henry rubbed his red nose, as he looked quizzically at Judge.

"Well, well!" he exclaimed. "What is the legal procedure?"

"There is no legal procedure, Henry. Most of the land south of the river is state land—and the state recognizes the rights of the sheep men."

"I see. But have the cattlemen any legal rights, which entitles them to—er—make corpses of sheep-herders?"

"The law, I believe, would deem it murder, Henry."

"Justly so," nodded Henry. "And just what would be my duty in this matter, Judge?"

"Your duty, my dear Henry, would be to stand firmly between the warring factions."

"Between? You mean—between?"

"You represent the law, Henry."

Henry blinked and caressed his nose. Suddenly he dived back to his desk and began pawing papers wildly.

"Looking for something?" queried Judge.

"I'm looking for that damnable telegram—wherever it is.

Even five shows a day in picture houses—where the devil is that telegram, anyway?"

"You are forgetting your sworn duty, Henry."

"Sworn? I swore to uphold the law. But there is a precedent, sir; a precedent older than the mustiest law book on earth."

"What is that, sir?"

"Self-preservation. Ah, here it is!"

As Henry started to read the telegram, a group of horsemen stopped in front of the office and dismounted from their tired horses.

Five dusty cowboys, headed by George Bellew, owner of the Seventy-Six cattle outfit, came tromping into the office.

Bellew, a tall, swarthy cowboy, glared at Henry.

"Well, what are you goin' to do about it?" he demanded.

"I haven't made up my mind yet," replied Henry, "but I think I shall accept it."

"Accept what?" snarled Bellew.

"Yust wait a minute," begged Oscar coldly. "If you fallers are looking for trouble—"

"Suppose we are?" snarled Bellew belligerently.

"Ay vars yust goin' to ta'l you that you won't find it ha'r."

"All right. Conroy, I suppose you have heard that Bill Grimes has moved a few thousand of his damned woolies into the valley."

"Ay yust told him," replied Oscar.

"I'm talkin' to the sheriff."

"Oscar just told us," nodded Henry. "The law says—"

"Damn the law! Do you think we're goin' to pay any attention to the law, in a case like this, Conroy?" asked Bellew hoarsely. "We want to know where you stand."

"And you better stand right," added a grim-faced cowboy.

"He has sworn to uphold the law," interposed Judge solemnly.

"Let me tell yuh somethin'," said Bellew. "This here office is goin' to keep its nose out of this deal. All you've got to do is set here and keep still. What yuh don't know won't hurt yuh. C'mon, boys."

THEY TROOPED outside and rode away.

"Do you know, Judge," said Henry whimsically, "they even intimate that my nose is the dominating feature of this office. This here office is going to keep its nose out of this deal, they say."

"You will do your duty, as prescribed by law, Henry."

Henry squinted at Judge for several moments, his nose twitching.

"Judge," he said softly, "some day you are going to quote law and duty to me once too often. And when I get through with you, you and the surrounding scenery will make a picture of Custer's Last Stand look like a still-life picture of a bowl of violets. In order to defer this holocaust, I suggest that we go across the street and have a drink."

"Suggestion sustained," nodded Judge. "As I have always contended, no man is so mentally deranged that he does not, at times, make rational suggestions. By the way, Henry, isn't it about time for Frijole Bill to bring us in some of his prune whisky?"

"Ay have gallon in stable," stated Oscar. "Free-holey says it is not so good as usual, because das last boonch prunes have vorms."

Henry grimaced and turned toward the door.

"After all," said Judge, "we know nothing about the vices nor virtues of a distilled worm; so why worry about it? My advice is for all of us to concentrate on sheep."

"Short jumps, in picture houses," muttered Henry. "At least, they won't shoot you—not with anything worse than eggs. Hm—m-m!"

"About that reference regarding red noses," said Judge, as he adjusted his sombrero. "The man is wrong when he says that a red nose is not funny. When I look at you—"

"Concentrate on sheep," interrupted Henry, and stalked out.

Judge turned and looked at Oscar Johnson.

"What are your reactions to this sheep menace, Oscar?" he asked.

"Ay don't know what the ha'l you are talking about," admitted Oscar, "but Ay can ta'l you dis much: Ay t'ank Free-holey lied about dem vorms. Ay can't taste damn one in das prune yuice."

CHAPTER II

PRUNE JUICE RAVINGS

DANNY REGAN, THE young, red-headed foreman of the J Bar C, heard about the sheep, and lost no time in coming to Tonto City to confer with Henry Harrison Conroy. He found Henry and Judge in the sheriff's office, quite mellow, thank you.

"So you heard about the sheep, did yuh?" remarked Danny.

"They have been mentioned in my hearing, Danny," admitted Henry. "In fact, the entire valley is agog."

"Yo're damn right!" snapped Danny. "You know what it means, if them sheep ever get a foothold?"

Henry cleared his throat and leaned back in his chair.

"Until recently, my knowledge of sheep was confined to that delightful little poem about Mary's Little Lamb, Danny. Did it not say, 'Let 'em alone and they'll come home—'"

"Wrong as usual," interrupted Judge. "That was Little Bo Peep."

"I stand corrected, Judge. However, they were not listed as a menace."

"Henry, don't yuh understand that a few thousand sheep can

ruin the cattle range in this valley?" asked Danny. "Don't yuh realize that the J Bar C is in danger?"

"I am beginning to understand something of the situation."

"Well, what are you goin' to do?"

"According to my three dominating senses, I am confused, Danny. My legs tell me to run, my brain tells me to fight to the last ditch in defense of my cows—and my lawyer tells me that the law says I must stand between the two warring factions.

"I'm afraid that if it comes to a showdown—my legs will dominate the situation."

"I don't figure the law in on this deal," declared Danny. "We've got to stop them sheep. Shepherds don't like hot lead."

"Do any of us?" asked Henry wearily.

"You can't deliberately shoot a sheep-herder," said Judge.

"It's the only damn language they understand," declared Danny. "Grimes has planned for years to sheep out this valley. It's Bellew's fault that they ever got in here. That Seventy-Six outfit was supposed to watch that side of the river, because of Saw Tooth Pass; but I reckon they got careless."

"Yes," sighed Henry, "and Bellew is the most indignant man in Wild Horse Valley. You would almost believe that I personally directed that band of sheep into this valley."

"He was prob'ly too busy gamblin' to watch for sheep," said Danny. "They tell me he lost the price of a whole train-load of beef in Los Angeles last month, playin' roulette."

"Well, I wish I knew what to do," sighed Henry.

"You can't do a thing, until trouble starts," replied Danny. "But don't worry—it'll start. There's goin' to be a meetin' tonight at the Broken Wheel ranch. Slim Pickins brought me the word, I sent Slim down to keep an eye on the sheep; along with Jones and Barber, from the Seventy-Six outfit."

"We will not countenance war, Danny," warned Judge.

Danny spat disgustedly and got to his feet.

"We're not lettin' sheep in here, Judge," he declared.

"The idea suits me fine," agreed Judge. "As long as things are done in a lawful and orderly manner, you understand. As counsel for the J Bar C, I advise—"

"Horsefeathers!" snorted Henry. "Judge, there are times when I feel that I must massacre you. When you start advising—"

"Henry," said Judge soberly, "do you want to see a holocaust?"

"Well, I wouldn't go out of my way to see one," replied Henry soberly, "even if I knew it was an original, and not some imperfect imitation."

"Henry," declared Judge wearily, "there are times when I almost believe you are a fool."

"I love that word 'almost,' Judge. It leaves a lingering doubt. However, I have no illusions about myself. But hasn't it been said that no man is wise, until he realizes what a fool he is? Something like that, I believe. You would never realize such a thing about yourself, because it probably isn't legal."

The door to the jail corridor banged open, and Oscar lurched in.

"Ay bet ten dollar there ain't a vorm in de whole yug," he said.

"How do you know?" asked Henry.

"Ay yust strained all de prune yuice t'rough my old hat."

"I believe," said Henry soberly, "I would prefer the worms."

"Hal'o, Danny," grinned Oscar. "How you vars, eh?"

"Pretty good, Oscar; how are you?"

"Ay am yust as good as anybody, Ay skal ta'l you. You hear 'bout dem ships, Danny?"

"Yeah, I heard about 'em, Oscar. What are we goin' to do about 'em?"

"Val, Ay skal ta'l you," Oscar cuffed his hat over one eye and looked owlishly wise. "Ay skal take t'ree more drinks of prune yuice, and den Ay skal go dere and vipe up Grimes."

"**THERE** yuh are!" snorted Danny. "The boy's constructive. Lawful and orderly! Turn Oscar loose with a jug of that prune whisky, a six-gun and a war-whoop—and the sheep menace is over."

"Oscar was born two hundred years too late," said Judge.

"Or two hundred years too soon," added Henry.

"How's Josephine?" asked Danny. Josephine Swensen was the waitress and chambermaid at the Tonto Hotel.

"Just another blighted romance," said Henry.

"You don't mean to say that it's busted up already?"

"Ay skal ta'l you!" snorted Oscar. "Seven dollar for new wheel."

"Wheel?" queried Danny. "The wheel of a romance?"

"Boggy wheel," explained Oscar. "Ay hired hurse and boggy to take Yosephine to a dance at Scorpion. Ay get dronk and have t'ree fights. Ay ta'l you, Ay have fine time. Yosephine get mad at me on de vay home, and Ay ron front wheel off bridge."

"And was Josephine hurt?" asked Danny quickly.

"Yust hu-meel-i-ated," said Oscar. "Ay don't know what dat varse, but dat is what she ta'l me."

"She won't even speak to him now," said Henry sadly.

"Das is not true," denied Oscar. "She speak to me las' night."

"She did? Maybe she's forgiven you, Oscar."

"Yah, su-ure. Last night Ay valk into the hotel, and she say: " 'Vat in ha'l are you doing here, you big Svede?'"

"Ah!" exclaimed Henry softly, his eyes brimming. "Let 'em alone and they'll come home—"

"I'm goin' up and see Leila and her mother, before I have a breakdown," said Danny, and walked out, holding his waist-line.

Judge stretched his long legs, shut one eye and looked curiously at Henry, who sat there, rubbing his nose and staring at the ceiling.

"Thinking?" queried Judge.

"Just polishing," replied Henry. "It is a habit of long standing."

Judge grunted and caressed his chin.

"You might spare a few moments to consider the sheep, Henry."

"The sheep have nothing to do with it, Judge; but I shall give Mr. Grimes my earnest consideration. It has suddenly occurred to me that sheep do not fight back. Non-combatants, as we might say.

"It also occurs to me that we might go down there and have a heart-to-heart talk with Mr. Grimes. I would represent the law, with my stalwart bearing, while you, my dear Judge, you would represent the letter of the law."

"Ay skal go, too," nodded Oscar.

"Assuredly," nodded Henry. "You—let me see—why, yes, of course! Oscar would be the symbolic figure, representing that asininity of the whole proceedings."

"I see nothing asinine about it at all," declared Judge.

"In that case," said Henry seriously, "you and Oscar better switch make-ups. There is no use of both being dumb."

"Yah, sure," agreed Oscar heartily. "Ay vant odience."

"You want an audience?" queried Henry. "An audience to see you do—what?"

"To see how far Ay can kick a ship-horder," replied Oscar blandly.

"Listen to me, you ingrown Viking," said Judge severely. "We are not going down there to kick any sheep-herders."

"That's right," agreed Henry. "You see, Oscar, we are going down there with the dove of peace and an olive branch."

OSCAR was not a little puzzled. He fought his hat for several moments, his little blue eyes narrowed in thought.

"Yust what in ha'l is a ship-horder goin' do with olive branch?" he wanted to know.

"He'll probably feed it to the sheep—after we're dead," said Henry.

"Yah, sure," nodded Oscar. "And eat de dove, too."

"If that is ignorance, I'll eat my hat," sighed Henry.

"You have the outlook of a confirmed pessimist, Henry," said Judge. "You forget that we go down there, armed with the majesty of the law."

"Which does not make us invulnerable, sir," declared Henry. "The majesty of the law!"

"Of course, no one is forcing us to go down there," reminded Judge. "We could sit here in perfect safety, our heads bowed with shame, while the cowboys and sheep-herders slaughter each other."

"You almost spellbind me, Judge," said Henry solemnly. "I can almost hear the tramp of feet, the distant notes of a bugle, the creak of gun caissons, the shrill neighing of frightened sheep—"

"Sheep do not neigh, sir!"

"I did not say they neighed," protested Henry. "I said I could almost hear them.

"Almost, but not quite, I suppose—if they do not neigh. Damn it, Judge, I've a mind to turn Oscar loose on the enemy."

"Yah, sure," agreed Oscar. "Ay take shotgun and—"

"That's out!" snapped Henry. Oscar's last escapade with a shotgun nearly cost the lives of some of the county commissioners, when Oscar accidentally fired both barrels through the corridor door.

"Ay don't need shotgun," Oscar declared. "All Ay need is—"

"Prune juice," finished Judge disgustedly.

Henry stepped over to the doorway, turned and looked back at Judge.

"If I'm not mistaken, it's here," he said.

"Trouble?" asked Judge quickly.

"No, not trouble; merely Frijole Bill Cullison, with a jug."

Frijole Bill was sixty years of age, five feet three inches tall, and weighed about a hundred pounds.

His face was small and skinny, with big bushy brows and a huge mustache.

Frijole was a cook at the J Bar C, and spent most of his time distilling a queer concoction from prunes which he drank in preference to fairly good whisky.

"Hyah, Henry," he said, as he dismounted carefully, with a heavy object inside a flour-sack.

"Greetings, Frijole," replied Henry gravely. "Any news from the front?"

"The front of what?" queried Frijole blankly.

"Merely a quip, my friend. Come in and bring your jug."

"Yeah, I—I cooked up a mess for Oscar. Is he in?"

"Yah, sure," called Oscar. "How are you, Free-holey?"

"Purty good. I run out of prunes on this batch; so I used up a few pounds of appercots and some raisins. It's shore in-vigger-a-tin' stuff. Couple shots of this, and yuh can see in the dark."

"How old is it?" asked Henry.

Frijole took out his watch and squinted thoughtfully.

"It doesn't matter," said Henry quickly. He picked up the jug, weighing it in his hand.

"Born this morning and weighed ten pounds," he observed.

"Yeah," grinned Frijole. "Bill Shakespeare, the rooster, ate some of the mash; and when I left there he'd already killed three chicken-hawks and one turkey-buzzard, and was down in a dry wash, trackin' a wild-cat in the sand."

Henry nodded solemnly.

"I'd like to see the fight, if they meet," he said.

"So'd I," agreed Frijole. "Every time Bill Shakespeare gits a crack at some of that mash, he goes war-pathin' after that bobcat. Once he came back minus his tail-feathers, but he had a bobcat's ear in his beak and a satisfied look on his face. I went out and looked for the rest of the hide, but couldn't find it."

"**FRIJOLE,** did anyone ever call you a liar?" asked Judge.

"I've been tried seven times for manslaughter, ain't I?"

"I stand rebuked. But what about the sheep situation?"

"I dunno, except what Slim said this mornin'. I was too busy with that liquid lightnin' to pay much attention. Anyway, I'm only a cook."

"That was well said," remarked Henry. "In this day and age, when everyone is trying to do something of which they know nothing, or giving advice on things of which they know less, it is refreshing to hear a man say, 'Anyway, I am only the cook.' Frijole, to me you will always have a place in the sun."

"Thank yuh, Henry; but I'd a damn sight rather be in the shade."

"Well," sighed Henry, "I suppose it would be more comfortable."

He adjusted his hat. "I believe I shall go up to Harper's place, Judge. Perhaps I shall find Danny there."

"Love's young dream," said Judge solemnly.

"With Danny—perhaps," replied Henry.

"Yuh better pack yore slicker," advised Frijole. "If we don't have rain tonight, I'm the worst prophet in Arizona."

But Danny Regan was not at the Harper home, nor the Harper Millinery Store, which was in the front room of the home. Leila met Henry at the door. She was twenty years of age, tall and slender, and quite the prettiest girl in Wild Horse Valley. Leila had been engaged to Danny Regan for several months. Mrs. Laura Harper had been a beautiful girl, and was still a handsome woman, in spite of a hard struggle to make a living and educate her daughter.

"Danny went home," Leila told Henry. "He said they were holding a meeting at the Broken Wheel ranch tonight. I believe Danny was going down to the river and see how the boys were holding the sheep. Slim Pickins is down there, with Ed Jones and Lew Barber, of the Seventy-Six."

"I suppose that Danny was disgusted with me, as usual," remarked Henry.

"Not disgusted," said Mrs. Harper quickly. "Danny loves you like a son should love his father—but he does get exasperated, Henry."

"He says you don't understand—about sheep," added Leila.

"That is very true," agreed Henry. "Except for roast lamb, my only experience with sheep was in the Canadian Provinces one winter. It was terrible, I assure you."

"You had experiences with sheep in Canada?"

"Well, not—er—exactly; and still, the contact was close. Those accursed suits of woolen underwear—will I ever forget them, I wonder?"

Grimes

MRS. HARPER looked accusingly at Henry.

"That is your failing, Henry—everything is a joke. I have seen what sheep will do to a cattle country. You have no idea what it means."

"It means the end of the cattle ranges," nodded Henry solemnly. "My dear Laura, I was born to wear the cap and bells. The immortal Shakespeare said, I believe, that all the world is a stage. It is very true. We are all playing a role. Tragedians are not always tragic. Heroes can't always be heroic. No one expects them to be. But the painted fool must always be a fool—outwardly."

"But, Henry," protested Mrs. Harper, "when you quit the stage—"

"But have I? Judging from local opinions, I am still chasing a paper butterfly on a stick and string."

Henry shook his head sadly and sighed audibly.

"But what are you going to do about the sheep?" asked Leila.

"I wish I knew, Leila. But what can I do? As long as the sheepmen are not breaking the law, I can do nothing.

"And, after the law is broken, I can still do nothing, except to arrest the breakers of the law; which does not remove the sheep from this valley."

"That is exactly what I told Danny," declared Mrs. Harper. "He said he hoped you'd keep out of it entirely."

"I've hoped that ever since I heard about them," said Henry.

"You won't go out to that meeting at the Broken Wheel, will you?" asked Leila.

"I haven't been invited. No, I'll leave that to Danny."

"Oh, I do hope there won't be any bloodshed," said Mrs. Harper.

"Amen," sighed Henry. "At least, I hope there won't be any of mine."

He put on his hat and sauntered back to the office. Judge was standing in the center of the floor, his right hand shoved inside the front of his shirt, reared back, his left hand raised in an emphatic gesture. Frijole Bill was backed in a corner, eying Judge with a mixture of amazement and fright, while Oscar sat on the cot, holding the jug between his knees.

Henry stepped in the doorway, his eyes traveling slowly from face to face. Slowly Judge lowered his left hand, and relaxed.

"Va'l," said Oscar, "Ay suppose it vars a good speech, but Ay don't know vat in ha'l it vars good for."

"So you were making a speech, eh?" queried Henry.

"I was rehearsing my speech to Mr. Grimes," replied Judge stiffly.

"Grimes?" blurted Frijole. "That sheep owner? What the hell does he care about Free Silver?"

"Judge," said Henry seriously, "you are drunk, sir."

Judge blinked, scratched his head thoughtfully and licked his lips.

"I deny the implication, sir," he replied. "On two cups?"

"Frijole," said Henry soberly, "will you please apologize to Bill Shakespeare, the rooster, for what I thought? And you might search further for the hide of that wild-cat; I'm sure it must be around there somewhere. Pour me a drink, will you, Frijole?"

CHAPTER III

SHOT IN THE BACK

TWO DOZEN MEN crowded the main room of the Broken Wheel ranch-house that night. Outside, the moon and stars had been blotted out by storm clouds, and a sharp wind whistled through the branches of the sycamores which surrounded the old ranch-house.

Scotty McDonald, owner of the Broken Wheel ranch, scowled at the circle of grim faces, indistinct in the smoky light of the oil lamps. His gaze singled out the swarthy face of George Bellew, owner of the Seventy-Six outfit, and he said:

"Bellew, you told me a week ago that yore men were ridin' far in on Saw-Tooth Pass, keepin' an eye out for sheep. And yet ye let 'em come in. Why?"

Bellew shrugged and smiled sourly.

"They caught us asleep—I'll admit it," he replied. "Me and Jones and Barber happened to be ridin' along the river, and met Slim Pickins of the J Bar C and Werlin of this Broken Wheel, just as the front end of the herd came pourin' out of the pass.

"Well, we unlimbered our guns, and stopped 'em on the far side. That's the whole story. Now, what's to be done?"

"Send 'em back the way they came," suggested Dave Meek.

"Wait a minute," said McDonald. "I've been examinin' some of the county maps, in reference to land down there around the river.

"And the good Lord knows, I've rode that country often enough in the years I've been here to know every blade of grass by its first name.

"The north bank of that river—if ye might call that almost-dry gut a river, is high and sharp, except for a spot perhaps a hundred and fifty yards wide, which is opposite where the sheep are now situated. Without the aid of dynamite or a steam shovel ye can't send sheep across any other place.

"And now," he turned to Bellew, "the map shows that the land owned by the Seventy-Six extends to that north bank, and is one mile in width at that point. There is a mile-wide strip, which extends six miles to the north, joining the four sections, which surround yore home ranch. In all, ye have ten sections."

"Correct," nodded Bellew.

"The law," continued McDonald, "does not allow sheep to pass over cattle ranches; so we can legally block them. Grimes can keep his sheep there until they starve and then go home."

"Go tell the sheriff," chuckled a cowboy.

"That damn fool!" snorted Bellew. "He wouldn't know a sheep from a pole-cat."

"Just a moment," said Danny Regan. "I believe that Henry Conroy has proved to this county that he's no damn fool. In fact, he's showed a lot more brains than the men who elected him."

"I figured you'd have some remark to make, Regan," laughed Bellew. "Yuh naturally would, because he's yore boss. But I still think he's a damn fool."

"It's yore privilege, George," grinned Danny. "But speakin' of him not knowin' the difference between sheep and pole-cats—was you in to see him this mornin'?"

"I was," replied Bellew.

"I thought as much," nodded Danny soberly. "Which proves he does know the difference."

"How do yuh figure that, Regan?"

"Well, he didn't call yuh a sheep, George."

"Wait a minute, now," interrupted McDonald. "The first thing we know, this meetin' is goin' to be personal. Whether the sheriff is right or wrong, it is his duty to go down to Grimes, explain the situation to him, and let Grimes decide if he wants to have both the law and the cattle interests against him."

"Why call in the law?" asked a Circle N cowboy. "Let's go down there and pistol-whip that whole outfit."

"Easier said than done," stated Bellew. "Grimes is all set for trouble—or I don't know Grimes."

"Do you know Grimes?" asked Danny quickly.

"I know him by reputation," replied Bellew.

"We are not gettin' anywhere," reminded Meek. "What's to be done? Shall we follow Mac's suggestion of havin' the sheriff talk with Grimes—or go down there, shootin'?"

"I think McDonald is right," said Bellew. "We can't get anywhere by goin' down there, lookin' for trouble. If Grimes won't listen to reason—well, that's different."

"Is that the decision of the majority?" asked McDonald.

There were no dissenting voices.

"Meetin' is closed," declared McDonald. "In the mornin'—"

ONE OF the men had opened the front door, and above the whine of the wind came the drumming sound of a running horse. It was Frijole Bill Cullison, the little cook at the J Bar C. He flung himself off his horse, and came into the house.

"Them dud-damned shepherds got Slim Pickins!" he blurted. "They tied him on his horse and sent him home. I—I gu-got him to the doctor in Tonto. Shot twice—in the back."

Danny Regan grasped Frijole by the shoulder.

"You say the sheep men got Slim, Frijole?"

"They shore did—twice. But he ain't dead, Danny. The doc said he had a fightin' chance. I'll bet they thought he was dead."

The rain was drumming hollowly on the roof as they stood there looking at each other. Bellew laughed shortly, harshly.

"Is this funny to you?" asked Danny softly.

"Funny—hell! But you'll find out that Slim—"

"I'll find out that Slim done what?"

"He prob'ly crossed the river, huntin' for trouble. I told yuh that Grimes was set for war."

"What about Jones and Barber?" queried Meek. "They were supposed to be down there with Pickins, wasn't they?"

Bellew nodded, scowling heavily.

"All right," said Danny harshly, "I'm goin' to town. Slim wasn't just a J Bar C puncher—he was my friend. If Slim can tell what happened—and it was a Grimes man—I'll kill Grimes, if it's the last thing I ever do."

"Don't be a hot-headed fool," advised Bellew. "Don't forget that they hang men for murder in this state—even the murder of a sheep-herder. Grimes don't do any shootin'—he's too smart."

Danny halted in the doorway and looked back at Bellew.

"It seems to me that you know a lot about Grimes," he said. "Is there any special reason why yuh don't want him killed?"

"Not likely—when I own the biggest cattle spread in this valley. Don't be a fool, Regan. I'd be the heaviest loser, if the sheep ever got a foothold around here."

"Listen, gents," said McDonald. "Let's wait a while—now. If Slim recovers and can talk—well, it might make a difference. I'll send a man or two down to the river, and—Bellew, you better investigate yore two men; they mebbe got what Slim got. Hell, as far as we know, they're runnin' sheep across now."

"Not in the dark," said Bellew.

Danny closed the door and went out to his horse, followed by Frijole. There was no conversation, as they raced back to Tonto City. The sheriff's office was closed and locked. Danny went down to the doctor's home to see Slim. Doctor Bogart, a newcomer in town, allowed Danny to see Slim, who was still unconscious.

"Certainly, he has a fighting chance," admitted the doctor.

"When will he be able to talk?" asked Danny.

"Who knows? The man lost a lot of blood, and the severe shock from those two bullets was terrific. Luckily for him, both bullets went through. But I can assure you that I shall not let him do any talking for some time—even if he pulls through."

Danny went up to Harper's place. They had heard about Slim, but neither of the women knew where Henry, Judge and Oscar had gone.

"I wonder if they were foolish enough to go down to the sheep camps," said Danny. "It's raining hard, and so dark you can't see a foot in front of yore nose."

"Won't this put water in the river?" asked Mrs. Harper.

DANNY nodded grimly. He knew what Wild Horse River was like during a heavy downpour. It was treacherous, with its drifting silt and crumbling banks.

"Stay here tonight, Danny," begged Leila. "There is no reason for you going home in the dark and rain."

"I reckon I will stay in town, Leila. But I'll get a room at the hotel for me and Frijole."

"I had forgotten Frijole. But, Danny, why do you suppose they shot Slim?"

"I ain't got any idea on that subject, Leila. They got him— that's all we know. And if he lives, mebbe we can put a rope around the neck of the man who shot him."

"Perhaps he didn't see who shot him, Danny."

"Yeah, that might be true—he wasn't lookin'."

"Listen to it pour!" exclaimed Mrs. Harper.

Danny nodded slowly, thoughtfully.

"They won't he crossin' Wild Horse River in the mornin'."

IT WAS nearly dark that evening, when Henry, Judge and Oscar left Tonto City. No one saw them leave. Silently they rode away in single-file, with Henry in the lead, followed by Judge, with Oscar at least a hundred yards in the rear. Henry was armed with a six-shooter, Judge carried the shotgun, while Oscar had a suspicious-looking burlap-covered object dangling from his saddle-horn.

As it grew darker, they halted to allow Oscar to overtake them. He untied the object, and they drank deeply.

"We must not forget that we are on matters of diplomacy," reminded Judge. "We are not here to show force of arms."

"Va'l," replied Oscar, "what in ha'l are you goin' to do with dat shotgun—hunt docks?"

"Not a bad suggestion," said Henry. "Oscar, you have been down here before; suppose you take the lead."

"Yah, su-ure. Yust where do you want to go, Hanry?"

"God help poor sailors on a night like this," sighed Henry. "Oscar, you vitrified Viking, have you any idea why we are here, and where we are going?"

"Yah, su-sure. Ay heard you say, 'Val, ha're ve go—looking for Little Bo Pip.'"

"Oh, yes. I believe I did mention such a thing. You don't happen to know where Little Bo Peep is camped, do you, Oscar?"

"Does he vork for Grimes?"

"You are beginning to see the light. We want to go to visit Mr. Grimes, the sheep man."

Oscar scratched his head thoughtfully.

"Das is crazy idea," he declared.

"Belated decision," said Henry. "You lead the way, Oscar."

"Va'l," said Oscar, "Ay am not sure. But, of course, at de same time, you must remember dat this is a ha'l of a big country, and yust as dark as de inside of a black hurse."

"Opinion sustained," replied Judge. "Proceed, Oscar. Unless I am the worst prophet in Arizona, we are going to get wet."

"Ay vish," stated Oscar, "Ay vars home."

A gust of rain swept into their faces, hissing through the mesquite, and causing the three horses to shift around.

"If wishing would do any good," sighed Henry, "I'd do a lot of it myself. Oscar, which way is Tonto City?"

"From ha're?" queried Oscar.

"Of all the asinine questions!" snorted Judge. "Oscar, without a doubt, you are the dumbest person I ever met."

"Yah, su-ure," admitted Oscar meekly. "But, Yudge, you must remember, Ay didn't came ha're alone."

In spite of his discomfort, Henry chuckled.

"Va'l," observed Oscar, "ve may as vell go. Ay can't see damn t'ing."

THE RAIN was coming in gusts, and in a few minutes they were wet to the skin. Mesquite branches ripped at their clothing and slapped them across their faces. Oscar found the riverbed, which was still nearly dry, and they went blundering southward, with no idea just where they might be.

For at least another hour they circled in the murk, getting wetter every moment. Finally they held another conference, and drank from the jug.

"If you want an opinion from me, I'd suggest that we go home," stated Judge miserably.

"An unsolicited opinion, but one of your best, Judge," replied Henry. "In fact, it is one of the first I ever heard you utter that wasn't based on some damnable precedent of law. And if you can guess within ninety degrees of a way home, I'll hail you as the greatest navigator since Columbus."

"Ay smell ships," declared Oscar.

"Take another whiff, and see if you can smell Tonto City," suggested Henry. "I don't see how in the devil you can smell anything—after drinking prune whisky—I can't."

"Don't belittle the product of Frijole Bill," said Judge. "It is the only silver lining we have with us. Oscar, I wish you would stop sniffing, and lead us back to Tonto City."

"Ay don't know where de ha'l Ay am," confessed Oscar. "Ay am lost. One t'ing looks yust like two."

"Prune juice," said Judge dismally. "Are we going to sit here and drown? Damn it, my boots are even full of water! In all sincerity, I must say, to hell with Grimes."

"I am just wondering, Judge," said Henry.

"Wondering what, sir?"

"Wondering if we are still in Arizona. Even a state of this size has its boundaries, sir. I suggest that we go north for a while, in order to not invade Mexico."

"Gladly," agreed Judge, "Go north and we will follow."

Henry sighed and moved soggily in his saddle.

"Yumpin' Yee-rusalem!" exploded Oscar. "Ay see light!"

"Where?" asked, Henry and Judge, in chorus.

"Ay can find it," assured Oscar.

Oscar led the way, ignoring mesquite, cactus and cat-claw, and drew up in front of a tent, inside of which a dim light was glowing. Stiffly they dismounted in the mud. The dim figures of two men were outlined against the dirty canvas, as the three men walked up.

But their reception was by no means a cordial one. They found themselves looking into the muzzles of two rifles, held in the hands of two bearded, evil-looking men.

"Drop that shotgun!" snapped one of the men, and Judge promptly dropped it on Henry's toes.

"That was uncalled for," murmured Henry.

"What'd yuh say, feller?" asked one of the men harshly.

"Merely a thought," replied Henry painfully, as the man took his gun, and made a search of Oscar for more weapons.

"Take a look at him, will yuh, Painful?" asked one of the men, pointing at Henry's insignia of office. "The sheriff!"

"Well, clog my cats!" snorted Painful. "Whatcha know about that, Edgar? Darned if he ain't almost as funny lookin' as they said he was."

"Thank you," said Henry dryly. "It is rarely that an act lives up to its advance billing."

"What do yuh mean, feller?" asked Painful.

"It's a long story," replied Henry. "In fact, it is too long to tell and our time is valuable. We seek Mr. Grimes."

THEY STARED at their three captives, and grinned a little.

"So yo're lookin' for the boss, are yuh?" said Painful.

"Your boss—not ours," said Judge.

"Yea-a-ah? Well, that's shore nice. But I'm scared that Grimes don't care to talk with yuh. Anyway, he ain't here; and what's the idea of sneakin' down here in the dark, packin' shotguns, anyway? We ort to sock hell out of all three of yuh, sneakin' in on honest, hard-workin' men this-a-way. Edgar, will you collect them three horses, while I watch these three whip-poorwills?"

"Collect the horses?" queried Henry. "Why, if I may ask?"

"Yuh may, Big Nose. As soon as Edgar has collected, we're goin' to kick you three jiggers in the general direction of Tonto City, and let yuh walk home. All my life I've hankered for a chance to boot a sheriff. Sorry to have to start in on a poor specimen like you, but I reckon a feller has to start at the bottom."

"Be sure about the direction," said Henry dryly.

"Are you tryin' to be funny?"

"No—merely accurate. By the way, Mr. Painful, do you ever expect to get anywhere, as they say, through kicking sheriffs?"

"I don't quite git yuh, Smart Feller."

"Well, it doesn't seem to me that there is any advancement. Of course, you might, later on, after experience, kick a United States Marshal. You might even get to a point where kicking a United States Senator might pall upon yuh. I can understand how you feel, of course. But, all joking aside, if I were you, I'd curb that obsession."

"I think yo're loco as hell," declared Painful.

"He has lucid moments," sighed Judge.

"I'd practice on deputy sheriffs first," said Henry maliciously. "This tall party is my deputy, Mr. Painful."

"Mebbe you think this is a joke," sneered Painful.

"Not at all," assured Henry. "As far as I know, it is the proper procedure, in a case of this kind."

"They said you was dumb; but they didn't tell half of it," said Painful. Judge snickered audibly.

"Yeah, and they said a few things about you, too," remarked Painful. "They said you didn't have sense enough to come in out of the rain."

"Page Diogenes," chuckled Henry.

Edgar came back and announced that the horses were removed.

"I've got a good idea," grinned Painful. "Take that shotgun, Edgar. We'll count ten—and fire. Back out, you three fool-hens. Line up there in front of the tent. When I say for yuh to go— yuh better go fast. Ready, Edgar? Cock both barrels, and hold a little high. Ready? Go!"

"Wait a minute!" snorted Judge. "You are carrying the joke a little too far, my friends. Do you realize who we are?"

"All right," said Painful. "We'll start all over again. Are yuh ready, Edgar?"

"M' finger's itchin'," replied Edgar, grinning wolfishly.

"I represent the law," panted Judge.

"Then yuh better show her how damn fast yuh can run! Ready! Go!"

HENRY grabbed his hat with both hands and went galloping, with Judge at his heels. Fifty feet from the tent, Oscar went sprawling in the mud, leaped to his feet and came galloping while from in front of the tent came the crashing report of the shotgun, and a choking yelp from one of the men.

Henry slapped both hands behind him, as though to intercept any stray shot, but none came. Judge tried to avoid a yucca clump, crashed into Henry and they both went down, with Oscar tripping over them and hitting the ground with a heavy thud.

"Ay hope to ha'l it ain't bruk!" he exclaimed, spitting mud.

"Your back?" queried Henry, pawing in the dark for his hat.

"No—das yug!" blurted Oscar.

"Heavenly days!" exclaimed Judge. "Have you still got that jug, Oscar?"

"Yah, su-ure. When ve rode up to das tent, Ay dropped de yug out in de dark. You b'at you, Ay am not furnishing prune yuice to ship-horders."

"Well, come on, Solomon," grunted Henry.

Geo. Bellew

They went far away from that tent and stood on the slope of a hill in the drifting rain. Oscar chuckled hollowly.

"Really," said Judge wearily, "your sense of humor is badly warped, Oscar."

"He might as well laugh as cry," said Henry. "I wonder if they really shot at us, Judge. Why, even a blind man could hit at least one of us at that distance, with a shotgun."

"Ay'll bet das ship-horder got big surprise," said Oscar.

"You'll *bet* he got surprised?" queried Henry. "What would surprise him?"

"Das shotgun."

"How would that surprise him?"

"Val, you see, it vars like dis, Hanry; when Ay cleaned das shotgun, Ay left de muzzle full of oil rags; so she von't get rosty. And Ay forgot to take 'em out."

"Good Lord!" blurted Judge. "Why—why that would cause a gas-check in the barrel—and explode the gun! Oscar, you dumb Swede, you might have killed me."

"You knew it all the time, Oscar?" choked Henry.

"Yah, su-ure, Ay knew it; but Ay forgot. Every once in a vile, Ay forget to remember."

"Dumb Swede!" snorted Judge.

"We'll ask Edgar—if we ever see him again," laughed Henry. "But where are we going? They promised to kick us toward Tonto City, but did not keep their words."

"There is no use trying to find home on a night like this," declared Judge. "Anyway, it would be too far to walk in the dark. If we could only find a dry place to spend the rest of the night, I'd be fully satisfied."

"A dry place would be of little use to me," sighed Henry, listening to the sugg-g-g-g of water in his boot.

"I am too civilized to enjoy sitting down in the mud," declared Judge. "Let us seek a sheltered nook, Oscar."

"What in de ha'l is a nook, Yudge?"

"A shelterd nook is a dry spot."

"I hope," sighed Oscar.

"What do you hope?"

"Ay hope ve find it. Coom on, yentlemen."

For another thirty minutes they followed Oscar, while the rain hissed down upon them. They stumbled, slid and skidded into a cañon, where house-size rocks reared up through the brush; and more through luck than design, Oscar found a huge, overhanging rock, under which the ground was dry.

They huddled under this, unable to find enough dry brush to make a fire. Oscar uncorked the jug and they drank.

"If I ever get out of this alive, they can have my heartfelt resignation," declared Henry. "I would rather do seven shows a day, and follow a dog act all the rest of my life. At least, picture theaters are dry inside."

"Oh, we'll get out of it alive," assured Judge, but added, "I hope."

"What do you hope, Oscar?" asked Henry.

"Ay hope Free-holey buys some prunes. Das ha're stuff taste yust like hurse liniment."

"I noticed—" began Judge. "Oscar, did you get the jugs mixed?"

"Ay am yust vondering," replied Oscar.

CHAPTER IV

EAVESDROPPERS

DANNY AND FRIJOLE were out early next morning, in spite of the fact that it was still raining hard. They ate breakfast with Leila and her mother, all of them genuinely worried about Henry, Judge and Oscar.

They had started for the livery stable to get their horses, when George Bellew, Ed Jones and Lew Barber rode into town, clad in dripping slickers.

"How's Slim this mornin'?" asked Bellew anxiously.

"Well, he's still alive, Bellew," replied Danny. "Anythin' new?"

"Nothin', except that the river is runnin' full. We're safe, as far as the sheep are concerned."

"I don't *sabe* about Slim," said Barber. "He was with me and Ed until almost dark. He said he was goin' to ride down the river a ways, before goin' back to the J Bar C. We never heard no shots."

"Mebbe he went over to get a close look at the sheep," said Ed Jones. "That's the only way I figure it."

"Well," sighed Danny, "we can only hope for the best. Slim's the only one that knows where he went."

Danny and Frijole rode down to the river, where they halted at the north bank and looked across the roily flood. There was no sign of the sheep, which had been herded into a more sheltered place. Danny looked grimly across there.

"I'm plumb scared to death that Henry, Judge and Oscar are over there somewhere, Frijole," he said.

"They're crazy enough," admitted Frijole.

"Aw, it ain't a case of bein' crazy. I'll betcha they've gone down there to try and talk Grimes out of bringin' in sheep. Grimes has a bad reputation. He's been mixed up in a lot of shady stuff. Tried twice for murder, I've heard.

"They can't fight. Damn it, they ain't the fightin' kind. If things went against 'em, they'd be helpless. Anyway, they couldn't come back across the river for a couple days, after the rain quits. I'll tell yuh, Frijole—" Danny straightened in his saddle.

"I'm goin' back and get some of the boys. I know a place over nearer the Seventy-Six where we can swim that flood. The boys from the Broken Wheel and the Circle N will take a chance. If Henry, Judge and Oscar are down there, we'll find 'em. And if them shepherds try to stop us, there'll be coyote food around them hills."

"I'll go with yuh, Danny," said Frijole. "I've been tried seven times for manslaughter—and not one was a shepherd. Might as well make it a full-house, I reckon."

They went straight back to Tonto City, where they found all the men from both the Broken Wheel and Circle N. Bellew and his two men had gone back to the Seventy-Six. Scotty McDonald and Dave Meek were a little bit dubious about leading their boys across the river.

"After all," said McDonald, "we'd be invadin' the sheep. And under them circumstances Grimes might start shootin'."

"What's yore opinion, Meek?" asked Danny.

"I'm kinda inclined to string with Mac, Danny," replied the owner of the Circle N. "As far as Conroy, Van Treece and Johnson are concerned—well, I'd kinda let nature take its course."

"In other words," said Danny seriously, "yo're a couple of yaller pups. Henry Conroy went down there to try and prevent trouble. He went down there to talk things over with Grimes— to show him how foolish he would be to try and sheep out this valley. Henry never went down there to start trouble, but was workin' in the interests of every cattle spread in this valley.

"I believe he was trapped down there by the flood, and is

now in the hands of Grimes and his men. I'm goin' after 'em—if I have to go alone."

"Conroy is a fool," declared McDonald stubbornly.

"Mebbe he is," said Danny. "But he's too much of a man to refuse to help another man, just because the man wasn't smart."

Meek scratched his head thoughtfully for several moments. "Yeah, I reckon I never thought of it that way," he admitted. "Anyway, he's our sheriff, Mac. We elected him, yuh know."

"I'm not goin' to ask my men to—" began McDonald.

"Yuh won't try to stop 'em, will yuh?" interrupted Danny.

"If they want to go—nope."

"Thank yuh, I don't reckon I'll need an army."

"Yuh might need a navy, though," laughed Meek. "Wild Horse must be runnin' bank-full about now."

"I know a place," said Danny. "It's toward the Seventy-Six. The flood spreads pretty wide—unless she cut a new channel. If she did, we can't make it. See yuh later."

HENRY, Judge and Oscar, wet, hungry and generally depressed, sat under the dripping rock and watched the cold, gray dawn creep across the brushy hills. Gray shapes bestirred themselves in the gray dawn. The swale was full of big rams, the dim light glinting on their corkscrew horns.

"The first animated bock beer signs I have ever seen," declared Henry.

"He-ships," stated Oscar.

"What?" queried Henry.

"He-ships."

Henry cocked one eye at Oscar. "Are you trying to talk English, or have you hiccups, Oscar?"

"Male sheep," explained Judge painfully. Being wet had given him a touch of rheumatism.

"I could lick the frost off a bakery window," declared Henry. "Gentlemen, in all my life I have never been so hungry."

"I told you, before we ever started—" began Judge.

"Pause a moment," interrupted Henry. "You and your judicial utterances are what brought us down here, sir. If I remember correctly, you said something about us staying at home, our heads bowed in shame, while men fought and bled down here. Well, if I ever get back home—"

"Das ha're yug is pretty damn light," interrupted Oscar. "Ay guess we better go home, yentlemen. If you vant my opinion, I say, 'To ha'l with Little Bo Pip.'"

"Shall we proceed, Judge?" sighed Henry.

"The spirit is willing, but the flesh is weak, Henry. This damnable rheumatism—ah-h-h! Catches me in the knees. I may not be able to walk—but I can still shuffle."

"Even a shuffle in the right direction is not to be sneezed at, Judge. Speaking of sneezes—I hope I do not get a head-cold from this exposure. I have never been so wet since I fell into a stage-tank, with a pair of trained seals. Shall we go, Oscar?"

Oscar tucked his beloved jug under one arm, made a comprehensive survey of the country, and started out. Big rams moved slowly aside, as the three men walked in single file, with Judge bringing up the rear.

"Friendly creatures," observed Henry. "So innocent and unspoiled."

"Not too fast," panted Judge. "My rheumatism is terrible."

He stopped, stooped over to rub his knees.

"Yeeminy!" yelped Oscar. "Don't do it, Yudge!"

But the warning came too late. A swift-moving ram smacked him square in the seat of the pants, and with a yelp of surprise and pain, Judge turned completely over and landed on his back in the brush, while the belligerent ram stopped dead still and began cropping leaves off a bush.

"Didn't Ay ta'l you—" began Oscar accusingly, and the next moment he was coming down on the back of his neck, feet in the air, when a big ram struck him behind the knees.

HENRY cuffed his hat over one eye and looked at Oscar, who had been knocked unconscious for the moment.

"Well, my goodness!" exclaimed Henry. "Of all the—"

And just then he realized that he was surrounded by animated battering rams; that every sheep-eye in the vicinity seemed to be glaring at him.

He heard the thudding of hoofs, and whirled just in time to be missed. But the big ram stopped dead, when there was no impact, and began backing up, half-twisting, possibly wondering at his poor marksmanship. Rams are more inclined to back up and make another try, rather than to turn and make a return charge.

The ram was against Henry, still backing up, when Henry, half-hysterical over what had happened—and what might happen—threw his left leg over the ram, and grabbed wool with both hands.

The next thing Henry knew he was reared back on that sheep, both hands hooked deep in the heavy wool, while the sheep went down through that swale, with frightened sheep scattering on either side, like waves from the prow of a speed-boat.

Fifty yards of high-speed traveling took them out of the herd, where the ram went through a mesquite thicket, leaving Henry all tangled up, breathless and battered. He shucked off part of his wet clothes, in trying to get loose from the thorns, and turned to see what might be happening to Judge and Oscar.

Things were a bit hazy for Henry, but gradually he was able to discern Oscar, armed with a huge club, seemingly gone berserk with rage. He was clearing a path for Judge, who was humped over and limping badly.

"Yump onto me, vill you?" yelped Oscar. "Yust try it. You let Yudge alone, too, or Ay'll knock your handle-bors off. Hanree-e-e!"

Oscar halted his attack long enough to yell loudly. "Hanree-e-e-e!"

"Yoo-hoo!" replied Henry, in a voice which greatly resembled the weak toot of a pop-corn vender's machine.

"He von't answer, Yudge," informed Oscar. "Ay saw him ridin' a ship."

Judge tried to straighten up and peered around.

"I don't see him," he said peevishly. "Like a good General, he rode away at the first attack. Oscar, where is that jug?"

"Bruk," replied Oscar. "Smashed all to ha'al on a rock."

"And just when I needed a dram or two—even if it is horse-liniment."

"Same ha're," agreed Oscar. "Ay could drink carbolic acid—and enjoy it. Han-ree-e-e-e!"

"Over here!" piped Henry.

"Over there by that bush—unscathed," groaned Judge. "Standing there, laughing at our sorry plight."

"Laughing?" wheezed Henry. "I have been hit so hard that I have a permanent leer. By the gods, I can easily understand why shepherds go crazy."

"I can't," declared Judge. "It will always remain a mystery to me, sir."

"Why?"

"Because I don't understand how they can live long enough to lose their minds." Henry's laugh brought a deep groan from Judge.

"Do not jest with a dying man, Henry. I—I have a feeling that I am on my last legs."

"**NOT EXACTLY** on them, Judge; just a bit off-set, as I see them. Not very good legs either, as far as walking is concerned. But now that we have passed the inner defense of the Ancient Order of Battering Rams—or is it the outer defense?—what is to be done? Oscar, suppose you make a suggestion."

"Ay have good notion to take club and knock ha'l from more ships," declared Oscar. "They bruk my yug."

"Well, never mind, lead the way, Oscar—we are going home," sighed Henry.

Again, in single file, they went down through the wet bushes, sliding in the mucky ground.

"Judge," said Henry, "you look like that ad for some sort of kidney pills."

"Your levity is ill-placed, sir," declared Judge.

It was beginning to rain again, which did not brighten their prospects. They came out on a point where they could see Wild Horse River. It was running, almost bank-full, a tumbling flood of yellow water. They grouped and looked at it. Judge turned a haggard face to Henry and said painfully:

"Sir, do you realize that it will require at least a week for that flood to subside?"

"If it quits raining," nodded Henry.

"And in the meantime starvation faces us—unless we can gain the confidence of the sheep men. We might throw ourselves on their mercy."

"We did that last night, Judge. I don't believe I should care to meet Painful and Edgar again."

"Ay don't like das ha're t'ing," declared Oscar gloomily. "Ay vant to go home, and Ay can't svim. Ay have seven brodders in Sweden, and every von is goot svimmer."

"Even with the fastest boat, it would take too long to bring them here," said Henry. "By that time the water would have gone down. However, you might bring one over later, in case we should get crazy again."

"My sister is good svimmer, too."

"This expedition is not coëducational," declared Henry.

"Yah, su-ure," agreed Oscar. "Ay never learn to svim."

"I hope you have convinced us, in that respect," sighed Judge. "Personally, I never doubted you. But, damn it, Henry, what are we going to do about our dilemma?"

"I have no answer real handy," replied Henry. "The prospect of starving to death has no appeal to my imagination."

"Aye," said Judge dramatically. "Starvation, exposure—insanity."

"No, Judge," replied Henry mildly. "Only starvation and exposure need be feared. Insanity only attacks people who have at least a vestige of brains—which we haven't. Of all the idiotic—"

"Ay smell somet'ing!" exclaimed Oscar.

"Maybe we are beginning to mold," said Henry. "What does it smell like to you, Oscar?"

"Vood smoke!"

THEY SNIFFED collectively.

"Let Henry do it," suggested Judge. "With that nose—"

But Oscar was working up-wind, like a hunting dog, and the other two followed him. Over the next small ridge they saw an old cabin, with a trickle of smoke coming from the sagging stove-pipe.

"Ay su-ure smell!" declared Oscar triumphantly.

"At times," agreed Judge, "you certainly do, Oscar."

They grouped together and considered the situation.

"There is one thing that worries me," said Henry.

"What is that one thing, sir?" queried Judge.

"The possibility that they might not count ten, before firing. It really was, as the English say, a sporting thing to do, Judge. But there is the cabin. Smoke from the pipe indicates warmth and cheer within—perhaps food, and liquor. But what to do?"

"Ay skal t'al you," replied Oscar. "Ay am going down to das cabin—to ha'al with ship-horders. Ay am honest Svedeman, and no ship-horder can make me storve. Coom along, yentlemen."

"Fools rush in," sighed Judge.

"Ay am no Russian," denied Oscar. "Ay'll show you how Ay can handle ship-horders."

Perhaps Oscar realized how desperate their situation was,

because he went straight to the closed door, and with a bellow of defiance, kicked it almost off its hinges.

"Ay am Oscar Yohnson, lookin' for fude and shalter!" he shouted. "No damn ship-horder can stop me, Ay t'al you! Ay vould also say that—" Oscar hesitated, peering into the cabin.

"Not a soul at home," said Henry, peering past Oscar.

They went in and looked around. It was a two-room cabin, and—judging from the scattered gear—had been recently occupied. A portable, sheet-iron stove was still warm from breakfast, and there were a number of dirty dishes and skillets on the table. Bed-rolls had been thrown into corners. Evidently the cabin leaked, judging from pools of water on the dirt floor.

Nothing had been moved into the rear room, which leaked badly. Across one side of this room, and about ten feet from the floor, was a pole-loft, with only a center pole to support it.

There was a makeshift ladder leaning against the loft, which had probably been used as a storage space at some time. Oscar spied a demijohn, and fell upon it with a whoop of joy. The others watched anxiously, as Oscar took a swallow. He smacked his lips several times, and recorked the jug.

"Yust kerosene," he said blandly.

"But you swallowed some of it!" exclaimed Henry.

"Yah, su-u-ure," admitted Oscar.

Judge shook the coffee pot, but it only contained moist grounds. There was no water for making more coffee, and very little wood for the stove. Judge went over to the door and looked out across the dripping landscape.

"Three men coming!" he blurted. "All armed with rifles, too!"

Henry thought quickly.

"Up on the loft!" he exclaimed. "They may not look. Quick!"

UP THE RICKETY ladder they went and sprawled on the creaking loft, which swayed dangerously under their weight. A few moments later the three men entered the cabin.

"Stir up that fire," ordered one of the men.

"We don't want to make much smoke, Boss," replied another. "We had a hell of a time cookin' breakfast with wet wood."

"Damn it, I'm soaked through! Why, I never thought of a slicker. I'd like to break Bellew's neck. The fool! We could have been all set, if he'd done as he promised."

"Yeah, I reckon that's right, Mr. Grimes."

Grimes? Henry pricked up his ears. So this was the sheep man himself. And what did he have to do with Bellew, owner of the Seventy-Six, wondered Henry? The man was talking again.

"Painful shoved a hundred rams across, before dark, and one of the J Bar C punchers started shootin' at 'em. He got a few of 'em, and drove Painful back, when one of Bellew's men downed this jigger from the J Bar C."

"Killed him, eh?"

"Yeah, I reckon so. They tied him on his horse, and turned the horse loose."

Grimes swore bitterly. "The crazy fools! I'll get the blame for that. Just when I've got everythin' set to move onto the Seventy-Six, legally. At the north end of the Seventy-Six is a strip of State land, which I've leased. Why, damn it, I can drive every cow out of this valley within two years."

"I don't guess the sheriff will try to do anythin', Grimes."

"That dumb fool!"

Henry winced, and was sure he heard Judge chuckle softly.

"Bellew told me all about this sheriff," said Grimes. "He was one of them actors. Good for nothin', except drinkin' whisky and makin' faces. His deputy is a broken-down lawyer; not worth the price of powder to blow him to hell. And his jailer has half the brains of a chickadee."

"That's what I've heard, Grimes. Bellew ort to be here any minute now—if Casey found him home."

The other men called from the doorway: "Here comes Painful—alone."

The three men on the loft heard Painful enter the cabin, and Grimes spoke sharply to him.

"We've gotta git a doctor for Edgar," said Painful. "Early last night, the whole damn sheriff's office came to our camp. Me and Edgar took their horses away from 'em, figurin' on sendin' 'em home on foot. We took their shotgun, and said we'd count ten, before salivatin' of 'em. Edgar done the shootin'."

Painful paused and cleared his throat.

"Yuh see, Mr. Grimes—it—it was all kinda in fun. But Edgar pulled both triggers, and the gun blowed out the back end. He—he lost all his front teeth, one ear, and he's got a busted nose."

"He has, eh?" growled Grimes. "Painful, I told you fellers to not start any trouble. I wanted this done quietly."

"I know yuh did—but we kinda got scared, havin' the sheriff bust in on us thataway."

"I see. He scared you into stealin' horses, eh?"

"Oh, that was more or less of a joke."

"Just a little joke, eh? I suppose the sheriff returned the compliment, when he plugged the barrels of his shotgun and let Edgar shoot at him."

"Edgar's really in bad shape," insisted Painful. "I cain't hardly understand what he says."

"What a damn mess we've made of things!" rasped Grimes. "I've planned this deal for months—and this has to happen."

"Here comes Casey and Bellew," said the man at the doorway.

There was no conversation in the cabin, as Bellew and Casey rode up and dismounted. Bellew came in.

"Hyah, Grimes," he said.

"Glad to see yuh, Bellew."

"I'm glad to see you, too, Grimes."

"Yuh are, eh? Yore outfit acted like they did. What's the idea of blockin' me like that? Damn it, you've just about queered the whole deal."

"Oh, I don't think so, Grimes," replied Bellew easily. "Yuh must remember that our deal ain't closed. I told yuh it would have to be all settled, before I let a sheep cross the river. I meant it. Don't you realize that the cattlemen of Wild Horse Valley would boil me in oil, if they knew I was sellin' out the Seventy-Six to Grimes? Why, it gives you a right-of-way through to the north ranges, which don't belong to the cattlemen—not legally. Without me, you can't get in; and you know it."

"Painful," said Grimes, "git some water and put on the coffee while me and Bellew talk over this proposition."

CHAPTER V

RATS IN A TRAP

FAR BACK IN the hills a slicker-clad posse sat on their horses in the rain. Dave Meek, owner of the Circle N spread, hunched forward, a pair of old field glasses glued to his eyes, while the rest of the posse waited his decision.

"The light's damn bad," he told them, "but I'm sure that one of the men is George Bellew. Anyway, it's his white horse. The other horse is dark-colored. And they're ridin' damn fast."

"Sounds kinda queer," said Danny Regan. "They're headin' down to the sheep. Suppose we foller 'em, boys?"

"Why foller George Bellew?" queried one of the men.

"Just a crazy hunch, I reckon."

"Might as well," said Meek. "Yuh know, Danny, I've been doin' a lot of thinkin', ever since McDonald talked about that map, and the Seventy-Six property. If Grimes brought his sheep across the river, he'd be on Seventy-Six ground."

"I know," nodded Danny grimly. "And I figure Bellew knows too much about Grimes—too much for the good of Wild Horse Valley."

"And Bellew needs money," said Meek.

"And don't forget that somebody shot Slim Pickins. Meek, I'm plumb scared that Henry and company have run up against a snag."

"I'm jist wonderin' if they haven't," nodded Meek.

WHILE the men in the cabin discussed things, the tantalizing odors of coffee and frying bacon came to the nostrils of the three men on the loft.

"All the arguments on earth won't change me, Grimes," declared Bellew. "I've got the law behind me. As long as I own the Seventy-Six, you can't put a damn sheep across the river. When you pay the price—it's yore ranch."

"That's plenty plain, Bellew," replied Grimes slowly. "Have you got the deed with yuh?"

"Have you got the money with yuh?" countered Bellew.

"I've got the money, when you produce the papers."

"Thirty-five thousand in cash?"

"Every dollar of it. Want to see it?"

"I shore do."

Grimes was as good as his word. Swiftly he counted the huge bundle of bills on the rough table, while Bellew watched narrowly. It was all there. Bellew drew out the papers.

"How'd yuh get a notary seal, without signatures?" asked Grimes curiously.

"He's a friend of mine," laughed Bellew. "It's just as legal. Some of yore men can witness the signatures, I reckon."

There was no conversation, while the signatures were being written.

"That settles it," said Bellew thankfully. "You own a ranch, Grimes—and I've got—wait! Grimes, you damn—"

A revolver shot shook the old cabin. One of the men cursed explosively—and everything was quiet for a space of time.

"You didn't suppose I was goin' to let Bellew get away with all that money, did yuh?" queried Grimes coldly.

"It—it was kinda sudden," said Painful weakly. "Yuh see, I never seen a man killed before."

"That's all right. Each one of you fellers will get five hundred dollars. Here yuh are—I'll pay it right now."

Henry squinted at Judge, who seemed rather sick. They had known Bellew for quite a while; and both of them realized what might happen to them, if Grimes discovered them.

"Man, that's plenty," said one of the men.

"More than you'd ever have in one lump," agreed Grimes. "Now, I want you three fellers to take that body and throw it in the river. Give it a good heave. By the time they find him—well, they won't know who he is, anyway."

Judging from the sounds, all four men went outside with the body. Henry realized that this cabin would be a death-trap for them, if discovered. Craning his neck dangerously, he was able to see a rifle leaning against the wall, where one of the men had left it.

AS CAUTIOUSLY as possible Henry got to his hands and knees. If he could get that rifle—The loft creaked softly.

"Careful!" hissed Judge.

And almost before they realized it, Grimes stepped into the room, directly under where Henry crouched. There were no windows, and in the dim light Grimes looked quickly about. With a sudden lurch Henry dived off the loft, landing his two hundred and a few pounds square on top of Mr. Grimes' head and shoulders.

And almost at the same moment the flimsy loft broke loose, and down came Judge and Oscar in a tangle of flying poles. Henry rolled weakly off Grimes, and sat there panting wind into his tortured lungs. Judge sat up among the poles, looking vacantly around. Oscar sneezed violently, removed a pole off the back of his neck, and said:

"Yee-e-e-e—zus!"

"Quick!" panted Henry. "Bar the door and get the rifles."

"The case is dismissed," wheezed Judge. "Lack of evidence—"

Oscar got up, a vacant expression in his eyes, and walked right over Henry and Grimes. He sprawled almost in the other room.

"Excoose, please," he said. "Ay am going avay from ha'ar yust as fast as Ay can valk."

He approached the door, and was reaching for it, when a rifle shot cracked viciously outside. Oscar jumped back and whirled around. Again the shot sounded near the doorway. Oscar reached out and picked up a roughly-made three-legged stool. As he swung it up in one hand, the door was flung open and a man sprang inside.

Ignoring the fact that the cabin might be occupied, he turned and swung up his six-shooter. And just at that moment Oscar Johnson tunked him over the head with the stool. As he fell, he fired a shot straight up through the flimsy roof.

Oscar stood there with uplifted stool, until a bullet came through the door and showered splinters out of the stool. Then Oscar shut the door and dived headlong for the connecting doorway, barely missing Henry, who was heading for one of the three rifles.

"Yumpin' Yee-rusalem!" he yelped. "Ay have killed Ed Yones!"

"Ed Jones?" queried Henry vacantly. "Why, why, the sheep-men must be after him. Judge, are you ossified? Grab a rifle—and die for Arizona!"

"I beg your pardon," replied Judge stiffly. "I have no intentions—"

From near the cabin came a fusillade of shots, and Judge ducked to safety behind a pile of bed-rolls. Oscar had a Winchester rifle, which he pitched over to Judge, and narrowly missed hitting him on the head.

"Shades of David Crockett," whispered Henry, examining the mechanism of his rifle. "It looks like the finish, Judge."

Zin-n-n-ng—splop! A bullet ripped its way through the door, hit a cast-iron skillet on the table and sent it spinning into a corner.

Spa-n-n-ng! Another one came through a window, and a tin cup, half-full of sugar, fairly exploded off the table.

"Do you know any prayers, Judge?" asked Henry, crouching in the middle of the floor.

"Das is no time for asking help," interrupted Oscar. "Das is time for sinking and fighting."

OSCAR slid over near the broken window, lifted his rifle and began shooting methodically. A bullet blew splinters in his face, but he worked the lever, until the gun was empty.

"Kuk-kill anybody?" asked Judge.

"Ay tank Ay kill six," replied Oscar blandly. He reached over and took the rifle out of Judge's unresisting hands.

"Wait a minute!" exclaimed Henry. "All the ammunition we have is in these two guns, Oscar."

"Yah, su-u-ure," agreed Oscar.

"God help us, when that is gone," said Judge.

"You might at least ask for help, before it is gone," suggested Henry.

More splinters blew off the old door, and a section of chinking blew out of a space between the logs.

"Rats in a trap," said Henry bitterly. "And I laughed, when they offered me seventy-five dollars a week."

"You said they didn't know who you were," reminded Judge.

"Don't use 'were,' Judge," replied Henry. "It is still 'are.' Let me have a try at 'em, Oscar."

Henry crawled carefully over to the window, poked the muzzle of his gun through the smashed window-frame, and lifted his head. And, as though yanked by a spring, his Stetson went across the room, the top of it practically shot off.

Judge shivered and looked at the hat.

"Almost 'were,' sir," he said slowly.

"Oh, yee-e-e!" choked Oscar, and Henry turned his head.

In the connecting doorway stood Grimes the sheep man. They had forgotten his six-shooter, which he had in his right hand. He was still groggy, dazed, but dangerous. Apparently he did not see Judge, hunched against the bed-rolls, only a few feet away, because he had eyes only for Henry and Oscar.

"Trapped," he muttered. "What's wrong? Who the hell are you, anyway? Who's doin' the shootin'? Talk, damn yuh, before I kill both of yuh."

"Gladly," said Henry in a thin voice. "What subject do you wish to discuss?"

"Discuss? Huh? What the hell happened to me? Who are you? I'll shoot you so damn full of holes—"

Unsteadily he lifted the big six-shooter, his head hunched forward. The muzzle wavered on Henry, wavered away, back again—

With a wide swing of one leg, Judge kicked Grimes behind the left knee, throwing him off balance. The gun went off, the bullet smashing into the wall above the window, and Judge, in one desperate lunge, caught Grimes around both legs, upsetting him completely.

They crashed to the floor, and Oscar dived into Grimes, who was almost as big as Oscar. For a moment there was a fierce struggle, as Oscar tried to secure the gun. A muffled shot, as the gun was discharged again.

Oscar yanked Grimes' right hand from beneath him, and jerked away the gun. But Grimes did not move. Slowly Judge slid away, one eye beginning to discolor, a trickle of blood from his nose.

SUDDENLY the front door crashed open, and they turned to look into the muzzles of a dozen guns.

"Don't move!" snapped a voice. "Drop yore guns, you damn fools, before we salivate yuh!"

"Why, good afternoon, Danny—or is it morning?" said Henry.

"Well, I'll be a liar by the watch!" snorted Danny Regan, as he came slowly into the cabin, followed by the boys from the Broken Wheel and Circle N. They stared at Henry, Judge and Oscar. They looked at the man near the doorway and at Grimes.

"I'm glad you came, gentlemen," said Henry. "It—well, it was getting beyond control. It seems that we were besieged from without and within. But it is all right now."

"Well, my gosh!" exclaimed Danny. "So this is where you are."

"This is where we are now," corrected Judge. "We have been other places, you know. You don't happen to have a drink with you, do you?"

"Not a drop," admitted Danny. "We came down here to rescue you, and—"

"Das is a ha'al of a way to rascue anybody," declared Oscar.

"Wait a minute," begged Meek. "Perhaps Henry can throw some light on what happened. What happened to Grimes?"

"Well," began Henry, "it seems that Mr. Grimes and Mr. Bellew had something in common. In fact, Mr. Bellew intended selling the Seventy-Six to Mr. Grimes, but in an altercation Mr. Grimes killed Mr. Bellew. When the burial party went out with the body, I—well, I landed upon Mr. Grimes, and captured this fort.

"Later, Mr. Ed Jones arrived, acting somewhat belligerent toward some outside party or parties, and Oscar knocked him down with that three-legged stool. He hasn't moved since."

"So it was Mr. Jones, eh?" muttered Meek grimly. "I suppose he came here to bring a warning. He fired upon us, possibly to sound a warning to the men here, and we fired back."

"Yeah, and we got him twice!" called a cowboy, who had been examining Jones. "He's dead as a fried tick."

Henry sighed deeply.

"He's not the first man to die under an anaesthetic."

"Anaesthetic?" queried Danny.

"The one Oscar administered with a three-legged stool. But what about that burial party?"

"Still swimming the river, I suppose," replied Danny. "They were a long ways down the river, when we saw them last."

"Wait a minute," said Meek. "You say Jones was knocked down, as he came in here, and—"

"Precisely, sir," nodded Henry. "Mr. Grimes came back to life, tried to recapture the fort, but in the struggle, it seems, he shot himself."

"Then who in the hell was shootin' at us?" asked Meek. "If Jones and Grimes—sa-a-ay! Was you fellers—"

"Just a moment," interrupted Henry. He picked up his sombrero and held it out to them.

"Well, what about it?" asked Meek.

"Rats never done that," replied Henry.

Danny chuckled and shook his head.

"Meek, I reckon we're all even. How damn lucky that none of us got killed! Henry, we thought this place was full of shepherds. We trailed Bellew down here, and I reckon Jones follered us."

"Either Jones or Barber shot Slim," said Henry.

"I figured that," nodded Danny. "They had to get rid of Slim, to let a bunch of rams across. Man, this was a close call for Wild Horse Valley."

"But they're blocked for keeps now," said Meek. "With Grimes dead, the outfit is sunk."

"Thanks to a damn fool sheriff," said Danny softly.

"Thanks," murmured Henry. "But don't overlook the other two damn fools. It was team work, my boy. But," Henry squinted at Danny, as he rubbed his nose carefully, "about that river. It—it seems impassable."

"**WELL,** I reckon it is," replied Danny. "We figured on tryin' to cross it up by the Seventy-Six. Mebbe we'd have made it—I doubt it though, 'cause she's runnin' wild."

"You—you doubt it, Danny?" queried the puzzled Henry.

"Anyway," grinned Danny, "I'm glad we found you three fellers on this side of the river. We was shore afraid you'd gone across."

Henry, Judge and Oscar looked queerly at each other.

"Val," drawled Oscar, "Ay skal ta'l you dis much; when das shoriff's office stort to do somet'ing, it is yust as good as done. Ve know das shoriff business by hort. But yust now Ay could use some fude and prune yuice."

"I shore reckon you've earned it," said Meek. "Some of you boys take the officers back to Tonto City, while a few of us check up on things down here. It's possible there's more of the Grimes gang on this side."

"At least one," said Henry. "He will answer to the name of Edgar. His description is about five feet ten inches, weight a hundred and seventy. One ear is missing, his front teeth are gone, and I believe his nose is broken."

"My Gawd!" gasped a cowboy. "You mark 'em, don'tcha, Sheriff?"

"One must be firm," said Henry.

WHEN Tonto City learned what the three officers had done, they were greeted with great acclaim. Liquor flowed over the Tonto Saloon bar, and Judge made a speech. Not a connected discourse, but who cared? Warmed, fed and liquored, the three sat in the sheriff's office—heroes, in spite of themselves.

From inside his shirt Henry removed a crumpled, legal-looking paper. Taking another paper from his desk, he put them together, lighted a match to them and sat there, eyes squinted, while they burned to a pile of ashes. With a sigh of relief, he managed to elevate his feet to the top of his desk—and relaxed.

"What were those papers, if I may be so bold as to ask, Henry?" queried Judge, slightly owl-eyed.

"The larger one, my dear Judge, was a document, which, when in ashes, removed all chances of a sheepman's heirs from claim-

ing an estate in Wild Horse Valley. I secured it from the pocket
of a fallen king. The other paper was that damnable telegram,
which offered me seventy-five dollars a week—in picture
houses."

"I see," nodded Judge stiffly. "Whether legal or not, I applaud
your judgment in destroying them, sir. By gad, sir, they do not
know who you are. My dear Henry, you have been underesti-
mated."

"True, Judge—true. But without your keen, legal brain—well,
sir, I shudder to think what might have happened. What is your
opinion, Oscar?"

"Val," declared Oscar, "Ay don't know what de ha'al dis talk
is all about. Three crazy fules, sax miles from home, without
brains enough to mind our own business. Yust as crazy as Yones'
mule, who swam a river to get a drink of al-ka-li vater, and den
left t'ree acres of al-fal-fa to storve to death in cactus patch."

"That Swede has no sense of proportion," sighed Judge.

BY SAI SHANKAR

W.C. TUTTLE WAS born in Glendive, Montana, on 11 November 1883, on what he called the coldest day of the coldest month of the coldest winter. He was the son of Henry and Anna Tuttle, the first of at least four children. Henry was from Connecticut, and Anna was from Germany. Henry had a job as a sheriff, and Tuttle was born "in jail," where the sheriff's quarters were in the same building as the jailed men.

His full name was the dark secret of his life, it being Wilbur Coleman Tuttle. Glendive was an agricultural hub with charming weather (cold winters and hot, humid summers) and pleasant scenery—the local chamber of commerce describes it as "good people surrounded by badlands." It was like the Des Moines Bill Bryson describes ("I was from Des Moines, Iowa. Someone had to be.")

The family seems to have moved around a little. The 1900 census shows them in Ravalli, Montana, a place that exists only so that the Census authorities have something to put against the place of residence.

It was a bleak place that Tuttle grew up in, with limited facilities for education. It is hard to imagine his childhood in this place, but he makes fun of it:

> Grew up normally, giving my parents and the neighbors plenty of grief, keeping out of jail by the grace of God and a friendship with the sheriff. Went to what was known as the toughest school on earth, where I did not add any soothing

influence, it seems. General appearance was a split lip, one black eye and a torn shirt.

I was one of 60 kids in a one-roomed school. We had five readers and different sized desks. When a youngster got too big for the primer class desks he was promoted to a higher reader and a bigger desk. When he got so even the biggest desks left corns on his knees he was graduated.

W.C. Tuttle

Expelled four times during final term. The first three times it did not take. Fourth time I found out that the Board of Trustees was not kidding me, so I went away, deciding to be a travelling salesman.

No diploma. In fact, there were no diplomas given. It wasn't even a graded school, except we had featherweight, lightweight, middleweight and heavyweights.

He was medium tall (5'10") with blue eyes. Once he quit school, he drifted further westward, taking a variety of jobs. He claimed to have been a sheep herder, a cow herder, harness and saddle salesman, cigar salesman, streetcar conductor and driver, railroad man, picture seller, poker game organizer, accountant, cook, prospector, miner, forest ranger and trapper. He didn't think that cowboy life was as attractive as it was made out to be by some authors:

> What a job! Forty-a-month plus frostbite. Out of the sack about five o'clock in the morning, the temperature about zero in the bunkhouse, outside ten or twelve below, and a wind blowing. You shiver into frozen overalls, fight your way down to the stable, where you harness a team of frosted horses, take 'em out and hitch them to a hayrick wagon.... Man, it was romantic!

He also spent some time as a cartoonist in Montana:

I'd always liked to draw, just for fun. In the heat of a political campaign a little daily paper in Montana needed a cartoonist. I was out fishing and the fellow who came after me had to pack in three days to find me. I drew cartoons for five months and made every Democrat in Montana hate me, because I drew what the boss wanted and he wanted the bitterest and most insulting stuff he could get. After he was elected the paper couldn't afford a cartoonist, so I drifted out to Tacoma, and became mining editor, cartoonist and staff photographer on a paper there.

This was in 1907, and he moved again the same year, this time to Tacoma, Washington, where he became a cartoonist on the *Spokane Chronicle*. He was staying with his uncle in Tacoma. This was the beginning of a more settled life for him, and he spent the next ten years with the *Chronicle*. He was married sometime between 1910 and 1914 to Bertha M., with a son, Gene Edward Tuttle being born 15 March, 1914. Gene would go on to also write westerns, with more than a hundred books to his credit.

He used to read many magazines, including *Adventure*. In 1915, he saw a statement by Arthur S. Hoffman on the cover of *Adventure* to the effect that a particular story was the best humorous story that he—Hoffman—had bought. Tuttle decided that he could write better than that, and sent off a story to *Adventure*. Hoffman bought it and paid Tuttle more for the story than he was earning per week on the staff of the *Chronicle*. He continued working at the *Chronicle* for a couple more years before deciding to quit and become a full-time author.

In 1918, he moved with his family to Hollywood, California, trying to break into the movies as a writer. He succeeded, with Universal Studios making more than twenty short movies based on his Piperock stories and characters. He continued to write for the pulp magazines, writing at least ten stories a year for *Adventure* alone from 1917 to 1924. He also wrote for *Short Stories* and *Argosy*, pulps aimed at a similar readership.

A lifelong lover of baseball, Tuttle also served as president of the Pacific Coast Baseball League from 1935 to 1943.

He kept writing, publishing more than fifty books and a thousand stories in his career. One of his last books was his autobiography, *Montana Man*. He also wrote the scripts for the radio show *Hashknife*, based on his characters, Hashknife Hartley and Sleepy Stevens.

He passed away on June 6, 1969.

THE ARGOSY LIBRARY ™

SERIES 1 INCLUDES:

* DENT * KETCHUM * KLINE *
* MacISAAC * ROSCOE *
* ROUSSEAU *
* SELTZER *
* TUTTLE *
* WIRT *
WORTS

THE BEST FICTION
FROM THE FRANK
A. MUNSEY LINE

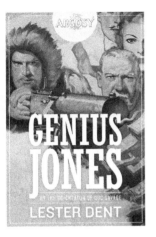

GENIUS JONES
BY THE RE-CREATOR OF DOC SAVAGE
LESTER DENT

WHEN TIGERS ARE HUNTING
THE COMPLETE ADVENTURES OF CORDIE,
SOLDIER OF FORTUNE, VOLUME 1
W. WIRT

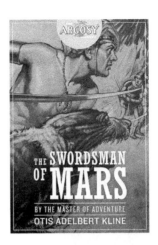

THE SWORDSMAN OF MARS
BY THE MASTER OF ADVENTURE
OTIS ADELBERT KLINE

THE SHERLOCK OF SAGELAND
THE COMPLETE TALES OF
SHERIFF HENRY, VOLUME 1
W.C. TUTTLE

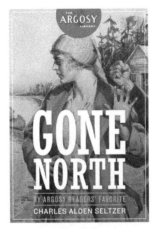

GONE NORTH
BY ARGOSY READERS' FAVORITE
CHARLES ALDEN SELTZER

THE MASKED MASTER MIND
BY THE AUTHOR OF PETER THE BRAZEN
GEORGE F. WORTS

BALATA
BY THE AUTHOR OF THE RAMBLER
FRED MacISAAC

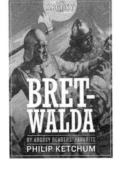

BRET-WALDA
BY ARGOSY READERS' FAVORITE
PHILIP KETCHUM

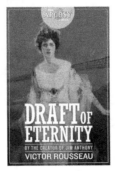

DRAFT OF ETERNITY
BY THE CREATOR OF JIM ANTHONY
VICTOR ROUSSEAU

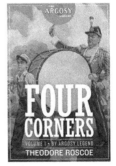

FOUR CORNERS
VOLUME 1 · BY ARGOSY LEGEND
THEODORE ROSCOE

SERIES 1 • AVAILABLE SPRING 2015

CPSIA information can be obtained
at www.ICGtesting.com
Printed in the USA
LVHW082139030820
662325LV00014B/514